Benito Pérez Galdós

DOÑA
PERFECTA

Translated by Alexander R. Tulloch

PHOENIX HOUSE
London

First published in Great Britain in 1999
by Phoenix House

Translation © Phoenix House 1999

A CIP catalogue record for this book is available from the British Library.

ISBN 1 861591 31 4 (cased)
ISBN 1 861591 32 2 (trade paperback)

Typeset by SetSystems Ltd, Saffron Walden, Essex
Printed in Great Britain by
Clays Ltd, St Ives plc

Phoenix House
An imprint of the Weidenfeld and Nicolson Division of
The Orion Publishing Group Ltd
Orion House
5 Upper Saint Martin's Lane
London, WC2H 9EA

CONTENTS

NOTE ON THE AUTHOR

Benito Pérez Galdós was born on 10 May 1843 in Las Palmas in the Canary Islands. At nineteen, he left the Canaries, ostensibly to study law in Madrid, but devoted himself instead to experimenting with creative writing and becoming a journalist and editor. In 1867 he travelled to Paris, where he discovered the work of Balzac. The following year, which saw the overthrow of the monarchy in Spain, he translated Dickens's *Pickwick Papers*. Inspired by his reading of the great masters of European Realism, he decided that Spain needed Realist novels of its own, and devoted the rest of his life to creating them. Galdós's writing bears witness to the tumultuous events of the 1868 revolution, the rise and fall of the First Republic, and the Restoration of the Bourbon Monarchy. He displayed amazing tenacity and productivity as a writer, publishing a total of seventy-eight novels, twenty-four plays and numerous articles and essays. He is famous for two panoramic series: the *National Episodes*, which trace Spain's history through the nineteenth century, and the *Contemporary Novels*, which centred on Madrid in his own time. *Doña Perfecta* was published in 1876 when Galdós was thirty-three. His signature works date mostly from the 1880s and 1890s, including *The Disinherited* (1881), which marks his appropriation of Naturalism, after an intense encounter with Zola's works in 1878; *Inferno* and *That Bringas Woman* (1884), and his masterpiece novel of adultery, *Fortunata and Jacinta* (1887).

From 1910 on, he had to dictate his work, and had become functionally blind by 1912. In that year, tragically, he was denied a nomination for the Nobel Prize for political reasons. His finances were in such a dire state that a national subscription fund was launched to help him out. He died on 4 January 1920.

DOÑA PERFECTA

CHAPTER I

Villahorrenda! . . . Five minutes!

When the coast-bound, combined freight and passenger train number 65 (it is not necessary to specify the line) stopped at the small station between the 171 and 172 kilometre posts, almost all the second and third class passengers stayed inside the carriages, asleep or yawning, because the penetrating cold of the early morning was not conducive to strolling along the platform, open as it was to the elements. The only passenger who had travelled in the first class compartment got off quickly and, addressing the railway employees, asked if this was the Villahorrenda halt. (This name, like many of the others which you will encounter here, is the property of the author.)

'We are in Villahorrenda,' answered the driver, whose voice merged with the clucking of the hens which at that moment were perched on top of the goods wagon. 'I forgot to call you, Señor de Rey. I think they're waiting for you with the horses.'

'It's freezing cold here!' said the traveller, wrapping himself up in his cape. 'Is there nowhere in the halt where I can rest and gather my strength before I begin my ride through this frozen landscape?'

The words were hardly out of his mouth when the driver, called away by the pressing onerous duties of his office, departed, leaving the stranger with another question on his lips. The latter saw that another employee was approaching, in his right hand a lantern which swung from side to side in time with his footsteps, casting a succession of geometrical undulations of light. The light fell onto the platform itself and formed a zig-zag pattern similar to that etched out by water as it falls from a watering can.

'Is there an inn or somewhere I can sleep in this station?' the traveller asked the man with the lantern.

'There's nothing here,' the latter answered curtly, running towards those people who were loading the train and weighing into them with such a torrent of invectives, curses and blasphemous invocations that even the hens, shocked by such coarse rudeness, murmured in their baskets.

'The best thing I can do is get away from here as quickly as I can,' the gentleman said to himself. 'The driver told me the horses were here.'

As this thought was running through his mind he became aware of a gentle, respectful hand tugging almost imperceptibly at his coat. He turned round and saw a dark bundle of tightly wrapped brown cloth from which peered the astute, nut-brown face of a Castillian farm labourer. He took in the ungainly stature, which reminded him of a black poplar growing among vegetables; the sagacious eyes which flashed beneath the broad brim of an old velvet hat; the dark-skinned, iron hand clinging to a green stick and the broad foot which jangled a steel spur every time it moved.

'Are you Don José de Rey?' he asked, touching his hat.

'Yes. And you,' the gentleman replied cheerfully, 'must be Doña Perfecta's servant, come to meet me and take me from this halt to Orbajosa.'

'The very same. When you're ready to set off . . . The pony moves like the wind. I imagine, sir, that you're a good horseman. It runs in the family . . .'

'Which is the way out?' said the traveller impatiently. 'Come on, let's get out of here . . . What did you say your name was?'

'My name's Pedro Lucas,' replied the man in the brown cloth, gesturing again as if to take his hat off. 'But they call me Licurgo. Where's your luggage, sir?'

'Over there, I can see it beneath the clock. Three pieces.

Two suitcases and a pile of books for Don Cayetano. Here's the receipt.'

A moment later man and servant had turned their backs on the shack which passed for the station and were looking out along a road which began at the halt and disappeared into the barren nearby hills where the hazy outline of the miserable hamlet of Villahorrenda could be seen. Three horses had to transport everything: the men and their worlds. A fine-looking pony was assigned to the gentleman. Old Licurgo was to strain the back of a venerable nag which had known better days but was still sure-footed, and the mule, whose reins were in the hands of a swift-footed and hot-blooded shepherd lad, was to transport the luggage.

Before the caravan set off the train pulled out, crawling over the tracks at the leisurely pace of a combined passenger and freight train. As the train disappeared into the distance its wheels produced a rumbling echo deep beneath the earth and when it entered the tunnel near the 172 kilometre mark, it propelled a jet of steam through its whistle and an ear-splitting screech cut through the air. The tunnel, exhaling a whitish smoke from its black maw, resounded like a trumpet, its stentorian voice awakening villages, towns, cities and provinces. Here a cock crowed and, a little further away, another. Dawn was breaking.

CHAPTER 2

A journey through the heart of Spain

Having set off on their journey they left the mean little
houses of Villahorrenda behind them and the gentleman,
who was young and very good-looking, said the following:

'Tell me, Señor Solon . . .'

'Licurgo, at your service . . .'

'Yes, of course, Licurgo. I knew that you had the same
name as a wise law-giver of antiquity. Forgive my mistake.
But let's get to the point. How's my aunt?'

'Beautiful as ever,' replied the farm labourer, moving the
horse on a few paces. 'It's as though the years have no effect
on Doña Perfecta. Not for nothing do they say that God
grants long life to the good. Which means that this angel of
the Lord should live for a thousand years. If all the blessings
which have been showered upon her in this world were
feathers she would have enough for wings to carry her up to
Heaven.'

'And my cousin, Señorita Rosario?'

'God bless those who take after their own kind,' said the
villager. 'What can I tell you about Señorita Rosario, except
that she's the living image of her mother? If what they say is
true and you have come here to marry her, Don José, then
you have found yourself a little darling. And she has nothing
to complain of either. You're well suited. It'll be a good
match.'

'And Don Cayetano?'

'Still buried in his books. His library is bigger than the
cathedral and he also pokes about in the earth looking for

stones with devilish scratch marks on them which are supposed to be Moorish writing.'

'How long before we reach Orbajosa?'

'We'll be there by nine, God willing. There's no telling how happy Doña Perfecta's going to be when she sees her nephew! . . . And Señorita Rosario, who spent all day yesterday getting your room ready. As they have never seen you, mother and daughter have done nothing but wonder what you would be like. The time has arrived for the letters to cease and the talking to begin. Cousin will see cousin and all will be feasting and rejoicing. God will send us another dawn and all will be well, as they say.'

'As my aunt and cousin don't know me yet it would be unwise to make plans,' said the gentleman, smiling.

'That's true. That's why they say that it takes two to tango,' answered the farm labourer. 'But faces don't deceive. What a jewel you've found yourself! And what a find lad she's getting!'

The gentleman did not hear the last words spoken by Old Licurgo because he had become distracted and somewhat thoughtful. They were just coming up to a bend in the road and the farm labourer, turning the horses in another direction, said:

'Now we have to take this path. The bridge is down and we can only ford the river at Cerillo de los Lirios.'[1]

'Cerillo de los Lirios?' said the gentleman, emerging from his meditative state. 'What an abundance of poetic names in such ugly places! Throughout my whole journey here I've been struck by the dreadful irony of the place names. A place distinguished only for its barren aspect and the desolate sadness of its mournful landscape is called "Valle-ameno".[2] A one-horse town consisting of mud huts, sprawling out over an arid plain and revealing its poverty in a variety of

---

[1] The Mount of Lilies

[2] Pleasant Valley

ways, has the audacity to call itself "Villa-rica".[1] And there's a stony, dusty ravine where not even the thistles can find any moisture but which, nevertheless, calls itself "Valdeflores".[2] And now we're coming up to the "Cerillo de los Lirios", but where in God's name are the lilies? I can't see anything but stones and parched grass. If they called this place "Cerrillo de la Desolación"[3] they would be closer to the truth. Except for Villahorrenda, which seems to have acquired a name in keeping with reality, everything here bears the stamp of irony. Beautiful words, prosaic and miserable reality. The blind would be happy in a place like this which is such paradise for the tongue and such hell for the eyes.'

Señor Licurgo either did not understand the words uttered by Señor Rey, or he paid no attention to them. As they had forded the river, muddy and flowing with indecent haste as if trying to escape from its own banks, the farm labourer stretched out his arm in the direction of some property which extended over to their left, and said:

'That place is called Los Alamillos de Bustamente.'[4]

'My property!' exclaimed the gentleman with delight, surveying the desolate fields bathed in the first light of morning. 'This is the first time I have seen the inheritance my mother left me. The poor old soul had such grand plans for this land and told me such wonderful things about it when I was a boy, and I thought that to be here would be to be in Paradise. Fruit, flowers, big and small game, mountains, lakes, rivers, poetic streams, pastoral slopes – they were all here at "Los Alamillos de Bustamente", in this blessed countryside, the best and most beautiful land of all . . . Damnation! The people around here live in a world of fancy! If I had been brought here in my childhood, when my head was full of the ideas and enthusiasm my mother

[1] Rich Town
[2] Flower Valley
[3] Desolation Hill
[4] Bustamente's Poplars

had instilled in me, all these barren hills, the dusty or flooded
plains, the old labourers' cottages, the rickety irrigation
wheels with buckets that can hardly raise enough water for
half a dozen cabbages, and the miserable, indolent desolation
I see before me now would have appeared enchanting.'

'It's the best land for miles around,' said Señor Licurgo.
'And you won't find any better for chickpeas.'

'I'm glad to hear it, because since I inherited it this
marvellous property hasn't yielded me a penny.'

The wise Spartan law-giver scratched his ear and sighed.

'But I've been told,' the gentleman continued, 'that some
of the neighbouring landowners have been ploughing into
these great estates of mine and that they're being nibbled
away. There are no boundary lines or markers here, nor any
real sense of ownership, Señor Licurgo.'

The farm labourer, after a pause during which his subtle
mind seemed engrossed in profound contemplation,
expressed himself thus:

'Old Paso Largo, whom we call "The Philosopher"
because of his great wisdom, did do some ploughing on Los
Alamillos, above the hermitage, and he's bitten off six acres,
bit by bit.'

'Some school of philosophy!' the gentleman exclaimed,
laughing. 'I'd lay odds that he's not the only . . .
philosopher.'

'Well, as the saying goes, the cobbler should stick to his
last, and if there's plenty of food in the dovecote there'll
always be plenty of doves . . . But you, sir, could quote the
saying that the cow looks fatter in the eye of the owner and
now that you're here you can set about getting the estate
back.'

'That may not be so easy, Señor Licurgo,' the gentleman
answered as they started along a path bordered on both
sides by beautiful wheatfields whose lush, early maturity
made them a joy to behold. 'This field seems better culti-
vated. I can see that Los Alamillos is not all sadness and
misery.'

The farm labourer pulled a long face and assumed a certain air of disdain towards the fields chosen by the traveller, then said with great humility:

'This one's mine, sir.'

'Forgive me,' answered the gentleman with alacrity. 'I was already thinking of setting to with my sickle on your estates. Obviously, philosophy is contagious here.'

They descended abruptly into a gulley which formed the bed of a stagnant, pathetic little stream and, once beyond it, entered a field full of stones without even the slightest trace of vegetation.

'The land here's very poor,' said the gentleman, turning round to look at his guide and companion who had fallen behind somewhat. 'You'd have a hard job making any profit here, it's all mud and sand.'

Licurgo, meekness personified, replied:

'This is yours.'

'I can see that everything that's bad here belongs to me,' said the gentleman, laughing jovially.

As they were having this conversation they came back onto the main road. The morning sunlight which was now stealing merrily through the windows and skylights on the Spanish horizon, bathed the fields in brilliant splendour. The immense cloudless sky seemed to increase in size and pull away from the earth in order to get a better view of it and to derive pleasure from its contemplation on high. The desolate countryside, devoid of trees, here the colour of straw, there the colour of clay, all divided into yellow, blackish, or pale green triangles or quandrangles, resembled a tattered patchwork cloak which had been laid out in the sun. And on that miserable cloak Christianity and Islam had engaged in epic battles. These were indeed glorious lands but the battles of yesteryear had left them in a sorry state.

'I think we're in for a blistering hot sun today, Señor Licurgo,' said the gentleman, partially loosening the cloak which enveloped him. 'What a miserable road! Not a single tree to be spotted for as far as the eye can see. Everything here is the opposite of what one would expect. There is nothing but endless irony. Why call the place "Los Alamillos" if there are neither large nor small poplars here?'

Old Licurgo did not reply to the question because he was listening with his whole being to certain noises which suddenly resounded in the distance and, with a gesture of disquiet, brought his horse to a halt and scanned the road and distant hills with a look of agitation in his eyes.

'What's the matter?' asked the traveller, who also stopped in his tracks.

'Are you armed, Don José?'

'I have a revolver . . . Ah, now I understand. Are there bandits about?'

'Could be,' answered the farm labourer, apprehensively. 'I think I just heard a shot.'

'Let's find out . . . Walk on!' said the gentleman, spurring his pony. 'They won't frighten me.'

'Careful, Don José,' exclaimed the villager, restraining him. 'These people are worse than the devil. Only the other day they murdered two gentlemen who were on the way to catch the train to . . . This is no time for games. Gasperón the strong, Pepito Chispillas, Merengue and Ahorca-Suegras won't cast eyes on me as long as there is breath in my body. Let's take the path.'

'Lead on, Licurgo.'

'After you, Don José,' replied the farm labourer in a shaky voice. 'You don't know what these people are like. They were the ones who only last month stole the ciborium, the Virgin's crown and two candlesticks from the Church of St Carmen. They're also the ones who held up the Madrid train two years ago.'

When Don José heard these terrible accounts he felt his bravery subside somewhat.

'Can you see that high steep hill in the distance? Well,

that's where these rogues hide away in some caves called
"La Estancia de los Caballeros".'[1]

'De los Caballeros!'

'Yes, sir. They come down to the main road when the
Guardia Civil relaxes its guard and rob whatever they can.
And can you see over there, just past the bend in the road, a
cross which was erected in memory of the Mayor of Villahorrenda who was killed during the elections?'

'Yes, I can see it.'

'There's an old house there where they hide and lie in wait
for wayfarers. The place is called "Las Delicias".'[2]

'Las Delicias!'

'Yes, and if everyone who has been murdered or robbed
on their way past that spot could be brought back to life
there'd be enough of them to form an army.'

While they were having this conversation closer shots rang
out, undermining somewhat the travellers' outward show of
courage, but the young shepherd boy was undisturbed; jumping for joy, he asked Señor Licurgo for permission to go on
ahead and observe the battle that had broken out so close to
them. Having witnessed the youngster's decisiveness, Don
José felt ashamed at having felt fear of, or at least respect
for, the robbers, and exclaimed, spurring on his pony:

'Let's all go! We may be able to render assistance to the
unfortunate travellers who have landed themselves in a tight
spot and teach the "Caballeros" a lesson!'

The farm labourer tried to convince the young man of the
temerity of his intentions and of the futility of his generous
thoughts, because the travellers had probably already been
robbed, and possibly killed, so that nobody could help them
now. But the gentleman was still insisting and paying no
heed to the wise counsel being offered to him, when the
appearance of two or three carters, calmly driving a wagon
along the road, put an end to the discussion. The danger

[1] The Gentlemen's Residence
[2] The Delights

could not have been all that great if these people could come along with such abandon and singing their jaunty songs.

And such indeed was the case because the shots, according to the carters, had not been fired by bandits but by the Guardia Civil, attempting in this way to prevent the escape of half a dozen thieves, handcuffed together, who were being conducted to the town prison.

'Now I understand what was going on,' said Licurgo, pointing out a wisp of smoke rising up some distance away and over to the right. 'They've done them in. This does happen from time to time.'

The gentleman did not understand.

'I assure you, Don José,' the Lacedaemonian law-giver added emphatically, 'that it's a good job well done. It doesn't do any good to bring that scum to trial. The judge shakes them up a bit and then lets them go. If one of them does end up in gaol after six years of litigation he'll probably get away, or be pardoned, and head straight back to La Estancia de los Caballeros. It's best just to shoot them. When they are being taken off to gaol you can find a suitable spot and say "So, you dog, try to escape, would you?" . . . Then, "bang! bang!" That takes care of the preliminary hearing, summoning the witnesses, listening to the evidence and the verdict . . . All over in one minute. Not for nothing do we say that the fox may be clever but the huntsman is even cleverer.'

'Well, let's move on faster, then. Besides being long, this road has nothing attractive to offer,' said Señor de Rey.

As they passed close to Las Delicias they spotted, some distance from the road, the members of the Guardia Civil who some moments earlier had carried out the extraordinary sentence with which the reader is already familiar. The shepherd boy was very disappointed because he had not been allowed to get a close look at the twitching bodies of the bandits, thrown together into a gruesome pile and visible in the distance as they all continued on their way. But they had not walked more than twenty paces when they heard a horse galloping up behind them so fast that it was only a

matter of moments before it reached them. Our traveller
turned round and saw a man, or rather a centaur, since no
greater harmony between horse and rider could possibly be
imagined. The rider was of coarse and ruddy complexion,
with large, passionate eyes, a mass of unkempt hair and a
black moustache. He was middle-aged and of generally
brusque and provocative appearance, and strength seemed
to ooze from his every pore. He was riding a magnificent,
robust beast, like a Parthenon horse, saddled and bridled
after the picturesque style of the region, and on its hindquar-
ters hung a large leather bag with the word 'mail' in large
letters on the flap.

'Hello there, and good day to you, Señor Caballuco,' said
Licurgo, greeting the rider as he drew near. 'What a head
start we had on you. But you'll arrive ahead of us if you've
a mind to!'

'Let's rest awhile,' answered Señor Caballuco, slowing his
horse down to the pace at which our travellers were riding,
and paying attention to the most important of the three,
'since I'm now in such company.'

'The gentleman,' said Licurgo, laughing, 'is Doña Perfecta's nephew.'

'Ah! . . . I wish you a long life . . . my lord and master.'

The two men saluted each other and it was noticeable that
Caballuco paid his respects with an air of disdain and
superiority which revealed at least an awareness of his great
importance and high standing in the community. When the
proud rider moved to one side and entered into a brief
conversation with two representatives of the Guardia Civil
who had just arrived, the traveller asked his guide:

'Who's that chap?'

'Who do you think? It's Caballuco.'

'And who's Caballuco?'

'Come on! . . . Are you telling me you've never heard his
name?' said the farm labourer, stunned that Doña Perfecta's
nephew should be so ignorant. 'He's a very brave man, a
great horseman and he knows more about horses than

anyone else hereabouts. We're very fond of him in Orbajosa, since he – and this is the honest truth – is as good as Our Lord's blessing . . . He's a big noise around these parts, and the Provincial Governor takes his hat off to him.'

'During the elections . . .'

'And the Government in Madrid writes to him and lards its missives with frequent expressions of respect . . . He tosses the caber like a Saint Christopher and is as skilful with weapons as the rest of us are with our own fingers. When they had a tax office here they could do nothing with him and every night shots rang out at the entrance to the town . . . He has men worth their weight in gold, as there's nothing they can't turn their hands to . . . He stands up for the poor and anyone who comes from outside and dares to harm a hair on the head of one of Orbajosa's sons will have him to reckon with . . . Soldiers from Madrid hardly ever come here. On those occasions when they have been here blood has been spilt every day because Caballuco would go picking fights with them for one reason or another. Now it seems he lives in poverty and is reduced to delivering the mail, but he's been pestering the life out of the Local Administration to set up another tax office and to put him in charge of it. I can't understand how you've never heard of him in Madrid, because his father was Caballuco the famous guerrilla fighter and he in turn was the son of another Caballuco who was also a guerrilla fighter in another age. And as they say we're in for another uprising because the whole country is in such a mess, we're afraid that Caballuco will leave us to go off and finish the job started by his father and grandfather, who to our glory, were born in our town.'

Our traveller was amazed to see what kind of knight errantry could still be encountered in the places he was riding through. But he did not have the opportunity to ask any more questions because the person who would have been the subject of his enquiries joined their group, saying in a bad-tempered tone:

'The Guardia Civil has killed three men. I've warned the

corporal to proceed with caution. Tomorrow I'm going to
have a talk with the Provincial Governor . . .'

'Are you going to X?'

'No. The Governor's coming here, Señor Licurgo. A couple
of regiments are going to be stationed in Orbajosa.'

'Yes,' said the traveller, smiling. 'In Madrid I did hear that
they were afraid rebel bands would be formed around
here . . . It's as well to be prepared.'

'They talk a load of nonsense in Madrid!' the centaur
exclaimed violently, accompanying his outburst with a
stream of unsavoury invectives. 'They're cunning devils in
Madrid . . . What are they sending soldiers here for? To
extract more taxes and call us up into the army? By God, if
there's no rebellion there should be one! So you,' he added,
casting a sly glance at the young gentleman, 'are Doña
Perfecta's nephew, are you?'

The uncalled-for remark and insolent look in the speaker's
eyes enraged the young man.

'Yes, sir. Is there something I can do for you?'

'I'm a friend of Doña Perfecta's and I am very fond of
her,' said Caballuco. 'Since you're on your way to Orbajosa,
we'll see each other there.'

And without saying another word he dug his spurs into
his mount which shot off and disappeared in a cloud of dust.

After they had travelled for half an hour, during which
time Don José remained rather uncommunicative, as did
Señor Licurgo, an ancient hamlet comprised of houses hud-
dled together, perched on the side of a hill, came into view.
From the hamlet several black towers stood out, together
with the ruined stonework of a dilapidated castle at the
highest point. A mass of distorted walls, of adobe hovels
which were as brown and dusty as the earth on which they
stood, formed the base, together with the remains of some
crenellated fortress walls in the shelter of which a thousand
mean little cottages raised their earthen facades, like anae-
mic, hungry faces begging alms from the traveller. A pathetic
little stream girdled the village like a tin belt, bringing

refreshment to the few orchards, the only sign of fertility in the vicinity to gladden the eyes. People entered or left on horseback or on foot, and the movement of humanity, although small, lent a certain impression of vitality to that great heap, whose architectural appearance was more evocative of ruin and death than of progress and life. The countless, repulsive beggars who lined both sides of the road and begged pennies from the traveller were a pitiful sight. It would be impossible to imagine creatures who were more in keeping with, and more appropriate to the cracks in that tomb of a city which was not only buried but also decomposing. When our travellers approached a discordant peel of bells announced in its own peculiar way that the mummified corpse still had a soul.

This was Orbajosa, a town which is not mentioned in Chaldean or Coptic, but only in Spanish geography, with its population of 7324 inhabitants, a Town Hall, an episcopal see, a law court, a seminary, a government-run stud farm, a secondary school and other official institutions.

'They're ringing for High Mass in the cathedral,' said Old Licurgo. 'We've arrived earlier than I thought we would.'

'This country of yours,' said the gentleman, surveying the view before him, 'could not look more unpleasant. The historic city of Orbajosa, whose name must be a corruption of *urbs augusta*, looks like a vast rubbish dump.'

'That's because you can only see the slums from here,' the guide said with obvious displeasure. 'When you enter Calle Real and Calle de Condestable you'll see buildings which are every bit as beautiful as the cathedral.'

'I don't wish to speak ill of Orbajosa before I get to know it,' said the gentleman. 'Nor is what I just said a sign of contempt; no matter how humble and miserable or beautiful and grand the city may be, it will always be dear to my heart, not just because it's the place where my mother was born, but because there are people living here whom I love very much even though I haven't met them. Now, let's enter this "august" city.'

They were already making their way along one of the roads leading to the streets of the city, keeping close to the orchard walls as they did so.

'Do you see that great house at the end of this orchard?' asked Licurgo, pointing to a thick, rendered wall which belonged to the only dwelling which appeared a comfortable and pleasant place to live.

'Yes . . . is that my aunt's place?'

'It certainly is. The part you can see from here is the back of the house. The front looks out onto the Calle del Cond-estable and it has five iron balconies which look like five little castles. The beautiful orchard on the other side of this wall belongs to the house, and if you stand up in your stirrups you'll be able to see everything from here.'

'We're home, then,' said the gentleman. 'Can't we go in this way?'

'There's a little door, but Doña Perfecta had it sealed off.'

The gentleman stood up in his stirrups and, craning his neck as much as he could, looked over the top of the wall.

'I can see the whole orchard,' he said. 'There's a woman, a girl . . . a young lady over there, under the trees . . .'

'That's Señorita Rosario,' answered Licurgo.

And at that moment he too raised himself up in his stirrups to have a look.

'Eh, Señorita Rosario,' he shouted, making meaningful gestures with his right hand. 'We've arrived . . . I've got your cousin here with me.'

'She's seen us,' said the gentleman, stretching his neck that little bit extra. 'But, if I'm not mistaken, there's a clergyman with her, a priest.'

'That's the Father Confessor,' the farm labourer answered casually.

'My cousin can see us . . . she's leaving the priest and has started running towards the house . . . She's pretty.'

'She certainly is.'

'Her face is all flushed. Come on, come on, Señor Licurgo!'

CHAPTER 3

Pepe Rey

Before we go any further it would be fitting for me to tell you about Pepe Rey and the affairs that brought him to Orbajosa.

When General Rey died, in 1841, his two children, Juan and Perfecta, had just got married. The latter had married the richest landowner in Orbajosa and the former a young lady from the same city. Doña Perfecta's husband was called Don Manuel María José de Polentinos, and Juan's wife, María Polentinos. But despite the fact that their surnames were very similar they were only distantly and tenuously related. Juan Rey was a law graduate from Sevilla, where he practised as a laywer for thirty years, earning both fame and wealth. By 1845 he was already a widower with a son who was starting to get up to mischief. He was wont to amuse himself with building things out of earth on the patio – viaducts, mounds, reservoirs, dams and ditches – and then flooding his fragile constructions with water. His father never tried to stop him and would say, 'You're going to be an engineer.'

Perfecta and Juan stopped seeing each other after they got married because she went off to live in Madrid with the opulent Polentinos, whose wealth was matched only by his ability to spend it. He found gambling and women so irresistible that he would have squandered his whole fortune if death had not carried him off before he had time to do so. The days of the provincial tycoon, who had been bled dry by the Court leeches and the insatiable vampire of gambling, came to an abrupt end when death visited him one night after one of his orgies. His only heiress was a daughter who was but a few months old. With the death of Perfecta's husband the family's immediate concerns were at an end, but a great struggle lay ahead. The Polentinos house was in a state of ruin and the estates were in danger of being seized by creditors. There was total chaos: the debts were enormous, the administration in Orbajosa was catastrophic and in Madrid the family was discredited and ruined.

Perfecta appealed to her brother and he, answering the poor widow's plea for help, displayed so much diligence and common sense that within a very short space of time the greatest dangers had passed. He began by obliging his sister to live in Orbajosa, administering the vast estates herself, while he confronted the formidable pressures of the creditors in Madrid. Gradually the house managed to overcome the enormous burden of debt, because the good Don Juan Rey, displaying the greatest talent in the world for such matters, defended himself in court, drew up agreements with the main creditors, and came to an arrangement with regard to the period of repayment so that, as a result of his skilful negotiations, the considerable Polentinos inheritance was kept afloat and continued to provide splendour and glory to the illustrious family for many a long year.

Doña Perfecta's gratitude was so great that when she was writing to her brother from Orbajosa, where she had decided to live until her daughter had grown up, she said, among other expressions of affection, 'You have been more than a brother to me, and to my daughter more than her own father. How can she and I repay you for such kindness? Oh, my beloved brother! As soon as my daughter learns to talk and can pronounce a name I shall teach her to bless yours, and my gratitude will last for as long as I live. Your unworthy sister regrets not having had the opportunity of showing you just how much she loves you and of compensating you in an appropriate manner for your magnanimity and the immense goodness in your heart.'

At the time when these things were being written, Rosario was two years old. Pepe Rey, ensconced in a college in Sevilla, was drawing lines on pieces of paper, preoccupied with proving that 'the sum of the interior angles of a polygon is equal to the same number of right angles as the polygon has sides, minus two'. The tiresome formulae kept him very busy. The years passed and the boy grew and continued to draw lines. Finally he drew what is known as the Taragona–Montblanc railway line, and his first real toy was the 120-metre long bridge which spans the river Francolí.

Doña Perfecta went on living in Orbajosa for many years. As her brother never left Sevilla they went for several years without seeing each other. One letter every three months, punctually written and punctually answered, maintained the communication between their two hearts, joined by a tenderness which neither time nor distance could cool. In 1870, when Don Juan Rey was satisfied that he had paid back his debt to society and went off to live in his beautiful house in Puerto Real, Pepe, who had been working for several years on projects for various large construction companies, undertook a study trip to Germany and England. His father's fortune (which was as substantial as any which accrued from an honest law firm could be in Spain), allowed him to break away from time to time from the necessity of gainful employment. A man of lofty ideas with a deep love of science, he derived his greatest pleasure from observing and studying the wonders which the genius of the century had been able to contribute to the culture, physical well-being and moral improvement of Mankind.

When he returned from his travels his father announced that he had an important project for him. If Pepe thought that it was going to be a question of a new bridge, a dock or at the very least the drainage works for some swamp, Don Juan proved him mistaken by announcing, in the following terms:

'It's now March and Doña Perfecta's quarterly letter has arrived as expected. Read it, son, and if you are in agreement with what my sister, that saintly and exemplary woman, has written, you will afford me the greatest happiness I could wish for in my old age. If the proposal is not to your liking, reject it forthwith for, even though your refusal would sadden me, I have not the slightest intention of imposing my wishes on you. It would be unworthy of both of us if the proposal should be accepted because of the coercion of a stern father. You are free to accept or not, and if the dictates of your heart mean that your commitment would be less than total, I should not wish you, either on my account or for any other reason, to act other than in accordance with your free will.'

Pepe glanced at the letter, put it down on the table and said in a calm voice:

'My aunt wants me to marry Rosario.'

'She has answered accepting my suggestion with pleasure,' said his father, obviously moved. 'Because the idea was mine . . . yes. Some time ago, some time ago it occurred to me . . . but I did not wish to speak to you about it until I had found out how my sister felt. As you can see, Doña Perfecta is delighted with my plan and says that she had the very same idea but did not dare to suggest it because you are – didn't you see what she said? – "because you are an exceptional young man, and her daughter is a country girl of only average education and without worldly attractions" . . . She says that herself . . . My poor sister! What a good woman she is! . . . I can see that you're not angry and that my suggestion does not seem ridiculous to you, even though it is not unlike the officious precautions taken by parents of another age who married off their children without consult-ing them and at times entered them into unsuitable and premature unions . . . May God grant that this marriage be or promise to be one of the happiest. It is true that you do not know my niece, but you and I have heard about her virtue, her discretion, her modesty and her noble simplicity. And what is more, she is pretty . . . My opinion,' he added in a celebratory tone, 'is that that you should set off and tread the ground of this secluded cathedral city, this *urbs augusta*, and there, in the presence of my sister and her charming Rosarito, decide whether or not she is to be more than my niece.'

Pepe picked up the letter again and read it carefully. On his face there was an expression of neither joy nor sadness. He looked as if he were examining the plans for a junction between two railway lines.

'Surely,' said Don Juan, 'in a remote place like Orbajosa where, incidentally, you have estates which you can now examine, life must pass with sweet, idyllic tranquillity. What patriarchal customs! What nobility there is in such tranquillity! What rustic, Virgilian peace! If you were a Classics scholar instead of a mathematician you would enter that city repeating to yourself *"ergo tua rura manebunt"*: Therefore your fields shall remain. What a marvellous place for devoting to a contemplation of the soul and preparing for good works! Everything there is kindness and honesty. The lies and hypocrisy of our great cities are unknown there; those saintly inclinations which the hustle and bustle of modern life stifles are reborn there. That is where dormant faith can awaken and that indefinable impulse for life can make itself felt within the human breast, like youthful impatience, crying out from deep inside "I want to live".'

A few days after this conversation Pepe left Puerto Real. Months previously he had turned down a government offer of carrying out a mining feasibility study of the bed of the river Nahara, in the Orbajosa valley. But as he thought of the task facing him after the said conversation, he decided: 'I must make use of my time. God knows how long the engagement will last and just how boring it will be.' He headed straight for Madrid and requested the commission for surveying the Nahara river bed, which he had no difficulty in obtaining, despite the fact that he did not belong officially to the Mining Department. Then he set off and

after he had changed trains twice, the combined freight and
passenger train No. 65, as we have seen, brought him to the
welcoming arms of Old Licurgo.

This excellent young man was not quite thirty-four years
of age. He was of strong constitution, a real Hercules,
perfectly formed and so dashing that if he had worn a
military uniform he would have cut the most warrior-like
figure it is possible to imagine. Although his hair and beard
were fair, there was no sign in his face of that phlegmatic
imperturbability of the Anglo-Saxons, but, on the contrary,
there was such vivacity that his eyes appeared black even
though they were not. His appearance was such that he
could have served as a handsome and perfectly finished
symbol and, if he had been a statue, the sculptor might have
carved the following words on the pedestal: 'Intelligence,
strength'. If not in visible letters, these qualities found vague
expression in the brightness of his eyes, in the powerful
attractiveness which formed an integral part of his personality and in the sympathetic feelings his warm personality
evoked in others.

He was not the most talkative of men: only those minds
which harbour insecure thoughts and shaky opinions tend
towards verbosity. The profound moral convictions of this
outstanding young man made him economical with words
when taking part in his generation's continual debates on
diverse subjects. But in polite conversation he could display
a witty yet discreet eloquence which resulted from his good
taste and his considerate and fair appraisal of the affairs of
this world. He would not tolerate lies or ambiguities or those
convoluted thoughts which the intellectual devotees of Gongorism[1] find so fascinating, and in order to bring the conversation back to reality Pepe Rey would occasionally resort to
the weapon of ridicule, and not always in moderation. Many
of his admirers saw this as a defect in his character because

---

[1] Gongorism: extremely ornate speech (after the poet Luís de Góngora y Argote
[1561–1627] whose poetry was full of complex imagery and metaphor)

it made our young man appear disrespectful of many generally accepted truths. It has to be said, although it may have an adverse effect on his prestige, that Pepe Rey knew nothing of the sweet tolerance of the understanding century which has invented extraordinary linguistic and factual veils in order to cover up what might seem unacceptable to public opinion.

This, despite what slanderous tongues may say about him, is an accurate description of the young man whom Licurgo introduced to Orbajosa at that very moment when the cathedral bell was announcing High Mass. It was then that both men peeped over the wall and saw the young girl and the confessor and then her speedy dash towards the house. Then they prodded their horses to ride on into the Calle Real, where a crowd of idlers stopped to gaze at the traveller as if he were some strange intrusive visitor to the patriarchal city. Veering off to the right, in the direction of the cathedral which dominated the whole town with its massive bulk, they went along the Calle del Condestable. This was a narrow cobbled street and the noisy clatter of their horses' hoofs alarmed the neighbours who appeared at the windows and on the balconies in order to satisfy their curiosity. The venetian blinds opened with their characteristic rattle and several faces, nearly all of them belonging to women, peered out from above and below. By the time Pepe Rey arrived at the ornate threshold of the Polentinos house he had already been the subject of numerous comments concerning his appearance.

CHAPTER 4

The cousin's arrival

The Father Confessor, when Rosario had brusquely taken her leave of him, looked over at the wall and, seeing the heads of Old Licurgo and his travelling companion, said to himself:

'Well now, the prodigy has arrived.'

He stayed where he was for a moment, deep in thought, holding his cloak with both hands folded across his stomach. He stared at the ground while his gold-rimmed spectacles slid gently down to the end of his nose, with his lower lip drooping and moist and his eyebrows, in which the black mingled with the white, slightly frowning. He was a saintly man, uncommonly knowledgeable, who always behaved in a manner entirely befitting a man of the cloth. He was well into his sixties, with an affable nature and refined, obliging personality, and was a great purveyor of advice and warnings to men and women alike. For many years he had been a teacher of Latin studies and rhetoric in the Institute, and this noble profession had provided him with a wealth of quotations from Horace and a store of flowery turns of phrase which he combined with his natural wit whenever the opportunity arose. There is no point adding anything more here about this personage, other than to say that when he heard the horses trotting along to the Calle del Condestable, he smoothed out his cloak, straightened his hat which was all askew on that venerable head, and, striding out towards the house, murmured:

'Let's have a look at this prodigy, then.'

Meanwhile Pepe was dismounting from his pony and being received into the welcoming arms of Doña Perfecta. Her face was bathed in tears and she was unable to express her sincere affection in anything other than stammered monosyllables.

'Pepe . . . how tall you've grown . . . and you've got a beard! It seems like only yesterday I dandled you on my knee . . . now you're a man, a fine figure of a man . . . Good Lord! . . . How the years pass . . .! And this is my daughter, Rosario.'

As these words were being spoken the two had already reached the drawing room on the ground floor where guests were normally received, and Doña Perfecta introduced him to her daughter.

Rosario was a girl of delicate and fragile appearance which revealed a tendency to what the Portuguese call *saudades*.[1] Her genteel, virginal face possessed something of that pasty, mother-of-pearl pallor which the majority of novelists attribute to their heroines and without which sentimental veneer no Enriqueta or Julia could ever be interesting. But the main thing to say about Rosario is that she radiated such sweetness and modesty no observer would notice any imperfections she may have had. This is not to say that she was ugly, but, in truth, to call her beautiful, in the strictest sense of the word, would be an exaggeration. The real beauty of Doña Perfecta's daughter consisted of a kind of transparency which had nothing to do with mother-of-pearl, alabaster, marble or with any of the other materials resorted to when we wish to describe the human face. What I mean is that this was a kind of transparency through which the very depths of her soul could be clearly seen: not fathomless, awesome depths such as those found at sea, but rather those of a limpid, gently flowing river. But something was lacking to make the person complete: there was no river bed and no river edges. Her enormous spirit had overflowed and was

---

[1] melancholy

threatening to swamp its narrow banks. When greeted by
her cousin she blushed to the roots of her hair, and could
manage no more than a few clumsily spoken words.

'You must be faint with hunger,' said Doña Perfecta to
her nephew. 'We'll have elevenses straightaway.'

'With your permission,' answered the traveller, 'I'd like to
shake off the dust from the road.'

'A good idea,' said Doña Perfecta. 'Rosario, show your
cousin to the room we've prepared for him. Don't take too
long over it, nephew. I'm about to order elevenses.'

Rosario showed her cousin to a beautiful room situated
on the ground floor. The moment he stepped inside, Pepe
detected the diligent and loving hands of a woman in all the
details of the house. Everything had been positioned with
consummate taste, and the cleanliness and freshness of everything was conducive to sweet repose in that delightful nest.
The guest noticed minute details which made him laugh.

'Here's the bell,' said Rosario, taking hold of the pull-rope
with a tassel which reached the bedhead. 'You only have to
stretch out your hand. The writing table has been positioned
in such a manner as to allow the light to come in from the
left . . . And look, you can throw any scrap paper in this
basket . . . Do you smoke?'

'Unfortunately, yes,' answered Pepe Rey.

'Well, you can put your cigarette ends here,' she said,
touching a gilded brass article of furniture, filled with sand,
with her toe. 'There's nothing worse than seeing the floor
littered with dog-ends . . . And here's the washbasin . . . and
a wardrobe and chest of drawers for your clothes . . . I don't
think this is a very good place for the clock so I think you
should move it closer to your bed . . . If the light bothers
you you only have to draw the blind with this cord . . . See?
. . . swishh . . .'

The engineer was delighted.

Rosario opened a window.

'Look,' she said, 'this window overlooks the orchard and

it gets the sun in the afternoon. There's a canary in a cage over there and it sings like mad. If it annoys you we'll remove it.'

She opened the window on the opposite side of the room. 'This window,' she added, 'overlooks the street. Look, you can see the cathedral; it's very beautiful and full of treasures. Many English people come to visit it. Don't open both windows at the same time because there's a very strong draught.'

'My dear cousin,' said Pepe, his soul flooded with inexplicable pleasure. 'In everything which stands before me I can see the hand of an angel, which could only be yours. What a beautiful room this is! It's as though I've lived here all my life. It's invitingly peaceful.'

Rosarito did not reply to these affectionate expressions and went out of the room, smiling.

'Don't be long,' she said from the doorway. 'The dining room is downstairs also . . . halfway along the hall.'

Old Licurgo came in with the luggage. Pepe tipped him with a generosity to which the farm labourer was unaccustomed and he, humbly expressing his gratitude, raised his hand to his forehead, as if he were neither putting on nor taking off his hat, and in an embarrassed tone, chewing on his words, like somebody who speaks but has nothing to say, expressed himself in the following manner:

'When would it be convenient for me to discuss a little matter with you, sir?'

'A little matter? . . . Right now,' answered Pepe, opening a trunk.

'This is not the right moment,' said the farm labourer. 'When you've had a rest, sir, we've got plenty of time. No need to rush things. Tomorrow's as good as today. You have a rest, sir, then when you fancy going for a ride . . . the pony's in good shape. Good day, then, sir. May you live for a thousand years . . . Oh, I was forgetting . . .' he added, coming back in only seconds after taking his leave. 'Do you have anything you want me to say to the municipal judge? . . . I'm on my way there now to talk about our little matter . . .'

'Give him my regards,' he said jauntily, unable to think of a better way of getting rid of the Spartan law-giver.

'Well, God be with you, Señor Don José.'

'Goodbye.'

The engineer had not yet unpacked when Old Licurgo's shrewd, beady eyes and dirty face appeared for the third time in the doorway.

'Excuse me, sir,' he said, smiling affectedly and revealing his extremely white teeth. 'But . . . I wanted to say that if you would like this matter cleared up by arbitration . . . Although, as they say, if you ask advice over a personal matter, everyone will tell you something different.'

'Will you go away!'

'I mention it because I can't stand the law. I want nothing to do with it. The less I have to do with it the better. So, goodbye, then, Don José. May God preserve you to benefit the poor.'

'Be off, man, be off!'

Pepe turned the key in the lock and said to himself:

'The people around here seem rather fond of litigation.'

CHAPTER 5

Will there be a difference of opinion?

Soon afterwards Pepe made his appearance in the dining room.

'If you eat a lot for elevenses,' Doña Perfecta said to him in an affectionate tone, 'you'll spoil your appetite. We have lunch here at one. I suppose you don't like the customs of the country?'

'I find them charming, Aunt.'

'Then tell us which you would prefer to have: a substantial snack now or something light to keep you going till lunch time?'

'I'll take something light so that I can have the pleasure of lunching with you. If I'd found something to eat in Villahorrenda I wouldn't be eating now.'

'Of course, I don't need to tell you to speak frankly with us. Order whatever you wish, just as if you were at home.'

'Thank you, Aunt.'

'How like your father you are!' said Doña Perfecta, observing the young man with genuine fascination as he ate. 'It's as though I were looking at my dear brother Juan. He used to sit just like you and eat in the same way, too. And particularly when it comes to looks, you're as like as two peas.'

Pepe made a start on his frugal elevenses. The things his aunt and cousin said, their attitude and the way they looked at him, made him feel entirely at home.

'Do you know what Rosario said to me this morning?' said Doña Perfecta, staring fixedly at her nephew. 'She said

that you, being a man accustomed to the ceremony and
manners of the Court and to foreign fashions, would not be
able to tolerate the somewhat rustic simplicity of our way of
life, nor our lack of good taste, since we are very down-to-
earth here.'

'You couldn't be more wrong!' replied Pepe, looking at
his cousin. 'Nobody despises the insincerity and farce of
what is called high society more than I do. You must believe
that for some time now I have wanted to steep myself in
Nature, as somebody once put it, and live far away from the
hustle and bustle, in the solitude and tranquillity of the
country. I long for the peace of a life without conflict and
struggle, to be neither envious nor envied, as the poet said.
For a long time I was prevented, first by my studies and then
by my work, from finding the relaxation I need and which
my body and soul crave. But since I set foot in your house,
dear cousin, I have felt myself surrounded by the atmosphere
of peace I've been looking for. So there is no need to talk to
me of high and low society, or of great and small worlds,
for I would willingly exchange them all for this little spot.'

As he was speaking the panes of glass in the door giving
onto the garden from the dining room were obscured by a
large, black figure. The lenses of a pair of spectacles reflected
a fugitive ray of sunlight which had struck them. The latch
creaked, the door opened and in walked the Father Confessor, looking very serious. He greeted those present and
bowed, removing his hat and almost sweeping the floor with
its brim.

'This is the Father Confessor from our holy cathedral,'
said Doña Perfecta, 'a person for whom we have the greatest
respect and with whom, I hope, you will become close
friends. Please be seated, Don Inocencio.'

Pepe shook the venerable clergyman's hand and the two
men sat down.

'Pepe, if you are used to having a smoke after your meal,
please carry on,' said Doña Perfecta, graciously, 'and that
includes you, too, Father.'

At that moment the good Don Inocencio was reaching under his cassock for a large leather tobacco pouch which bore the undeniable signs of long use. He opened it and removed two long cigarettes, one of which he offered to our friend. Rosario drew a match from one of those small cardboard boxes which Spaniards refer to jokingly as 'wagons', and in no time at all the engineer and the priest were puffing smoke at each other.

'And how does Señor Don José like our beloved city of Orbajosa?' asked the clergyman, tightly closing his left eye as was his wont when he was smoking.

'I haven't come to an opinion as yet,' said Pepe. 'From the little I have seen I would say that half a dozen sizeable injections of capital wouldn't go amiss here, and neither would a couple of good brains to direct the renovation of the place and a few thousand willing hands. Between the entrance to the city and the front door of this house I saw more than a hundred beggars, the majority of whom were able-bodied and even robust-looking men. They form a pitiful army which makes a depressing spectacle.'

'That's why we have charities,' stated Don Inocencio. 'And moreover, Orbajosa is not a poor town. I am sure that you are aware that the best garlic in the whole of Spain is produced here. We have more than twenty wealthy families living in our community.'

'The fact of the matter is,' remarked Doña Perfecta, 'that we have had a rough few years on account of the drought, but, even so, the granaries are not empty and thousands of strings of garlic have been delivered to the market.'

'During the many years I've lived in Orbajosa,' said the clergyman, frowning, 'I've seen many people come here from Madrid, some drawn by the contests at the hustings, others by the desire to visit some abandoned property or to see the antiquities in the cathedral. And all have arrived talking about English ploughs, mechanical threshing machines, water-power, banks and Heaven knows how many other new-fangled ideas. They all sing the same song about how

bad everything is here and how much better it could be.
Well they can go to the devil. We're quite happy here and
we don't need these visits from gentlemen from the capital.
And we'd be even happier if we didn't have to listen to their
constant clamour about how poverty-stricken we are and
about how big everything is and what wonderful things can
be seen in other places. The fool in his own house knows
more than the sane man in someone else's, is that not so,
Don José? But of course you mustn't think that I'm referring
to you. Not at all! By no means! I know only too well that
we have among us one of the most eminent young men in
modern Spain; a man who would be capable of transforming
our arid plains into the most fertile of lands ... It doesn't
bother me that you're singing the old song about English
ploughs and forestry. Not at all. Men of such great talent
may be forgiven for the manner in which they look down on
our humility. It's quite all right, my friend, it's quite all right,
Don José. You have the authority to say anything and even
to tell us that we are no better than savages.'

This diatribe, which was impertinent from start to finish
and ended on a sarcastic note, was not well received by the
young man. But he abstained from showing the slightest
displeasure and continued the conversation, doing his best
to avoid any topic which might offer the clergyman's patri-
otic sensitivity the slighest reason for an argument. Don
Inocencio stood up while Doña Perfecta was talking to her
nephew about family matters and took a few turns round
the room.

It was a vast and spacious room, decorated with an old-
fashioned wallpaper with flowers and branches which,
although discoloured, still preserved their original design,
thanks to the cleanliness in each and every part of the house.
The grandfather clock, with its motley-coloured dial and
housed in a case in which the apparently immobile weights
and large pendulum, constantly saying 'no', were visible
from the outside, occupied the most prominent position
among the sturdy dining-room furniture. A series of French

engravings depicting the exploits of the man who conquered Mexico completed the wall decorations. These were accompanied by prolix captions which mentioned a certain Ferdinand Cortez and Donna Marine, names as unlikely as the figures depicted by the ignorant artist. Between the two glass doors opening out onto the garden was a brass object which needs no further description apart from saying that it served as a perch for a parrot which sat on it with all the gravitas and circumspection common to those little creatures which observe everything. The hard, ironical faces of parrots, their green plumage, red caps, yellow boots and, finally, the hoarse, comical words they enunciate, give them a strange, repulsive appearance in which the serious and the ridiculous are combined. They possess something of the pompous rigidity of diplomats. At times they resemble clowns and they always have something in common with those conceited people who, because of their desire to appear superior, descend into caricature.

The Father Confessor was very friendly with the parrot. When he left Rosario and her mother in conversation with the traveller, he went up to the parrot and, letting it chew on his index finger, said:

'You rascal, you rogue, why don't you say something? You wouldn't be worth much if you weren't a chatterbox. The world of both men and birds is full of chatterboxes.'

Then, with his own venerable hand, he picked up some chickpeas from the little dish and fed them to the parrot. The creature began calling to the maid, demanding chocolate, and his words distracted the ladies and the gentleman from a conversation which could not have been all that important.

CHAPTER 6

*Where we see that differences of opinion can
occur when least expected*

Suddenly Don Cayetano Polentinos, Doña Perfecta's brother-in-law, came in, his arms open wide, saying:
'Come here, my dear Don José!'
And they embraced cordially. Don Cayetano and Pepe were acquainted because the erudite and distinguished bibliophile made frequent visits to Madrid when it was announced that some book collector had died and that his estate was to be auctioned off. Don Cayetano was tall and thin, of middling years, although either a lifetime of study or ill-health had aged him. He expressed himself with a complicated correctness which was very becoming to him and he was kind and affectionate, if at times excessively so. On the subject of his vast knowledge, what can one say except that it was prodigious? In Madrid his name was never pronounced other than with respect, and if Don Cayetano had resided in the capital he would not have been able to avoid being a member of all the academies which exist and are still to come into existence, despite his modesty. But he enjoyed tranquil isolation, and that part of the soul which in others is occupied by vanity, in Don Cayetano's case was occupied by a pure passion for books, a love of solitary and quiet study with no incentive other than his love of books and study for its own sake.

He had gathered together in Orbajosa one of the best stocked libraries to be found throughout the length and breadth of Spain, and he spent long hours there, day and night, compiling, classifying, making notes and extracting precious snippets of information, or involved in some work of the type nobody had ever heard of or dreamed about before, but which was worthy of such a great mind. His habits were patriarchal: he ate little, drank less and his only foolhardiness consisted in taking a picnic at Los Alamillos on very special days and in going for daily walks to a place called Mundogrande where, after lying in the mud for twenty centuries, Roman medals, architrave stones, strange plinths of unknown architectural style, possibly an amphora or night-light of inestimable value, were often unearthed.

Don Cayetano and Doña Perfecta lived in a state of harmony which was beyond comparison even with the peace which reigned in Paradise. They never argued. It is true that he never interfered, for any reason whatsoever, in domestic affairs, just as she never became involved in the running of the library except to have it swept and cleaned every Saturday. And she always respected with religious admiration the books and papers in use at any given time which lay on his desk and elsewhere in the room.

After some questions and answers which were suitable for the occasion, Don Cayetano said:

'I have already looked at the box. What a pity you couldn't bring me the 1527 edition. I'll have to make a journey to Madrid myself . . . Will you be here long? The longer, the better, Pepe, my boy. How pleased I am to see you here! We can sort out part of my library together and compile an index of authors on the civet cat. It's not often one comes across a man with your talent . . . You will see my library . . . you can read to your heart's delight in there . . . anything you wish. You'll find wonderful things in there, real marvels, priceless treasures and rare items which only I possess and nobody else . . . But I think it's time to eat, isn't it, Rosarito? Is that not so, Don Inocencio? . . . Today you're Father Confessor twice over. I say that because you're going to accompany us in a penance.'

The canon bowed and, smiling, displayed his kind acquiescence. The meal was a cordial affair and all the dishes displayed that disproportionate abundance of country feasts which is achieved at the expense of variety, and there was enough to satisfy twice the number of people present. The conversation ranged over a variety of topics.

'You must visit our cathedral as soon as you can,' said the clergyman. 'There are few to equal it, Don José . . . But the truth is that you who have seen so many wonderful things abroad will see nothing remarkable in our old church . . . We, the poor yokels of Orbajosa, think it is divine. Master López de Berganza, its prebendary in the sixteenth century, called it the *pulchra augustina* . . . nevertheless, for a learned man like yourself it perhaps has no merit and any market built of iron would be more beautiful.'

The sarcastic remarks of the shrewd canon were becoming increasingly objectionable to Pepe Rey, but, determined to contain and disguise his anger, he limited himself to non-committal responses. Doña Perfecta immediately joined in the conversation, and said jovially:

'Take care, Pepito. I warn you that if you speak ill of our holy church you and I will fall out. You're a very know-ledgeable and eminent man with an understanding of every-thing. But if it turns out for you that that great building is not the eighth wonder of the world, keep your discovery to yourself and leave us alone with our ignorance.'

'Far from believing that the building is not beautiful,' replied Pepe, 'the little of its exterior which I've seen is, in my opinion, of imposing beauty. So there's nothing for you to be afraid of, Aunt. I'm no sage, not by a long chalk.'

'Steady on,' said the canon, showing the palm of his hand and giving his jaws a rest from chewing for the short time he was speaking. 'Stop there: don't come here pretending to be modest, Señor Don José, we've heard all about your marvel-lous talents, about the great fame you enjoy and the import-ant role you always play wherever you happen to be. Men like you are rather thin on the ground. But now that I've extolled your merits . . .'

He paused in order to resume his meal and, as soon as his tongue was free again, said:

'Now that I've extolled your merits, allow me to express another opinion with the frankness which is in keeping with my character. Yes, Señor Don José and yes, Don Cayetano; yes, madam and yes, my child; science, as it is studied and taught by modern thinkers, is the death of sentiment and sweet illusions. It brings about a withering of the spirit; everything is reduced to fixed rules and the sublime enchantments of Nature vanish. With science all that is marvellous in the arts is destroyed, as is the belief in the soul. Science says that everything is a lie and seeks to reduce everything to figures and lines, not only the *maria ac terras*, where we are, but also the *coelumque profundum*, where God is. The captivating dreams of the soul, its mystical capacity for enchantment, the very inspiration of poets, are all lies. The heart is a sponge and the brain a maggot farm . . .'

Everyone burst out laughing while he took a sip of wine.

'Come, now, Señor Don José, do you deny,' added the priest, 'that science, as it is studied and taught today, is heading straight towards a conversion of the world and the human race into one vast machine?'

'That all depends,' said Don Cayetano. 'All things have their pros and cons.'

'Help yourself to more salad, Father,' said Doña Perfecta. 'It's smothered in mustard, just the way you like it.'

Pepe Rey did not enjoy becoming embroiled in futile arguments. He was not a pedant and did not make great shows of learning, especially in the presence of ladies or at intimate gatherings. But he felt that the inopportune, aggressive verbosity of the canon demanded correction. But this would not be achieved, he thought, by expressing ideas which accorded with those of the priest and which the latter would therefore find flattering, so he decided to give vent to opinions which would contradict and irritate the scathing Father Confessor.

'Think you can entertain yourself at my expense, do you?'

he said to himself. 'You're about to find out that I can give you a hard time.'

And then he said aloud:

'Everything that the Father Confessor has said in jest is certainly true. But it is not our fault that false idols, superstition, sophistry, the thousand lies from the past (some beautiful and some ridiculous) are being destroyed by the hammer blows of science every day; everything grows in the vineyard of the Lord. The world of illusions, which is, if you like, a second world, is coming down with a crash. Mysticism in religion, routine in science, mannerism in the arts, are all falling about us in the same way that the pagan gods fell, surrounded by laughter. Farewell, incongruous dreams, humanity is awakening and sees with clear eyes. Vain sentimentalism, mysticism, fever, hallucination and delirium are disappearing. He who was sick yesterday is today healed and enjoying with unspeakable pleasure a proper appreciation of things. Fantasy, that terrible madness, which used to be the mistress of the house, is now becoming the servant . . . Look around you, Father, and you will see the wonderful totality of reality which has taken over from the fable. The sky isn't a vault, the stars aren't little lanterns, the moon is not a wayward huntress, but a hunk of opaque rock. The sun is no vagabond coachman in a resplendent livery, but a ball of fire in a fixed position. The sandbanks are not nymphs but two sunken reefs, the sirens are seals and in the world of humans, Mercury is Manzanedo; Mars is an old, sparse-bearded Count de Moltke; Nestor could be one of those gentlemen in a gabardine coat called Thiers; Orpheus is Verdi, Vulcan is Krupp, Apollo is any poet. Should I go on? Well, Jupiter, a god who would deserve to be in gaol if he were still around, does not send down flashes of lightning. Lightning occurs when electricity causes it. There is no Parnassus, no Olympus; there is no river Styx and the only Elysian Fields are in Paris. There are no depths of hell other than those familiar to geologists, and anyone who has been down there tells us that there are no condemned souls at the centre of the earth. All ascents into heaven are achieved by astronomy, which informs us that it has never detected the six or seven levels of paradise mentioned by Dante or the mystics and dreamers of the Middle Ages. Nothing is found there except asteroids, distances, straight lines, the vastness of space and nothing else. There are no more inaccurate estimates of the age of the earth because paleontologists and students of prehistory have counted the teeth of this skull in which we exist and have calculated its exact age. The fable, call it paganism or Christian idealism if you will, doesn't exist any more and imagination is awaiting its coffin. All possible miracles are reduced to those which I perform in my laboratory, whenever I please, with a Bunsen burner, a piece of wire and a magnetized needle. There are no more miracles involving loaves and fishes apart from those performed by industry with moulds and machinery, or the miracle of printing, which imitates nature by producing millions of copies from one text. In sum, my dear Father Confessor, redundancy notices have been issued for all those absurdities, falsehoods, illusions, daydreams, all that mawkishness and the preoccupations which cloud Man's understanding. Let us rejoice that this has happened.'

When Pepe Rey finished speaking, a faint smile appeared on the canon's lips and his eyes acquired an extraordinary animation. Don Cayetano fidgeted with a piece of bread, making odd rhomboid then prism shapes from it. But Doña Perfecta had turned pale and fixed her eyes on the priest, observing him intensely. Rosarito stared at her cousin in amazement. He leaned towards her and slyly whispered:

'Don't pay any attention to me, cousin. I said all this nonsense just to rile the priest.'

CHAPTER 7

The difference of opinion increases

'I suppose you think,' said Doña Perfecta, with a hint of vanity in her voice, 'that Don Inocencio is going to remain silent and not reply to each and every one of the points you have just made.'

'I certainly am not!' exclaimed the canon, arching his eyebrows. 'I have no intention of measuring my inferior strength against that of such a champion who is both valiant and has such an armoury to back him up. Señor Don José knows everything. That is to say that he has at his disposal the whole arsenal of exact sciences. I know very well that the doctrine he expounds is based on a false premise, but I have neither the talent nor the eloquence with which to confront him. I shall use the weapons of sentiment; I shall use the arguments of theology, drawn from revelation, from faith and from the Divine Word. But, I'm afraid that Señor Don José, who is an eminent sage, would laugh at theology, faith, revelation, the holy prophets and the Gospels . . . A poor, ignorant priest, a wretch who knows nothing of mathematics or German philosophy which talks of the Ego and Non-ego, a poor teacher who knows only the science of God and a little of the Latin poets, could not hope to do battle with these brave champions.'

Pepe Rey burst into spontaneous laughter.

'I can see,' he said, 'that Don Inocencio has taken all this nonsense of mine to heart . . . Come, now, Father, let's bury the hatchet and say no more about it. I'm certain that my real convictions are not so far removed from your own. You are a pious and educated man. I'm the ignorant one here. If I had a little joke with you, then please forgive me, all of you. It's just my nature.'

'Thank you,' replied the priest, visibly upset. 'Trying to get out of it now, are we? I know only too well, and we all do, that these are your ideas. And it couldn't be otherwise. You are a man of the century. There is no denying that your knowledge is prodigious, truly prodigious. While you were speaking, and I confess it openly, I could not help admiring the sublimity of your powers of expression, your undeniable eloquence, your astoundingly methodical reasoning and the power of your arguments . . . What brains, Señora Doña Perfecta! What a head this young nephew of yours has on his shoulders! When I was in Madrid I was taken to the Atheneum and I confess that I was engrossed by the astonishing ingenuity which God had bestowed on the atheists and Protestants.'

'Señor Don Inocencio,' said Doña Perfecta, looking alternately at her nephew and her friend, 'I think that you have exceeded the bounds of benevolence in judging this boy . . . Don't be angry, Pepe, and don't pay any attention to what I say, because I am neither a sage nor a philosopher nor a theologian; but it seems to me that Don Inocencio has just demonstrated his modesty and Christian charity by refraining from crushing you, as he could have done, had he had a mind to . . .'

'For Heaven's sake, Señora!' said the priest.

'That's the sort of man he is,' added Doña Perfecta. 'Always pretending that butter wouldn't melt in his mouth . . . And he has more wisdom than the three wise men. Oh, Señor Don Inocencio, how apt is the name that you bear! But there is no place here for your humility. My nephew has no pretensions . . . If he knows nothing more than he has been taught . . . If what he has learned is all a mistake, what more could he ask for but that you should point this out to him and rescue him from the hell of false doctrine?'

'Precisely, I could ask you for nothing more than to be

saved by the Father Confessor . . .' murmured Pepe, realizing
that he had unintentionally walked into a labyrinth.

'And I am a poor priest who knows nothing but ancient
science,' answered Don Inocencio. 'I recognize Don José's
immense, worldly, scientific value, and I prostrate myself
before such a brilliant oracle and have nothing to say.'

So saying, the canon folded his arms across his chest and
bowed his head. Pepe Rey was just a little perturbed by the
way in which his aunt had twisted a silly argument, begun
in jest and in which he had taken part merely to liven up the
conversation, so it seemed to him that the most prudent
thing to do would be to terminate such a dangerous dis-
course. He therefore asked Don Cayetano a question when
he saw him waking up from the hazy stupor which always
overcame him after the sweet course, and was offering the
diners the indispensable toothpicks in a little porcelain dish
shaped like a peacock with its tail fanned out.

'Yesterday I came across a hand grasping the handle of an
amphora which had several hieroglyphics on it. I must show
it to you,' said Don Cayetano, glad of the opportunity to
introduce a topic of his pleasing.

'I suppose Señor de Rey is also a great expert in matters
of archaeology,' said the canon, still relentlessly pursuing his
victim into his most hidden refuge.

'Of course,' said Doña Perfecta. 'What does the modern,
well-informed younger generation not know about? They
have all the sciences at their fingertips. The universities and
academies teach them everything in a flash and confer on
them diplomas testifying to their wisdom.'

'Oh, that's unjust!' replied the canon, who had noticed
the pained expression on the engineer's face.

'My aunt's right,' replied Pepe. 'Today we learn a little
about everything and come out of school with a rudimentary
knowledge of different disciplines.'

'I was saying,' continued the canon, 'that you must be a
great archaeologist.'

'I know absolutely nothing about that science,' the young

man replied. 'Ruins are ruins and I have never derived any pleasure from covering myself in dust among them.'

Don Cayetano grimaced.

'But that is not to condemn archaeology,' Doña Perfecta's nephew said quickly, becoming painfully aware that every time he opened his mouth he offended someone. 'I know full well that history emerges from underneath the dust. Such studies have their value and their uses.'

'You,' said the Father Confessor, poking his last molar with a toothpick, 'must be more inclined towards controversial subjects of study. I've just had a wonderful idea. Señor Don José, you should become a lawyer.'

'The legal profession is one which I detest,' Pepe Rey replied. 'I know some very respectable lawyers, amongst whom I include my father, the best of men. But despite such a fine example, I would never enter a profession which involves defending both the pros and cons of an argument. I can think of no greater error, blindness or cause for concern than the manner in which some families persist in pushing our best young people into the law. The most serious and terrible plague rampaging through Spain at the present time is the horde of young lawyers who depend on an unconscionable number of lawsuits to provide them with a living. Disputes increase in proportion to the demand. Even so, a great many of them are unemployed and, as a man qualified in the law is unsuited to taking up the plough or sitting at the loom, we have this brilliant army of layabouts, full of their own importance, seeking public office, rocking the political boat, influencing opinion and stirring up revolutions. They must eat somehow and it would be even worse if everybody got involved in litigation.'

'For heaven's sake, Pepe, have a care with what you say,' said Doña Perfecta in a noticeably severe tone. 'Please excuse him, Señor Don Inocencio ... he doesn't know that you have a nephew who, although straight out of university, is a promising lawyer.'

'I'm speaking in general terms,' Pepe declared firmly.

'Being as I am the son of a famous lawyer I cannot deny that there are some people who perform the duties of this profession with real distinction.'

'No . . . my nephew is still a child,' said the canon in tones of feigned humility. 'Nothing could be further from my mind than to state that he is an academic prodigy like Señor de Rey. In time, who knows? . . . He is neither brilliantly nor seductively talented. Of course, Jacintito's ideas are sound and he has very good judgement, but what he knows he knows thoroughly. He knows nothing of sophistry and hollow words . . .'

Pepe Rey was growing more and more uneasy. The knowledge that he was unintentionally contradicting the convictions of his aunt's friends mortified him and he decided not to say anything more for fear that he and Don Inocencio might end up throwing the dinner plates at each other. Fortunately the cathedral bell, summoning the priest to important choir work, saved him from a difficult situation. The venerable gentleman stood up and took his leave of everyone, addressing Pepe in such a flattering and friendly manner that one might have thought that a strong and intimate bond of friendship had long existed between them. The canon offered to help him in any way he could and then promised to introduce him to his nephew so that the latter could show him the town. He then spoke to him in the most affectionate terms and even patted him on the shoulder as he went out. Pepe Rey gladly received these conventional expressions of reconciliation, and felt that the atmosphere had cleared when the priest walked out of the dining room and left the house.

CHAPTER 8

At full speed

A little while later the scene had changed. Don Cayetano, relaxing after his sublime duties, was lost in blissful slumber as he sat slumped in an armchair in the dining room, and Doña Perfecta was walking about the house attending to her chores. Rosarito, sitting next to one of the windows giving onto the garden, looked at her cousin and spoke to him with the silent eloquence of her eyes.

'Sit here, cousin, next to me, and tell me all that you have to tell me.'

The latter, although a mathematician, understood.

'My dear cousin,' he said, 'how bored you must have been today by our argument! God knows that I had no intention of pontificating like that, but the priest drove me to it. You know, I think that priest is a bit odd.'

'He's an excellent man!' replied Rosarito, exhibiting the joy she felt at being in a position to give her cousin all the information and details he might need.

'Oh, of course, an excellent person. Anyone can see that!'

'When you get to know him better, you'll see . . .'

'That he's priceless. After all, it's sufficient that he's a friend of both you and your mother for him to be my friend also,' the young man said. 'Does he come here often?'

'Every single day. He spends a lot of time with us,' replied Rosarito ingenuously. 'How kind and good he is! And he's very fond of me.'

'I am beginning to take to this man.'

'He also comes in the evenings to play cards,' the young

lady added. 'Several people gather here in the early evening: the magistrate, the public prosecutor, the dean, the bishop's secretary, the mayor, the inspector of taxes and Don Inocencio's nephew . . .'

'Ah! Jacintito, the lawyer.'

'That's right. He's a poor boy, but worth his weight in gold. His uncle adores him. Since he came down from university with his Doctorate (he has doctorates from a couple of faculties, and with distinctions, too. What do you think of that?) . . . Well, since he came down his uncle has been bringing him here often. Mother likes him very much, too. He's a bit on the formal side, and he goes to bed at the same time as his uncle. He never goes to the Club in the evenings, he doesn't gamble or squander his money and he works in the law firm of Don Lorenzo Ruiz, the most important lawyer in Orbajosa. They say that Jacintito will make a fine barrister.'

'His uncle was not exaggerating when he praised him,' said Pepe. 'I very much regret having said those stupid things about lawyers . . . My dear cousin, I spoke out of place, didn't I?'

'Not at all. I think you were quite right.'

'But don't you think I was a bit . . .?'

'Certainly not.'

'What a load off my mind that is! The truth is that I just found myself arguing constantly and painfully with the venerable priest, but I can't give a reason why. I regret it very much.'

'What I think,' said Rosarito, looking tenderly straight into his eyes, 'is that you don't really fit in here.'

'What do you mean by that?'

'I don't know if I'm expressing myself very well, cousin. What I mean is that you won't find it easy to get used to what people say or how they think in Orbajosa. That's how it seems to me . . . but I'm only supposing.'

'Oh, no! I think you're wrong.'

'You're not from here, you're from another world where

people are very clever, very knowledgeable and have refined manners and clever ways of expressing themselves, a style . . . Perhaps I'm not explaining myself well. I want to say that you are used to living among the elite. You know a lot . . . You won't find what you need here; there are no educated people here, nor people with refined manners. People here are very simple, Pepe. I think that you will be bored, very bored, and in the end you will have to go away.'

The sadness which was the normal expression on Rosario's face now became so marked that Pepe Rey felt himself deeply moved.

'You're making a mistake, dear cousin. I have not come here with the preconceptions you have in mind, and my character and understanding are not all that much out of keeping with the people here or their opinions. But let's suppose for a moment that that were the case.'

'Let's.'

'If that were the case I am of the firm belief that between you and me, dear Rosario, perfect harmony could be established. I cannot be wrong about that. My heart tells me that I could not deceive myself.'

Rosarito blushed and in a effort to hide her blushes with smiles and glances directed anywhere but at him said,

'Don't try to sweet-talk me. If you're saying those things just because I always find that I approve of everything you say, you're right.'

'Rosario,' exclaimed the young man. 'From the moment I saw you I've had feelings of happiness deep down inside . . . but at the same time I've felt sadness for not having come to Orbajosa earlier.'

'I can't believe that for one moment,' she said, feigning joviality in order to partially hide her emotions. 'So soon? . . . You shouldn't say such things . . . Look, Pepe. I'm a country girl and I only know how to speak about ordinary, everyday matters. I don't speak French, I am not an elegant dresser and I can hardly play anything on the piano, I . . .'

'Oh, Rosario!' exclaimed the young man ardently. 'I wasn't sure if you were perfect, but now I know that you are.'

Suddenly the mother came in. Rosarito, who did not know how to reply to the last words spoken by her cousin, knew, all the same, that she had to say something, and looking at her mother, said:

'Oh! I forgot to put the food out for the parrot.'

'Don't bother with that now. Why are you both in here? Take your cousin for a stroll around the garden.'

Doña Perfecta was smiling with maternal kindness as she pointed out to her nephew a leafy grove which could be seen from the window.

'Let's go,' said Pepe, standing up.

Rosario shot over to the window like a bird which had just been set free.

'As Pepe is so knowledgeable, he must know all about trees,' said Doña Perfecta. 'He'll explain to you how grafting is done. And let's hear what he thinks about the pear tree saplings which are going to be transplanted.'

'Come on, come on,' said Rosarito from the garden.

She called to her cousin impatiently and they both disappeared into the foliage. Doña Perfecta watched them move further away and then saw to the parrot. While she was refilling its food dish she said in a whisper and with a pensive gesture:

'What a cold character he is! He didn't even stroke the birdie!'

Then, speaking aloud, thinking that her brother-in-law might be able to overhear her, she said:

'Cayetano, what do you think of my nephew ... Cayetano!'

A muffled groan indicated that the antiquarian was returning to consciousness of this miserable world.

'Cayetano ...'

'All right, all right ...' murmured the sage in a sluggish tone of voice, 'that young gentleman probably believes mis-

takenly, like everybody else, that the statues of Mundogrande date back to the first Phoenician invasion. I'll show
him . . .'

'But Cayetano . . .'

'But Perfecta . . . Bah! Now you'll be telling me that I fell
asleep.'

'No, I won't. Why should I say anything as foolish as
that? But tell me, what is your opinion of this young man?'

Don Cayetano placed his hand in front of his mouth so
that he could yawn more comfortably, then entered into a
long conversation with Doña Perfecta. The people who
provided us with the details necessary for the composition of
this story passed over this dialogue because, no doubt, it was
of too intimate a nature. With regard to what the engineer
and Rosario discussed in the garden that evening, it seems
obvious that it is not worthy of mention.

During the evening of the following day events occurred
which certainly cannot be passed over in silence since they
were so important. The cousins found themselves alone, at a
rather advanced hour of the afternoon, after conversing in
different parts of the garden, engrossed in each other's
company and wishing for nothing more than to gaze into
each other's eyes and listen to what each had to say.

'Pepe,' said Rosario, 'everything you have said to me is
pure fantasy, one of those yarns clever men like you know
how to spin so well. You think that I believe whatever
anyone says to me just because I'm a country girl.'

'If you knew me as I think I know you, you would
understand that I never say anything I don't feel. But let's
drop this silly repartee and lovers' banter as they only lead
to a distortion of feelings. I'll speak nothing but the truth to
you. Are you perhaps some young lady I met during a
saunter or at some social gathering and with whom I think I
can spend an entertaining few moments? No. You are my
cousin. You are more than that . . . Rosario, let's sort things
out once and for all. No more beating about the bush. I
came here to marry you.'

Rosario felt her face burn as her heart beat faster and faster.

'Look, dear cousin,' added the young man, 'I swear that if I'd not taken a liking to you I'd be miles away from here by now. Courtesy and good manners would have obliged me to make an effort, but it would not have been easy for me to hide my disappointment. That's the kind of man I am.'

'Cousin, you've barely arrived here,' Rosario said laconically, trying not to laugh.

'I've only just arrived and already I know all I need to know. I know that I love you and that you're the woman my heart has been telling me about, day and night, for some time now ... "Now she's coming, she's getting nearer, you're on fire." '

This last phrase gave Rosario the excuse she needed to release the laughter cavorting on her lips. Her jubilant soul seemed to evaporate in an atmosphere of bliss.

'You persist with this idea that you're a nonentity,' Pepe continued, 'but you're wonderful. You possess that admirable ability to constantly shed the divine light of your soul on your surroundings. From the moment anyone sets eyes on you, from the very first glance, your noble sentiments and the purity of your heart are evident. To look at you is to see a little bit of Heaven left on earth by an oversight of the Lord. You're an angel and I'm madly in love with you.'

It was as if, by saying these things, he had accomplished an important mission. Rosario was suddenly overcome by such powerful feelings that her limited natural stamina could not cope with the excitement her soul was experiencing. She felt faint and slumped down onto a stone which often served as a seat in that pleasant spot. Pepe bent over her and saw that her eyes were closed and that she was supporting her head with the palm of her hand. A short time later the daughter of Doña Perfecta Polentinos, with sweet tears in her eyes, looked tenderly at her cousin and uttered the following words:

'I've been in love with you since before I met you.'

Taking hold of the young man's hands she rose to her feet and then they both disappeared among the leafy branches of an avenue of oleanders. Dusk was falling and a soft shadow was creeping over the far end of the garden, while the last rays of the setting sun bathed the tree tops in a crown of resplendent colours. The noisy republic of birds clamoured in a cacophony of rejoicing among the uppermost branches. They had flitted through the happy immensity of the sky and now, when it was time for them to retire for the night, they were squabbling among themselves over which branches to sleep on. Their chatter seemed at times like recrimination and argument and at others like joking and relaxed banter. With their noisy chirping the little rascals hurled insolent remarks at each other and pecked each other, flapping their wings like orators who wave their arms about as they attempt to make people believe the lies they are telling. But words of love, so appropriate to the peaceful hour and the beautiful setting, could also be heard. A sharp ear might have been able to distinguish the following:

'I've been in love with you since before I met you, and if you hadn't come here I'd have died from grief. Mother let me read your father's letters and they contained so many words of praise for you that I said to myself, "This is the man I must marry." For a long time your father didn't talk of our marrying and this seemed to me to be a grave oversight. I didn't know what to think of such negligence . . . Cayetano, my uncle, used to say, whenever he heard your name mentioned, "Men like him are very thin on the ground. The woman who nets him can consider herself lucky." Eventually your father said what he could no longer stop himself from saying; no, he couldn't help saying what I'd been hoping to hear every day . . .'

Soon after these words had been spoken, the same voice said in an alarmed tone:

'We're being followed.'

Coming out from among the oleanders, Pepe saw two people approaching and, as he fingered the leaves of a tender young sapling growing there, said to his companion:

'It's not a good idea to prune trees as young as this one until their roots are well established. Newly planted trees are not strong enough to withstand the operation. I'm sure you know that the roots are only formed under the influence of the leaves, so if you remove the leaves . . .'

'Ah, Don José,' exclaimed the Father Confessor, laughing spontaneously, greeting the two young people as he drew near to them. 'Are you giving a lesson in horticulture? *Insere nunc, Meliboee piros, pone ordine vites*, as the great poet of work in the fields said. "Graft your pear trees, my dear Meliboeus, see to your vines . . ." And so, how are you, Don José?'

The engineer and the canon shook hands. Then the latter turned round and, signalling to a young lad who was following him, said smiling:

'I have the pleasure to present to you my dear Jacintillo . . . a good sort even if he is a scatterbrain, Señor Don José.'

CHAPTER 9

The differences of opinion continue to increase and threaten to develop into discord

A fresh, rosy-complexioned face stood out next to the black cassock. Jacintito greeted our young man, but not without a certain degree of self-consciousness.

He was one of those precocious young men despatched prematurely by lenient universities into life's bitter struggles, convincing them that they are men just because they are in possession of a doctorate. Jacintito had a delicate, chubby face, with rosy cheeks, like a girl's. He was a bit on the plump side, shortish if not small in stature, with no more of a beard than the soft down which precedes a real one. He was just over twenty years of age and had been educated since childhood under the tutelage of his excellent and discreet uncle, which is the same as saying that the tender sapling grew fine and straight. A strict moral code had kept him on the straight and narrow, and in the performance of his academic studies he scarcely faltered. He finished his university course with flying colours, as there was not a single class in which he did not gain excellent marks. When he embarked on his career he showed every promise of keeping the laurels he had won in the classroom fresh and green, such was his diligence and talent for the law. At times he could behave like a naughty little boy and at others he could behave correctly like an adult. In fact, if Jacintito had not been more than just slightly attracted to pretty girls, his good uncle would have believed him to be perfect. His uncle never ceased to lecture him at every opportunity, striving as he did to clip his audacious wings. But not even those worldly urges experienced by the young man succeeded in cooling the great love which the good canon felt for the charming offspring of his dear niece, María Remedios. In his dealings with the young lawyer he was totally indulgent and even his solemn, methodically observed routine would be altered at the drop of a hat if some matter arose involving his precocious pupil. His rigorous habits, which were as fixed as any planetary system, would be knocked off balance if Jacintito was ill or had to undertake some journey. So much for the celibacy of the clergy! If the Council of Trent forbids them to have children, God, not the devil, gives them nephews and nieces so that they might savour the sweet delights of parenthood.

When the hardworking youth's qualities were considered impartially, it was impossible not to recognize his worth. Generally speaking he was inclined to be honourable, and high-minded conduct awakened admiration in his soul. As for his intellectual ability and social graces, he possessed all the necessary attributes to become, in time, one of those notables who so abound in Spain: he could be what we are often pleased to call a *distinguished patrician* or an *eminent public figure*, types which, because there are so many of them, are scarcely appreciated for their true worth. At that tender age when a university degree serves to weld childhood to manhood, few young people, particularly when they have been mollycoddled by their teachers, are free of that irritating pendantry which, if it makes them seem more important in their mothers' eyes, gives rise to laughter among sensible, grown men. Jacintito had this defect, excusable not only because of his youth, but because his well-meaning uncle encouraged his childish vanity with imprudent applause.

After the four of them had met up with one another they continued on their walk. Jacintito said nothing. The priest, returning to their interrupted conversation about the *piros*[1] and *vites*[2] which have to be seen to, said:

'I have no doubt that Don José knows a great deal about farming.'

'Not at all; I don't know the first thing about it,' replied the young man, annoyed at encountering this mania for supposing that he was versed in all the sciences.

'Oh, yes. A great agronomist,' the Father Confessor continued, 'but in matters of agriculture, please don't quote me any of these new-fangled theories. As far as I'm concerned, Señor de Rey, everything you need to know about the subject is contained in what we call the *Bible of the Countryside*, that is to say the *Georgics* of the immortal Roman. It is wholly admirable, starting with that great sentence, *nec vero terrae ferre omnes omnia possunt*, that is to say that not all soil is suitable for all trees, Señor Don José. And it goes on to deal in detail with bees, when the poet explains everything about these clever little creatures and defines the drone as:

Ille horridus alter
desidia, latamque trahens inglorius alvum,

that is to say, a horrid, lazy creature which drags its heavy ignoble belly, Señor Don José . . .'

'I'm glad you translated it for me,' said Pepe, 'because I know very little Latin.'

'Oh, this modern generation! How could the young possibly derive any enjoyment from studying that old rubbish?' the canon added sarcastically. 'Moreover, only weaklings like Virgil, Cicero and Livy wrote in Latin. I, however, support the other point of view and my nephew, to whom I have taught the sublime language, can be my witness. The rascal knows more than I do. The problem is that he is forgetting it now with all the modern things he reads, but

[1] pears
[2] vines

one fine day he'll come face to face with his own ignorance
without even having suspected it. Because, Señor Don José,
my nephew has taken to entertaining himself with reading
new-fangled books with extravagant theories. Flammarion
explains everything in heaven and earth and to cap it all he
says that the stars are inhabited. Come now, I have a feeling
that you two are going to get on well together. Jacinto, ask
this gentleman to instruct you in the wonders of mathematics
and all about the German philosophers, it'll make a man of
you.'

The good priest was laughing at his own witticisms, while
Jacinto, happy to see the conversation turn to an area which
was so much to his taste, begged Pepe Rey's pardon and
then quite out of the blue, fired the following question at
him:

'Tell me, Don José, what is your opinion of Darwinism?'

Our young man smiled when he heard such inopportune
pedantry and would gladly have encouraged the young man
along the path of childish vanity. But he considered it wiser
not to get too closely involved with either the nephew or the
uncle, and answered simply:

'I am not in a position to hold any opinions on Darwin's
theories since I know very little about them. My professional
duties don't allow me much time for studying them.'

'Well,' said the priest, laughing, 'it can be summed up by
saying that we're all descended from monkeys . . . if he was
just talking about a few people I know, he would be right.'

'The theory of natural selection,' added Jacinto emphatically, 'is supposed to have a lot of adherents in Germany.'

'I don't doubt it,' said the priest. 'In Germany they won't
be sorry if this theory is true as far as Bismarck is concerned.'

Doña Perfecta and Don Cayetano appeared in front of the
four.

'What a beautiful evening it is!' said Doña Perfecta. 'How
are you, nephew? You're not too bored . . .?'

'Certainly not,' answered the young man.

'Don't deny it. Cayetano and I have just been saying you

must be. You are bored and you're trying hard to hide it. Not all young people today are willing to sacrifice their youth, like Jacinto, in a town without a Theatre Royal, music-hall, ballerinas, philosophers, clubs, trite newspapers, congresses or other diversions and pastimes.'

'I'm very happy here,' replied Pepe. 'I've just been telling Rosario that I like this city and this house very much and that I'd like to live and die here.'

Rosario blushed and the others remained silent. They all sat down in the arbour and Jacinto rushed to seat himself to the left of Rosario.

'Listen, nephew, I have to warn you of one thing,' said Doña Perfecta, with that smiling expression of kindness which emanated from her soul, like the bouquet from a flower. 'But don't run away with the idea that I am reproaching you or am trying to teach you a lesson. You're not a child and you will easily understand what I mean.'

'Scold me, dear Aunt, as there can be no doubt that I deserve it,' replied Pepe, already beginning to get used to the kind ways of his father's sister.

'No, this is nothing more than a warning. And these gentlemen will see that I am right.'

Rosarito was listening with her very soul.

'It's just that,' Doña Perfecta continued, 'when you visit our beautiful cathedral again I would like you to behave with a little more devotion.'

'But what have I done?'

'I'm not surprised that you don't even recognize your own mistake,' Doña Perfecta said with apparent joviality. 'It's only natural. You're used to frequenting such places as the Atheneum, clubs and academies and attending congresses, where you feel completely at ease and so you think that you can enter a temple of His Divine Majesty with the same nonchalant manner.'

'But, Señora, forgive me,' said Pepe in a serious tone of voice, 'I conducted myself with great decorum in the cathedral.'

'I'm not telling you off, my boy, I'm not telling you off. Don't take it like that otherwise I'll have to remain silent. Gentlemen, please forgive my nephew. We mustn't be shocked by a minor oversight, a moment's loss of concentration . . . How long is it since you set foot in a place of worship?'

'Señora, I swear to you . . . But, after all, it makes no difference what my religious convictions are, I am in the habit of always behaving correctly inside a church.'

'But I assure you . . . come now, if you're going to take offence I'll say no more . . . But I assure you that many people noticed it this morning. Señor and Señora Gonzáles, Doña Robustiana, Serafinita . . . they all noticed it. And I must tell you that you attracted the bishop's attention. His Grace complained to me this afternoon in my cousins' house. He told me that he didn't have you thrown out because people told him that you're my nephew.'

Rosario looked anxiously at her cousin's face, trying to guess in advance the answer he would give.

'They must have confused me with someone else.'

'No . . . no. It was you . . . But don't be offended. We're all friends here and we can confide in each other. It was you. I saw you myself.'

'You did?'

'Precisely. Do you deny that you set about examining the paintings as you passed through a group of worshippers who were listening to mass? . . . I swear I was so distracted by you to-ing and fro-ing that . . . Come now . . . you mustn't do it again. Then you went into the chapel of Saint Gregory where they were elevating the Host at the high altar and you didn't even turn round to make some gesture of religious devotion. Then you walked the whole length of the church, approached the Provincial Governor's tomb and placed your hands on the altar. After that you walked through the group of the faithful again, attracting attention. The girls were all looking at you and you seemed very pleased that you had made such a good job of disturbing the devotion and exemplary conduct of those good people.'

'My God! I did do all that!' exclaimed Pepe, half in anger, half smiling. 'I'm a monster and didn't even suspect it!'

'No: I know perfectly well that you're a good boy,' said Doña Perfecta, noticing the look of affected and unaltered severity on the canon's face, which looked more like a cardboard mask. 'But, my boy, it's one thing to think a thing and quite another to reveal it in such an arrogant manner. There is a line over which a prudent and moderate man should never cross. I'm well aware that your ideas are . . . don't be angry; if you get angry I won't say another word. What I mean to say is that it's one thing to hold religious convictions, but another to express them . . . I will not allow myself to condemn you for perhaps not believing that God created us in His image and likeness, but believing instead that we are descended from monkeys; nor because you may deny the existence of the soul, assuring us that it's a drug like the magnesium and rhubarb wrapped in little pieces of paper which they sell in chemists' shops . . .'

'Señora, for Heaven's sake . . .' exclaimed Pepe, showing his displeasure. 'I can see that I have a very bad reputation in Orbajosa.'

The others continued to say nothing.

'Well, as I was saying, I'm not going to condemn you for those ideas . . . Apart from the fact that I have no right to, if I got into an argument with you, you with your unusual talent, would be able to tie me up in knots . . . No, nothing of the kind. But what I will say is that the poor, unfortunate inhabitants of Orbajosa are pious and good Christians, even if none of them knows anything about German philosophy, so you must not belittle their beliefs publicly.'

'Dear Aunt,' the engineer said gravely, 'I have not belittled anyone's beliefs and I don't hold those beliefs which you attribute to me. I may have been a little disrespectful in church because I can be absent-minded. My thoughts and concentration were fixed on the architecture and, to be honest, I didn't notice . . . But that is no reason why the bishop should want to have me thrown out or for you to suppose me capable of attributing the functions of the soul to a chemist's concoction. I can take all this as a joke, but not if is meant as anything more than a joke.'

Pepe Rey could feel his emotions getting the better of him and, in spite of his prudence and moderation, could not hide the fact.

'Come now, I can see that you're getting angry,' said Doña Perfecta, lowering her eyes and crossing her hands. 'Let's leave it there. If I had known that you would take it like this I would not have said anything. Pepe, please forgive me.'

When he heard this and saw his kind aunt's submissive attitude, Pepe felt ashamed at the harshness of his words and tried to calm down. He was helped out of his embarrassing situation by the venerable Father Confessor who, smiling his usual benevolent smile, said:

'Señora Doña Perfecta, one must be tolerant with artists . . . Oh! I have known many of them. These gentlemen, if they see before them a statue, a rusty suit of armour, a mouldy old picture or an ancient wall, forget about everything else. Señor Don José is an artist and he visited our cathedral the way the English visit it who would gladly carry off the last of its flagstones to one of their museums. You say that the faithful were praying, that the priest was elevating the Sacred Host and that he arrived at the moment of greatest piety and devotion . . . so what? Of what importance is any of this to an artist? It's true that I know nothing of the value of art once it's separated from the feelings it's supposed to express . . . but, after all, today the fashion is to admire the form and not the idea. God save me from getting into an argument on this theme with Señor Don José. He is so knowledgeable and, with the neat subtlety of his modern reasoning, he would straightaway confuse my mind, which knows only faith.'

'The insistence of everyone here to consider me as the

wisest man in the world is a source of great embarrassment to me,' said Pepe, regaining a certain aggression in his voice. 'Take me for a fool, for I'd rather be called an idiot than possess the satanic knowledge which is attributed to me here.'

Rosarito began to laugh and Jacinto thought that an opportune moment had arrived for him to show off his erudition.

'Pantheism and panentheism are condemned by the Church, as are the doctrines of Schopenhauer and the modern Hartmann.'

'Ladies and gentlemen,' said the canon in a serious voice, 'men who so fervently make a cult of art deserve the greatest respect, even though they only pay attention to form. Far better to be an artist and to delight in beauty, even if it is only represented in naked nymphs, than to be indifferent and to believe in nothing. A mind dedicated to the contemplation of beauty cannot be all bad. *Est Deus in nobis . . . Deus*,[1] you understand. So let Don José continue to admire the wonders of our church and for my part, I shall willingly forgive his acts of irreverence, with all due respect to the bishop's opinion.'

'Thank you, Don Inocencio,' said Pepe feeling inside him a gnawing and rebellious sense of hostility towards the astute canon, and unable to control the need to rile him. 'And what's more, you needn't think that my attention was gripped by those artistic gems which are supposed to fill the church. Apart from the imposing architecture of one part of the main church building and that of the three sepulchres in the chapels in the apse, plus a few of the carvings in the choir, I don't see any beauty anywhere. What caught my attention was the deplorable decadence of religious art and I was not astonished but angered by the innumerable artistic monstrosities crammed into the cathedral.'

The others were stunned beyond belief.

[1] God is within us . . . God

'I cannot endure,' Pepe went on, 'those varnished, vermilion images which, and may God excuse the comparison, look just like the dolls upper-class little girls play with. And what can I say about the theatrical garb they're dressed in? I saw Saint Joseph in a cloak the appearance of which I wouldn't like to describe out of respect for the saintly patriarch and the church which adores him. The altars are piled high with images in the most appalling artistic taste and the stack of crowns, palm branches, stars, moons and other adornments made out of metal or gilt paper all add up to what looks like an ironmonger's shop. It is such an affront to religious sentiment and has such a depressing effect on the soul. Far from being elevated to religious contemplation, it sinks and is disturbed by a sense of the ridiculous. Great works of art, giving tangible form to ideas, dogmas, faith and mystical exaltation, fulfil a noble mission. Coarseness and perversions of taste, the grotesque forms with which poorly understood piety fills our churches also achieve their desired aim, but it is an unhappy one: they foment superstition, chill enthusiasm, and oblige the faithful to avert their gaze. But as they avert their gaze they also turn their souls away because they lack a profound, secure faith.'

'The doctrine of the iconoclasts,' said Jacintito, 'also seems to have spread far and wide in Germany.'

'I'm no iconoclast, although I'd prefer the destruction of all images to the coarse parodies which I'm concerned with,' said the young man. 'When one sees all this it's not unreasonable to uphold the idea that religion should regain some of the sombre simplicity of the ancient temples. But no: it's not necessary to do away with the admirable assistance that all art, beginning with poetry and finishing with music, lends to the relationship between Man and God. Long live the arts and let pomp be displayed in religious rites. I'm all for pomp . . .'

'An artist, an artist, nothing but an artist,' exclaimed the canon, shaking his head ruefully. 'Fine pictures, fine statues, fine music . . . a feast for the senses and the soul can go to hell.'

'And on the subject of music,' said Pepe Rey, taking no heed of the dreadful effect his words were having on mother and daughter, 'imagine how my soul was prepared for religious devotion during my visit to the cathedral when, out of the blue, when it came to the offertory at High Mass, the organist struck up a passage from *La Traviata*.'

'Señor de Rey is right,' said the little lawyer emphatically. 'Only the other day the same organist played the toast scene and the waltz from the same opera, and finished off with a rondo from *La Gran Duquesa*.

'But what really made my heart sink,' said the engineer implacably, 'was when I saw an image of the Virgin which was obviously the object of great veneration, to judge from the number of people in front of her and the great many candles which illumined her. They had dressed her in such a strange-looking, fluffed-up velvet garment embroidered with gold that it outshone the most extravagant fashions of the day. Her face was buried beneath a dense mass of innumerable types of lace which had been curled with crimping tongs, and her crown, over eighteen inches high, and surrounded by golden laurel leaves, resembled a misshapen catafalque which had been erected on her head. The Infant Jesus's breeches were of the same embroidered material . . . I won't go on because my description of the Mother and Child may cause me to be guilty of yet more irreverent remarks. I'll say no more, other than that it was impossible for me to contain my laughter and that I contemplated the profane image for a brief moment, thinking: "Holy Mother, what have they done to you?" '

As he finished speaking, Pepe observed his audience, and although their faces could not be seen clearly because of the evening shadows, he thought that he detected in them signs of bitter consternation.

'Well, Señor Don José,' the canon replied promptly, laughing and with an expression of triumph on his face, 'the image which seems so ridiculous to your philosophy and pantheism is that of Our Lady of Perpetual Succour, the patroness and protectress of Orbajosa, whose inhabitants venerate her so much that they would not be beyond dragging anyone who spoke ill of her through the streets. Our history and chronicles, my dear sir, are full of the miracles she has performed, and even today we are constantly presented with irrefutable proof of her protection. You must also be aware that your aunt, Doña Perfecta, is the chief handmaiden of Our Lady of Perpetual Succour, and that the clothing which seems so grotesque to you . . . well . . . I repeat, the clothing which appears so grotesque in your faithless eyes, came from this very house. And the Infant's breeches are the result of the marvellous needlework and pure faith of your cousin Rosarito, who is standing here listening to us.'

Pepe Rey was quite disconcerted. At that moment Doña Perfecta suddenly stood up and, without saying a word, walked back to the house, followed by the Father Confessor. The others also rose to their feet. The astonished young man was on the point of asking his cousin to forgive his irreverence, when he noticed that Rosario was crying. Staring at her cousin with a look of friendly and sweet reproach, she exclaimed:

'What strange notions you have!'

Doña Perfecta's agitated voice could be heard calling out: 'Rosario! Rosario!'

And the girl ran indoors.

CHAPTER 10

The discord is obvious

Pepe Rey felt disturbed, embarrassed and angry with the others and with himself as he tried to ascertain the reasons for the quarrel which, in spite of himself, had taken place because of the differences between his ideas and those of his aunt's friends. Pensive and sad, and seeing only discord ahead, he remained seated in the summer-house for a while with his chin resting on his chest, his brow furrowed and his hands crossed. He thought he was alone.

Then suddenly he heard the joyous sound of someone singing a refrain from an operetta. He looked up and saw Don Jacinto in the opposite corner of the summer-house.

'Ah, Señor de Rey,' said the youth suddenly, 'you cannot offend the religious beliefs of the overwhelming majority of the nation with impunity . . . if you don't believe me, just think about what happened during the first French revolution . . .'

When Pepe heard the buzzing of this insect he became even more irritated. However, he felt no malice in his heart for the young know-all. He found him a nuisance, as flies are a nuisance; nothing more. Pepe experienced that sense of annoyance which is aroused by all bothersome people and he replied like somebody shooing away a bee:

'What's the French revolution got to do with the Virgin Mary's cloak?'

He stood up and set off towards the house, but he had not gone four paces when he heard the buzzing insect again, saying:

'Señor Don José: I have to speak to you about a matter which you'll find very interesting and which may cause you some trouble . . .'

'A matter?' the young man asked, retracing his steps. 'Let's hear it, then.'

'You've perhaps already had an inkling of it,' said Jacinto, moving closer to Pepe and smiling in the way that business-men do when they are dealing with a difficult customer. 'I wish to talk to you about the lawsuit.'

'What lawsuit? . . . My friend, I don't have any lawsuits. You, as a good lawyer, dream of court cases and see fiscal papers everywhere.'

'What? But surely . . . Haven't you received notification about the lawsuit?' the boy asked in astonishment.

'My lawsuit! . . . Absolutely not. I am not involved in any lawsuits and never have been.'

'Well, if you haven't been notified then I'm glad to be able to warn you so that you can prepare yourself . . . Yes, sir, you're about to become involved in litigation.'

'With whom?'

'With Old Licurgo, and others with land adjoining the area known as Los Alamillos.'

Pepe Rey was dumbfounded.

'Yes, sir,' the young lawyer went on. 'Señor Licurgo and I had a long talk today and, as I'm such a friend of the family, I wanted to be sure to warn you so that, if you wish, you can get things sorted out quickly.'

'But what is there for me to sort out? What does the rogue want from me?'

'It seems that a stream with its source on your land has changed course and is now running onto the tile factory belonging to the aforementioned Licurgo and onto the mill belonging to another party. It has caused considerable dam-age. My client (who insists that I sort this problem out for him), my client, as I say, demands that you restore the stream to its former course in order to avoid further damage and that you indemnify him against the damage he has suffered through the negligence of the proprietor of the land upstream.'

'And I am the proprietor of the land upstream! . . . If I enter into litigation it will be the first fruit the famous Alamillos will have yielded during my whole life. These lands were mine but now, as I understand it, they belong to everyone, because this same Licurgo, together with other peasants in the region, has been nibbling away at my land, year after year, and it'll cost me a fortune to re-establish the boundaries.'

'That's another question.'

'It isn't another question. The point is,' said the engineer, no longer able to contain his anger, 'that I'm the one who should be entering a lawsuit against this rabble who are trying no doubt to frustrate me and make me give up hope so that I'll abandon everything and leave them to their ill-gotten gains. We'll see if there are any lawyers or judges who will go along with the clumsy machinations of these country lawyers who make a living out of lawsuits and are like woodworm to other people's property. Young sir, I thank you for warning me about the dreadful plans of these bumpkins who are worse than Cacus. If I tell you that the very tile factory and mill upon which Licurgo is basing his claim belong to me . . .'

'There will have to be a search of the property deeds to determine if the right of peaceful possession applies in this case,' said Jacintito.

'What do you mean by "possession"! . . . These rogues aren't going to make a fool out of me. I assume that the Department of Justice in the town of Orbajosa is honourable and above-board.'

'Oh, there's no doubt about that!' exclaimed the young scholar in tones of admiration. 'The judge is an excellent man. He comes here every night . . . But it's odd that you've not been informed of Señor Licurgo's claims. Hasn't the Arbitration Tribunal summoned you yet?'

'No.'

'It will do tomorrow . . . In short, I'm very sorry that
Señor Licurgo's haste has denied me the pleasure and honour
of acting in your defence, but what has to be has to be.
Licurgo has made up his mind that he wants me to get him
out of the quandary he finds himself in. I'll go through the
details with a fine-tooth comb. These petty domestic cases
are the bane of the legal profession.'

Pepe entered the dining room feeling very dejected. He
saw that Doña Perfecta was in conversation with the Father
Confessor and that Rosario was standing by herself, her eyes
riveted on the door. No doubt she was waiting for her
cousin.

'Come here, you prize specimen,' said Doña Perfecta,
smiling with forced spontaneity. 'You have offended us, you
great atheist, but we forgive you. I know that my daughter
and I are yokels incapable of venturing into the realm of
mathematics where you live. But, in brief . . . it is still
possible that one day you may kneel down before us and
beg us to instruct you in Christian doctrine.'

Pepe answered in vague, conventional expressions of
regret.

'For my part,' said Don Inocencio, as his eyes acquired an
expression of modesty and sweetness, 'if in the course of
these vain arguments I have said something to offend Don
José, then I beg his forgiveness. We are all friends here.'

'Thank you. There's no need . . .'

'In spite of everything,' said Doña Perfecta, now smiling
with greater sincerity, 'I am still just as fond of my dear
nephew, despite his extravagant and irreligious ideas . . .
And what do you suppose I have in mind to do this evening?
Well, I'm going to get Old Licurgo to forget these stubborn
notions he's pestering you with. I've told him to come here
and he's waiting for me in the corridor now. Don't worry,
I'll sort everything out, even though I know he's not entirely
in the wrong . . .'

'Thank you, Aunt,' replied the young man as he felt

himself engulfed by the profound generosity which flowed so effortlessly from his soul.

Pepe Rey directed his gaze to where his cousin stood and fully intended to join her; but a few of the canon's well-timed questions kept him at Doña Perfecta's side. Rosario was feeling sad as she listened with melancholy indifference to the words of the young lawyer who had planted himself next to her and was regaling her with his soggy theories, interspersed with inappropriate jokes and silly remarks in very bad taste.

'The bad news for you,' Doña Perfecta said to her nephew when she caught him observing the ill-matched pair, Rosario and Jacinto, 'is that you have offended poor Rosario. You'll have to do everything you can to make it up to her. The poor girl is so sweet!'

'Oh, yes, of course, she is so sweet,' added the canon, 'that I'm sure she will forgive her cousin.'

'I believe Rosario has already forgiven me,' asserted Rey.

'And if not, resentment does not last long in angelic hearts,' Don Inocencio said mellifluously. 'I have considerable influence over the girl and I'll attempt to rid her generous soul of any prejudice against you. It won't take more than a couple of words from me . . .'

Pepe Rey felt a cloud pass over his thoughts and he said pointedly:

'Perhaps that will not be necessary.'

'I won't say anything to her just at the moment,' added the canon, 'she's spellbound by young Jacinto's nonsense . . . The young are such imps and once they start nattering away there's no stopping them!'

The magistrate suddenly joined the gathering, together with the mayor's wife and the cathedral dean. They all greeted the engineer, their words and manner revealing that the meeting satisfied an intense curiosity. The judge was a youngish man with his wits about him, one of those who appear every day in the incubators of eminent people and

who, once hatched, aspire to the leading positions in administration and politics. He assumed an air of importance and,
when he spoke of himself and his recently acquired robes,
seemed angry that he had not been elevated to the rank of
President of the Supreme Court immediately. To those inex-
pert hands, that brain puffed up with wind and that ridicu-
lously presumptuous manner the State had entrusted the
most delicate and difficult functions of human jurisprudence.
He behaved like the perfect courtier and in all matters
concerning himself he revealed scrupulous attention to detail.
He possessed the irritating mannerism of constantly putting
on and taking off his gold-rimmed spectacles and he punc-
tuated his conversation with frequent references to his wish
to be transferred to *Madrith*, so that he might offer his
indispensable services to the Justice Department.

The mayor's wife was a kind-hearted lady whose only
weakness was that she had convinced herself that she had
good connections at Court. She asked Pepe several questions
about fashions, mentioning fashion houses where she had
had a shawl or a skirt made up during her most recent trip
which coincided with that of Muley-Abbas, and also mentioned a dozen or so duchesses and marchionesses, speaking
of them with the same familiarity as when speaking of her
old school friends. She said that the Countess of M. (famous
for her salons) was her friend and that she had visited her in
1860, when the countess had invited her to her box in the
Theatre Royal where she had seen Muley-Abbas in Moorish
dress and accompanied by his Moorish entourage. The
mayor's wife talked the hind leg off a donkey, as they say,
and was never at a loss for a witty remark.

The dean was getting on in years, overweight and red-
faced, full of life and apoplectic; he was a man who seemed
to bulge out of his own skin because he was so fat and
fleshy. He was a product of the trimming of the monastic
orders. He spoke only on religious matters and treated Pepe
Rey with the greatest disdain from the moment he met him.
The latter revealed himself as being increasingly inept at

adapting to a society which was so little to his taste. He had a firm, inflexible and unbending nature and he rejected the perfidy of spoken compromise which emulated harmony where none existed. During the course of the irksome salon he maintained an air of gravitas as he was obliged to endure the oratorical flow of the mayor's wife whose claim to fame was that, although not the Gossip of the fables, she was capable of exhausting the human ear and making it feel as if it has been lashed by a hundred tongues. If, during the brief respite which this lady allowed her listeners, Pepe Rey wished to join his cousin, the Confessor attached himself to him like a mollusc to a rock and, drawing him to one side with a conspiratorial gesture, would suggest a trip out to Mundogrande with Don Cayetano, or a fishing trip in the limpid waters of the Nahara.

At last it came to an end, as everything comes to an end in this world. The dean took his leave, making the house seem empty, and very soon afterwards nothing remained of the mayor's wife but an echo, similar to the buzzing noise which remains in the ear after a recent thunderstorm. The judge also absented himself from the salon and then, finally, Don Inocencio signalled to his nephew that it was time to leave.

'Come, my boy, it's late,' he said to him, smiling. 'How you've made poor Rosario's head spin! . . . Is that not so, young lady? . . . Come on, you young scamp, it's time for home.'

'It's time for bed,' said Doña Perfecta.

'Time for work,' answered the young lawyer.

'No matter how much I tell him to get his work done in the day, he pays no attention,' added the canon.

'But there's so much work to do . . . so much!'

'No there isn't. It's that fiendish work you've got involved in off your own bat . . . He doesn't want to mention it, Don José, but he has set himself the task of writing a book on *"The influence of women in Christian society"* and another entitled *"A glance at the catholic movement in . . ."* I don't

know where. What do you know of "glances" and "influences"? ... The young of today have nerve enough for
anything ... Bah! ... These young men ... Anyway, let's
go home. Goodnight, Don José ... Rosarito.'

'I'll wait for Don Cayetano,' said Jacinto, 'then he can let
me have his "*Augusto Nicolas*".'

'Always lugging books around! Sometimes when you
come home you look like a donkey. All right, then, let's
wait.'

'Señor Don Jacinto,' said Pepe Rey, 'takes his writing
seriously and is already showing his ability for producing
masterpieces of erudition.'

'But the boy will damage his brain, Don Inocencio,'
objected Doña Perfecta. 'For Heaven's sake, take good care
of him. I would limit his reading if I were you.'

'Since we're waiting,' said the young doctor of law in a
supercilious tone, 'I'll take the third volume of *The Vatican
Councils*. Isn't that a good idea, Uncle?'

'Why, yes, of course. Don't let an opportunity like this
slip through your hands.'

Fortunately Don Cayetano, who was a frequent visitor to
the Lorenzo Ruiz household, soon showed up and, when the
books had been handed over, the uncle and nephew took
their leave.

Pepe Rey detected in his cousin's sad face an urgent desire
to talk to him. He walked over to her while Doña Perfecta
and Don Cayetano were engaged in a tête-à-tête discussing a
domestic matter.

'You have offended my mother,' Rosario said to him.

Her features betrayed a certain fear.

'That's true,' replied the young man. 'I've offended your
mother, I've offended you . . .'

'No. You haven't offended me. I had already come to the
conclusion that the Infant Jesus should not be wearing
breeches.'

'But I hope that you will both be able to forgive me. Your
mother was so kind to me just a short while ago . . .'

Doña Perfecta's voice suddenly reverberated so stridently around the dining room that her nephew started as if he had heard a cry of alarm. The voice said imperiously:

'Rosario, go to bed!'

Shocked and pained, Rosario walked several times around the room as she pretended to look for something. As she passed close to her cousin and taking care not to be overheard, she murmured:

'Mother is angry . . .'

'But . . .'

'She's angry . . .; watch your step, watch your step.'

And she walked away. She was followed by Doña Perfecta, for whom Old Licurgo was waiting, and for a while the voice of the lady and the peasant could be heard as the two engaged in a private conversation. Pepe remained alone with Don Cayetano who, lifting up a lamp, said:

'Goodnight, Pepe. Don't think that I'm off to bed. I'm going to work. But why are you so pensive? What's the matter with you? . . . Right, yes, off to work. I'm making notes for a study I'm doing on *Orbajosan Genealogies*. I've found a lot of very interesting and useful information; absolutely no doubt about it. Throughout our whole history the people of Orbajosa have distinguished themselves with their sense of honour, their nobility, their valour and their high-mindedness. All this is borne out by the Conquest of Mexico, the wars of the Emperor and Philip's wars against the heretics . . . But, do you feel all right? What's the matter? . . . yes, eminent theologians, brave soldiers, *Conquistadores*, saints, bishops, poets, politicians and all sorts of illustrious men have flourished in this humble land of garlic . . . No; in the whole of Christendom there is no more illustrious town than our own. The whole of Spanish history is filled with her virtue and glory, with plenty to spare. Come now, I can see that you're feeling sleepy. Goodnight . . . Oh, no, I wouldn't change the glory of being a son of this noble land for all the gold in the world. *August* it was called by the ancients; *Most august* I call it now because now, as then, a sense of honour, generosity, valour and nobility are her heritage . . . Anyway, goodnight, Pepe my boy . . . I have the feeling that all is not well with you . . . Did dinner not agree with you? . . . Alonso González de Bustamante was right when he said in his *Floresta amena* that the inhabitants of Orbajosa could bestow greatness and honour on any kingdom. Don't you agree?'

'Oh, yes, sir, without a shadow of a doubt,' replied Pepe Rey, walking off abruptly towards his room.

CHAPTER II

The discord increases

Over the following days Pepe Rey made the acquaintance of several people in the village and visited the Club where he made friends with one or two of the habitués of that institution.

But the youth of Orbajosa did not spend all its time there, as malicious rumour may suggest. In the afternoons certain gentlemen, dashingly draped in their cloaks, could be seen near the Cathedral corner and on the little square at the junction of the Calle del Condestable and the Calle de la Tripería, like guards watching the people walk past. If the weather was fine these leading lights of Orbajosan culture, in their indispensable cloaks, would head for the promenade known as the Descalzas, formed from two rows of consumptive elms and a few faded broom bushes. There the dazzling Pleiad ogled the daughters of all and sundry, also out for a stroll, and so the afternoon would follow its normal course. When night fell, the Club would fill up again and, while some of the members concentrated their attention on the card tables, others would read the newspapers and yet others would sit in the coffee-room and discuss a wide variety of topics such as politics, horses, bulls and local gossip. The conclusion arrived at in all debates was always the supremacy of Orbajosa and its inhabitants over the rest of humanity.

These notable gentlemen were the cream of society in that illustrious town; some were rich landowners, others were very poor but all were totally lacking in lofty ambition. They possessed the imperturbable serenity of the beggar who asks for nothing so long as he has a stale crust to allay starvation and the bright sun to keep him warm. The Orbajosans who gathered in the Club were distinguished mainly by their antipathy to all outside influences. And if a distinguished stranger crossed the threshold of their august chambers, they believed he had come with the express purpose of casting doubt on the superiority of the 'garlic homeland' or, out of jealousy, to dispute the incontrovertible pre-eminence bestowed upon it by Nature.

When Pepe Rey appeared he was received with a certain amount of suspicion and, as the Club was awash with keen wits, all sorts of jokes had been cracked about the new member before he had been there a quarter of an hour. When he answered the members' repeated questions about his purpose in coming to Orbajosa by saying that he had been commissioned to examine the coal seams of the Nahara and the feasibility of constructing a road, everyone came to the conclusion that Don José was a fool who wanted to make himself look important by dreaming up coal deposits and railway lines. One of them added:

'But he's come to the wrong place. These clever gentlemen think that we're all idiots here and that they can pull the wool over our eyes with their big words . . . He's come to marry Doña Perfecta's daughter and anything he says about coal deposits is just an act.'

'And just this morning,' said another, a bankrupt business-man, 'they told me at the Domínguez house that this gentle-man hasn't a penny to his name and that he has come here to see if his aunt will support him and to land Rosarito at the same time.'

'I don't think he's an engineer or anything else of any importance,' added an olive grower who had mortgaged his estates for twice their value. 'It's as clear as day . . . these people who go hungry in Madrid think they have the right to pull a fast one on us provincials and think we walk round in loinclothes . . .'

'Everyone knows he's hungry.'

'Half in jest and half seriously he told us last night that we were lazy savages.'

'That we lived like Bedouins, taking the sun.'

'That we're living in a dream world.'

'That's right: living in a dream world.'

'And that there's no difference between this town and those in Morocco.'

'That's the last straw. Where could he have seen (unless it was in Paris) a street like Calle del Condestable, with seven houses in a row, all magnificent, from Doña Perfecta's to Nicolasita Hernández's? ... These bounders think that nobody else has ever seen anything or been to Paris ...'

'He also said with great finesse that Orbajosa is a town of beggars and implied that we live here in abject penury without even realizing it.'

'Heavens above! If he'd said that to me there would have been a scandal in the Club,' said the tax collector. 'Why did nobody tell him how many gallons of olive oil Orbajosa produced last year? Does the idiot not realize that in a good year Orbajosa provides bread for the whole of Spain and even for the whole of Europe? It's true that we've had bad harvests for God knows how many years; but that's not the norm. And what about the garlic harvest? I'll bet this gentleman doesn't know that garlic from Orbajosa left the judges at the London Exhibition speechless.'

Such were the exchanges which could be heard those days in the Club. In spite of such chatter, common enough in small towns where pride is in indirect proportion to the town's size, Pepe Rey did make some sincere friends among the learned society since not everyone was a scandalmonger or lacking in good sense. But young Rey was unfortunate enough, if unfortunate is the right word, to express his opinions with consummate frankness, and this attracted the antipathy of some of the inhabitants.

The days passed. In addition to the natural displeasure which the customs of that episcopal society aroused in him, various feelings of unease began to develop a deep sadness in his soul, the main cause of which was the pitiless swarm of lawsuits which engulfed him. And it was not only Old Licurgo. There were many other neighbours clamouring for damages or claiming reparations or demanding to see the accounts of lands administered by his grandfather. They also presented him with a claim for some sort of crop-sharing contract that his mother had signed but which apparently had not been adhered to. They also demanded recognition of a mortgage on the Alamillos estate, drawn up by his uncle in a manner which did not comply with the usual format. It was all a disgusting maggot-bed of lawsuits. He had thought of renouncing his ownership of the estates but in the meantime his sense of pride obliged him not to surrender to the machinations of the devious bumpkins; and as the Town Hall had also issued a claim against him for alleged encroachment of his lands onto those belonging to the town, the unfortunate young man found himself having to deal with new problems concerning his rights at every turn. His honour was at stake and he was forced to choose between litigation or death.

Doña Perfecta had magnanimously promised to help him extricate himself from his awkward situation by arranging an amicable compromise, but the days passed and the exemplary lady's good offices brought no result. The lawsuits increased in number with the frightening speed of a virulent illness. Pepe Rey spent long hours every day in the Law Court making statements and answering question after question, and when he returned home, tired and bad-tempered, he could see in his mind's eye the elongated, grotesque face of the notary who presented him with a constant stream of official documents couched in dreadful legal language . . . so that he could continue studying the matter.

Obviously Pepe Rey was not the kind of man who would deliberately put up with such setbacks if he could avoid them by absence. In his imagination he began to see his mother's noble city transformed into a horrible beast which had sunk its ferocious claws into him and was drinking his blood. He came to the conclusion that flight would be the only means of escape. But a deep, heart-felt interest held him back, lashed firmly to the rock of martyrdom. Nevertheless, he came to feel so out of place and to consider himself a foreigner (if we can put it like that) in that dismal city of lawsuits, outmoded customs, envy and malice, that he resolved to leave without delay, but at the same time clung to the original project which had brought him there.

One morning, deciding that the moment was the right one, he informed Doña Perfecta of his plan:

'Nephew,' replied the latter with her customary sweetness, 'don't be so impulsive. Goodness, you're like a fire! Your father was just the same; what a man! And you're like a flash of lightning . . . I've already told you that I'd gladly call you my son. Even if you didn't possess those fine qualities and talent which you do have (despite one or two shortcomings); even if you weren't an excellent young man, it is sufficient that this union was suggested by your father, to whom my daughter and I owe so much, for me to agree to it. And Rosario will not be opposed to it if it is my wish. So what else do we need? Nothing. Only a little time. We cannot go ahead with the marriage as quickly as you would wish as it might lead to somewhat unfortunate comments concerning my beloved daughter's honour. You think of nothing but machinery so you think that you can drive everything by steam. Be patient, my boy, be patient . . . What's your hurry? This dislike you have of Orbajosa is merely a passing whim. Evidently you can only live surrounded by counts, marquises, orators and diplomats. You want to get married and take my daughter from me for ever,' she added, as she wiped away a tear. 'And since that is the case, you inconsiderate young man, at least have the decency to delay this marriage which you so earnestly desire for a short time . . . Such impatience! Such ardour! I never dreamed that a poor country girl like my daughter could arouse such volcanic passion!'

Pepe Rey was not swayed by his aunt's arguments, but he did not want to annoy her. He therefore decided to wait for as long as possible. A new source of irritation soon joined those which were making his life miserable. He had been in Orbajosa for two weeks and during that time had not received a single letter from his father. He could not place the blame for this on the inefficiency of the Orbajosa postal service because the official in charge was a friend and protégé of Doña Perfecta, and she cautioned him every day to make sure that any letters addressed to her nephew should not go astray. Furthermore, the man who delivered the mail, a certain Cristóbal Ramos, nicknamed Caballuco, whom we have already met, came to the house every day and Doña Perfecta regularly admonished and reprimanded him in the following stern manner:

'A fine postal service you run! ... How is it that my nephew has not received a single letter all the time he has been in Orbajosa? ... What's the world coming to when the mail is entrusted to a dunderhead like you! I'll speak to the Provincial Governor and get him to consider carefully what kind of administrators he recruits.'

Caballuco, shrugging his shoulders, looked at Pepe Rey with the greatest indifference.

One day he entered carrying a wad of documents.

'Thank God!' Doña Perfecta said to her nephew. 'Here are your father's letters. I hope you're pleased now. What a fright we had because of my brother's laziness in writing ... What does he say? He's well, to be sure,' she added, seeing that Pepe Rey was opening the wad of documents with feverish impatience.

The engineer grew pale as he cast his eyes over the first lines.

'My God, Pepe, what's the matter?' exclaimed Doña Perfecta, standing up and showing signs of alarm. 'Is your father ill?'

'This letter is not from my father,' replied Pepe, abject consternation written all over his face.

'What is it, then?'

'It's an order from the Ministry of Public Works withdrawing a contract they had awarded me.'

'What? . . . Can they do that?'

'They've given me the sack, pure and simple, and in terms which are very unflattering to me.'

'Have you ever heard of anything so disgraceful?' exclaimed Doña Perfecta, emerging from her state of shock.

'How humiliating!' murmured the young man. 'It's the first time in my life I've been snubbed like this.'

'This government is just unforgivable! Fancy snubbing you like that! Do you want me to write to Madrid? I have very good connections there and could arrange for the government to correct this terrible mistake to your satisfaction.'

'Thank you, Señora, but I don't need recommendations,' replied the young man in a rather offhand manner.

'One sees such injustices, such outrages! . . . To dismiss such a capable young man, such an outstanding scientist! It makes me very angry!'

'I'll find out,' Pepe said passionately, 'just who it is who is so concerned to see me ruined . . .'

'That minister . . . but what else can you expect from these devious politicians?'

'There's someone here who is bent on making me die from despair,' said the young man, visibly angry. 'This is not the work of the minister. This and the other setbacks I'm experiencing are the result of some plan of revenge, some underhand plot, an implacable enmity. And whoever is behind this plan, this plot, this enmity is here in Orbajosa. You can be sure of that, Aunt.'

'You've taken leave of your senses,' replied Doña Perfecta, displaying feelings which resembled compassion. 'What enemies have you got in Orbajosa? Are you saying that someone wants to avenge himself on you? Come, now, Pepe, you're not thinking straight. Your brain has been addled by reading those books which say that we're descended from monkeys or parrots.'

She smiled sweetly as she uttered the last sentence and then, admonishing him in a friendly, affectionate tone, she added:

'My boy, we inhabitants of Orbajosa are rustics and rough, uneducated labourers who lack finesse and the social graces. But when it comes to loyalty and faithfulness we are second to none.'

'Do not think,' said the young man, 'that I'm accusing people in this house. But I insist that I have an implacable and ferocious enemy in this town.'

'I'd like you to show me who this traitor out of some melodrama is,' replied Doña Perfecta, smiling again. 'I assume you're not accusing Old Licurgo or any of the others who have issued lawsuits against you. The poor souls are only thinking of defending their rights. And by the way, they're quite justified in the present case. Also, Old Lucas is very fond of you; he's told me so himself. Since he got to know you he's had a soft spot for you.'

'Yes . . . a very soft spot,' murmured Pepe.

'Don't be silly,' Doña Perfecta said, placing her hand on his shoulder and looking at him closely. 'Don't think such foolish things and rest assured that your enemy, if one exists, lives in Madrid, that centre of corruption, envy and rivalries. He is not to be found in this peaceful, quiet corner where everything is sweetness and light . . . It must be somebody who's envious of your abilities . . . I'll just say one thing and that is that if you wish to go there to find out the source of this snub and demand an explanation from the government, don't let us stop you.'

Pepe Rey stared into his aunt's face as if he wanted to penetrate deep into the most hidden parts of her soul.

'I'm saying that if you want to go, don't let us stand in your way,' repeated his aunt with laudable calm and an expression of both frankness and genuine honesty in her face.

'No, Señora. I don't intend to go there.'

'That would be for the best, in my opinion. You're calmer here, despite the notions you're torturing yourself with. Poor

Pepe! Your extraordinary intellect is the cause of all your troubles. We, the people of Orbajosa, are poor rustics but we're happy in our ignorance. I'm very sorry that you're unhappy. But is it my fault if you're bored and agitated for no reason? Don't I treat you as if you were my son? Did I not receive you as my family's hope for the future? Is there something more I can do for you? If, in spite of all this, you do not love us; if you are so indifferent to us, mock our religious beliefs and look down on our friends, is it perhaps because we don't treat you well?'

Doña Perfecta's eyes grew moist.

'My dear Aunt,' said Pepe Rey, feeling his anger ebb away, 'I too have made some mistakes since I have been a guest in your house.'

'Don't be silly . . . What mistakes have you made? Anything can be forgiven among members of the same family.'

'But where's Rosario?' the young man asked, standing up. 'Am I not going to see her today, either?'

'That would be better. Didn't you know that she did not want to come downstairs?'

'I'll go up then.'

'Oh dear me, no. That girl is so stubborn . . . She insists on staying in her room all day and has locked herself in.'

'How strange!'

'It'll pass, that's for sure. We'll see tonight if we can get these silly notions out of her head. We'll organize a party for her entertainment. Why don't you go round to Don Inocencio's place and tell him to come tonight and bring Jacinto with him?'

'Jacinto!'

'Yes. When Rosario has these attacks of melancholy that young man is the only one who can bring her out of them . . .'

'I'll go upstairs . . .'

'Heavens, no.'

'I see that there are certain standards of behaviour in this house.'

'You're making fun of us. Do as I tell you.'

'But I want to see her.'

'Impossible. You don't know the girl very well, do you?'

'I thought I understood her very well . . . All right, then, I'll stay here . . . But this solitude is unbearable.'

'Here comes the notary.'

'The devil take him!'

'And I think the lawyer is with him . . . he's a fine man.'

'I wish they'd hang him!'

'When business matters are one's own they serve as a distraction. Someone else is coming . . . I think it's the expert in agricultural matters. You're going to be busy for some time.'

'Time spent in Hell!'

'Well now, if I'm not mistaken Old Licurgo and Paso Largo have just come in. They might have come to propose some compromise.'

'I'd as soon throw myself in the lake!'

'How heartless you are! They're all very fond of you! . . . Look, here's the constable to complete the picture. He's come to present you with a summons.'

'To crucify me.'

All of these people were walking into the drawing room.

'Goodbye, Pepe. Enjoy yourself,' said Doña Perfecta.

'If only the earth would swallow me up!' said the young man.

'Don José . . .'

'My dear Don José . . .'

'Don José, sir . . .'

'My dear friend Don José . . .'

When he heard these sugary greetings Pepe Rey sighed deeply and succumbed. He surrendered body and soul to his executioners as they brandished their awesome official documents while the victim, raising his eyes towards Heaven, said to himself with Christian meekness:

'My God, my God, why has thou forsaken me?'

CHAPTER 12

This was Troy

Love, friendship, an atmosphere conducive to spiritual well-being, light for the soul, sympathy and a relaxed interchange of ideas and sensations was what Pepe Rey was in greatest need of. In their absence the shadows enveloping his spirit increased and an inner depression lent a bitter and disagreeable tone to his treatment of others. On the day following the scenes described in the previous chapter, he felt especially irked by his cousin's excessively long and mysterious incarceration which, apparently, was partly due to her being slightly unwell, and partly the result of whims and nervous problems which could not easily be explained.

Pepe Rey was surprised by Rosario's behaviour, which was so unlike what he had come to expect from her. He had not seen her for four days, but this was certainly not because he did not wish to be by her side. So the situation was beginning to be humiliating and ridiculous for Pepe Rey and his only remedy lay in decisive action.

'Am I not going to see my cousin today, either?' he asked his aunt in a bad-tempered voice when they had finished dinner.

'No. But God knows how sorry I am about it! I've given her a good talking-to today. We'll see later . . .'

The suspicion that his dear cousin was the helpless victim of unreasonable incarceration and had not brought it upon herself with her own stubborn behaviour, induced him to show restraint and to be patient. Had it not been for his suspicion he would have left Orbajosa that very day. There was absolutely no doubt in his mind that Rosario loved him; but it was obvious that some unknown force was acting on them and trying to separate them. It seemed only fitting that an honourable man should attempt to discover the source of that malign force and resist it to the limit of human will-power.

'I do hope that Rosario's obstinacy will not last much longer,' he said to Doña Perfecta, hiding his real feelings.

On the same day he received a letter from his father in which he complained that he had not received any letters from Orbajosa and this only served to make the engineer feel more suspicious and ill at ease. Finally, after a long stroll alone through the garden of the house, Pepe went off to the Club and entered like a man in a state of desperation about to throw himself into the sea.

In the main rooms he found people chatting and engaged in arguments. In one group they were using subtle logic to analyse some difficult problems connected with bull-fighting while another group was arguing over which were the best donkeys, those of Orbajosa or those of Villahorrenda. Feeling thoroughly fed up, Pepe Rey paid no attention to these debates and walked into the periodicals room where he leafed through a few magazines, unable as he was to derive any pleasure from reading. A short time later he ambled through the rooms and stopped, without realizing why, in the gaming room. For almost two hours he remained in the talons of that terrible, yellow devil whose sparkling, golden eyes are the cause of torment and fascination. Not even the excitement of gambling could alter the despondent condition of his soul and the tedium, which earlier had driven him towards the green table, now pulled him away from it. Fleeing from the crowd he found himself in a room intended for meetings but which was deserted at the moment, and he sat down indolently by the window and looked out into the street.

The street, which was extremely narrow and contained more angles and bends than houses, was completely dominated by the pitted black wall of the awesome cathedral which loomed up at the far end of it. Pepe Rey looked all around, up and down, and observed the peaceful silence of the grave; not a footfall, not a voice, not a glance. Suddenly strange noises, such as whispers from women's lips, assaulted his ears, and this was followed by the rustling of curtains being drawn, a few words being spoken and then, finally, the soft humming of a song, the gentle barking of a lap-dog and other indicators of social existence, all of which sounded extremely strange in such a place. Taking a closer look, Pepe Rey noticed that the noises all emanated from behind the venetian blinds of an enormous balcony right opposite his window. Before Pepe Rey had had time to complete his observations a Club member suddenly appeared at his side, laughing and upbraiding him as follows:

'Aha! Don Pepe! You old rogue! Locked yourself up in here to make eyes at the girls, have you?'

The speaker was Don Tafetán, a likeable man and one of the few in the Club who had befriended Pepe Rey and shown genuine admiration for him. With his ruddy face, his moustache dyed black, his vivacious eyes, his diminutive height, his hair carefully and studiously combed so as to conceal his baldness, Don Juan Tafetán bore little resemblance to Antinoüs. But he was very sociable and witty and had a natural gift for recounting amusing adventures. He laughed a great deal and at such times his whole face, from his forehead right down to his chin, would be covered in grotesque furrows. Despite these qualities and the acclaim which might have made him temperamentally inclined to biting sarcasm, he was not at all malicious. Everybody liked him, and Pepe Rey spent some pleasant moments with him. Poor Tafetán, who had previously been employed in the Civil Administration department in the provincial capital, lived on his modest salary from the Social Welfare Department which he supplemented with his hearty playing of the clarinet in processions, on solemn occasions in the cathedral and in the theatre when a troupe of impoverished actors arrived in that

part of the country with the ridiculous intention of perform-
ing in Orbajosa.

But Don Tafetán's dominant characteristic was his fond-
ness for pretty girls. In the days before he had to disguise his
baldness with six well-pomaded hairs, before he dyed his
handlebar moustache, when he still had a straight-backed,
willowy gait unaffected by the passing of the years, he had
been a formidable Don Juan. He could make people laugh
until they cried with tales of his amorous conquests, for
there are Don Juans and Don Juans and he was one of the
most original.

'What girls? I can't see any girls anywhere,' answered Pepe
Rey.

'That's it. Pretend to be a hermit.'

One of the blinds on the balcony opened, revealing a
charming young and smiling face which instantly vanished
like a light blown out by the wind.

'Now I see.'

'Don't you know them?'

'No, I swear on my life.'

'They're the Troyas, the Troya girls. You've obviously
been missing out on something . . . they're delightful girls
. . . the daughters of a colonel on the General Staff who died
on the streets of Madrid in '54.'

The blind opened again and two faces appeared.

'They're making fun of us,' said Tafetán, giving the girls a
friendly wave.

'Do you know them?'

'Of course I know them. The poor girls are poverty-
stricken and I've no idea how they make ends meet. When
Don Francisco Troya died people were asked to contribute
towards their upkeep, but that didn't last long.'

'Poor girls! I suppose they can't be models of virtue . . .'

'Why not? . . . I don't believe what they say about them in
the town.'

The blind moved again.

'Good evening, girls,' shouted Don Tafetán to the three

girls who had appeared in an artistically arranged group. 'This gentleman says that the good should never be hidden from sight and that you should open the blind wide.'

But the blind closed again and a chorus of happy laughter spread a strange joy along the sad street, as though a flock of birds were passing overhead.

'Shall we go over there?' Tafetán suddenly asked.

There was a twinkle in his eye and a mischievous smile played about his crimson lips.

'But what sort of people are they?'

'Come now, Señor Rey . . . The poor creatures are honourable souls. What? Are they supposed to live on fresh air like chameleons? Tell me, can anyone be a sinner if he's dying of hunger? These poor wretches are virtuous enough. And if they have sinned they have atoned for it by their continuous fasting.'

'Let's go then.'

A moment later Don Juan Tafetán and Pepe Rey entered the building. Pepe was greatly affected by the vision of abject poverty, and the strenuous efforts to conceal it, which confronted him. The three girls were very attractive, particularly the two younger ones who were very pale with dark eyes and slender figures. If they had been well dressed and had decent shoes on their feet they could have passed for the daughters of a duchess and suitable brides for princes.

When the visitors arrived the three girls were overcome with shyness. But their frivolous, bubbly natures soon burst through. They lived in miserable conditions, like birds confined to prison life but still able to sing through the bars as if they were in the midst of a luxuriant forest. They spent their days sewing, thus revealing at least an honest upbringing; but in Orbajosa nobody of their social standing would have anything to do with them. They were, to a certain extent, exiled, degraded and banished from society and this became the basis of idle gossip. But, out of the respect for truth, it has to be said that the Troya sisters' bad reputation rested mainly on their fame as gossips, troublemakers and

naughty, easy-going pranksters. They used to send anony-
mous letters to respected members of the community and
they had a nickname for everybody in Orbajosa, from the
Bishop right down to the meanest layabout. They also threw
pebbles at passers-by and then made hissing noises as they
remained hidden behind the railings and observed the confusion and amazement of the persons walking past. They got
to know everything that was going on in the neighbourhood
by way of their constant use of the fanlights and openings in
the upper part of the house; they sang at night on the
balcony and put on masks in order to gain admission to the
best people's houses during carnival time. And they got up
to all sorts of other tricks which were typical of small towns.
But whatever the reason, there was no getting away from
the fact that the Troya sisters had been branded with that
stigma which, once bestowed by a suspicious neighbourhood, remains with one even beyond the grave.

'Is that the gentleman who people say has come to sink
gold mines?' said one of them.

'And to knock down the cathedral and make a shoe
factory with the stones?' added another.

'And to replace Orbajosa's garlic crop with cotton and
cinnamon?'

Pepe could not contain his laughter when confronted with
such ridiculous suggestions.

'He's only come here to round up some beautiful girls and
take them back with him to Madrid,' said Tafetán.

'Oh, I'd love to go!' exclaimed one of the girls.

'I'll take all three of you,' said Pepe. 'But let's clear one
thing up first. Why were you all laughing at me when you
saw me at the Club window?'

These words were the signal for another round of laughter.

'My sisters are stupid,' said the eldest one.

'We laughed because we said that you deserved something
better than Doña Perfecta's daughter.'

'It was because she said that you were wasting your time

and that Rosario only loved people connected with the Church.'

'The things you say! I never said any such thing! It was you who said that this gentleman was a Lutheran atheist and that he went into the cathedral smoking and wearing his hat.'

'Well, I didn't make it up,' said the youngest. 'Suspiritos told me so yesterday.'

'And who is this Suspiritos who says such dreadful things about me?'

'Suspiritos is . . . Suspiritos.'

'Girls, girls,' said Tafetán with a syrupy smile on his face. 'Here comes the orange seller. Call him, I want to treat you all to some oranges.'

One of them called out to the orange seller.

The conversation the girls had begun was not to Pepe's liking and it banished the slight feeling of contentment he had been experiencing since entering their jolly and convivial company. Nevertheless he could not help laughing when he saw Juan Tafetán take down a guitar and begin to strum it with skill and grace, as if reliving the years of his youth.

'People have told me that you have a marvellous singing voice,' said Pepe Rey.

'Let Juan Tafetán sing.'

'I can't sing.'

'Nor I,' said the second girl, offering the engineer some segments of the orange she had just peeled.

'María Juana, don't neglect your sewing,' said the eldest of the Troya girls. 'It's late and that cassock has to be finished tonight.'

'No work today . . . To hell with the needles!' exclaimed Tafetán.

And with that he began to sing.

'People are stopping in the street,' said the second Troya girl, leaning out over the balcony. 'Don Juan Tafetán's voice can be heard in the square . . . Juana, Juana!'

'What?'

'Suspiritos is walking down the street.'

The youngest girl flew out onto the balcony.

'Throw some orange peel at her.'

Pepe Rey leaned over the balcony too. No sooner had he spotted the lady walking along the street than the youngest of the Troya girls hit her bun with a superbly aimed piece of orange peel. Then they closed the blind quickly and the three almost choked on their laughter as they struggled not to let it be heard in the street below.

'No work today,' one of them said as she kicked her sewing basket over.

'That's the same as saying that we won't eat tomorrow,' said the eldest, gathering up the sewing things.

Pepe Rey instinctively thrust his hand into his pocket as he would gladly have given them some money. The sight of those unfortunate orphans, condemned by the world for their frivolity, saddened him greatly. If the Troyas' only sin and their only means of finding relief from their loneliness, poverty and isolation was to throw pieces of orange peel at passers-by, then he could easily excuse them for it. Perhaps the austere customs of the miserable town they lived in had protected them from vice, but the poor girls lacked breeding and a sense of decorum, the first and most obvious signs of modesty, so that one might have suspected that they had thrown more than just orange peel out of the window. Pepe Rey felt profound pity for them. He observed their tattered clothes which had been repaired, mended and darned in a thousand different ways so that they would look new. He saw their worn-out shoes ... and again his hand moved towards his pocket.

'It's possible that vice does reign here,' he said to himself, 'but their faces, the furniture and everything else suggests to me that these girls are the unfortunate vestiges of a noble family. If these poor girls were as bad as people say they are they would not be living in such dire straits and nor would they be working. There are rich men in Orbajosa!'

The three girls approached him one after the other. They walked from him to the balcony, from the balcony to him as they indulged in a racy, light-hearted conversation which indicated, it has to be said, a sort of innocence in the midst of so much carefree frivolity.

'Señor Don José, what an excellent lady Doña Perfecta is!'

'She's the only person in Orbajosa to whom we haven't given a nickname; the only person in Orbajosa who is not spoken ill of.'

'Everyone respects her.'

'Everyone loves her.'

The young man replied to each of these comments with praises in favour of his aunt. But he still experienced the desire to put his hand in his pocket and say: 'María Juana, take this and buy yourself some boots. Pepa, take this and buy yourself a dress. Florentina, take this so that you can all eat for a week . . .' And he was on the point of putting his thoughts into action. At a moment when the three girls ran out onto the balcony to see who was passing by, Don Juan Tafetán approached him and said in a low voice:

'They're really pretty, aren't they? . . . Poor things! Their happiness just has to be a facade . . . you can be sure they haven't eaten today.'

'Don Juan! Don Juan!' shouted Pepilla. 'Here comes your friend, Nicolas Hernández, or the *Easter Candle* in his three-cornered hat. He's saying prayers quietly to himself, no doubt for the souls of the people he's sent to the grave with his usury.'

'I'll bet you won't call him by his nickname!'

'You want to bet?'

'Juana, close the blind. Let's wait till he's gone past and then, when he reaches the corner, I'll shout *Candle, Easter Candle.*'

Juan Tafetán ran to the balcony.

'Don José, come here and see what this man is like.'

Pepe Rey seized his chance while the three girls and Don Juan were laughing and joking on the balcony and calling out the nickname which made Nicolas Hernández so furious. He cautiously walked over to one of the sewing baskets and placed in it the gold coin which he had left over from his gambling.

Then he ran to the balcony just as the two younger girls were shouting in a fit of uncontrollable laughter: *Easter Candle! Easter Candle!*

CHAPTER 13

A *'casus belli'*

After this little prank the three girls embarked on a lengthy conversation with the men concerning the affairs and personalities of the town. The engineer, suspecting that his ploy would be revealed while he was still there, made up his mind to leave, much to the displeasure of the Troya sisters. One of them, who had been out of the room, came back and said:

'Suspiritos has ventured outside and is hanging up the washing.'

'Don José will want to see her,' said another.

'She's a very pretty lady. And she does her hair in the Madrid style. Come on.'

They took the men through to the dining room (a room which was very rarely used) and out onto the terrace where there were some flower pots and more than a few discarded, broken pieces of junk. The sunken patio of the adjoining house could be seen from here with a passageway full of green vines and lovingly tended pot plants, all of which suggested that the house was owned by humble, meticulous and industrious folk.

The three Troya sisters, moving towards the edge of the flat roof, stared at their neighbours' house and, after telling the men to be quiet, returned to that part of the terrace from which nothing could be seen and there was no danger of being seen.

'She's coming out of the pantry carrying a bowl of peas,' said María Juana, straining her neck to see at least something.

'Bang!' said another, throwing a pebble.

The noise of the projectile could be heard as it struck the window panes of the porch, and then an angry voice exclaimed:

'Now they've gone and broken another pane . . .'

The three girls, hidden in the corner of the terrace, next to the two gentlemen, almost choked as they stifled their laughter.

'Señora Suspiritos is very annoyed,' said Pepe Rey. 'Why do you call her that?'

'Because whenever she speaks she sighs between each word and although she wants for nothing she is always complaining.'

There was a moment of silence in the house below. Pepita Troya maintained careful observation.

'She's coming back,' she murmured in a low voice, telling the others to be quiet. 'María, hand me a pebble. Now let's see . . . Bang! . . . there she goes.'

'You've missed. It landed on the ground.'

'Let me have a go . . . We'll wait for her to come out of the pantry again.'

'Now, she's coming out. Get ready, Florentina.'

'One, two, three . . . fire!'

A cry of pain was heard from below, then a curse in a male voice: it was a man who had been hit by the pebble. Pepe Rey clearly heard the words:

'What the devil! . . . They've put a hole in my head, those . . . Jacinto, Jacinto . . . what kind of rough neighbourhood is this?'

'Jesus, María and Joseph, what have I done?' Florentina exclaimed, full of anguish. 'I've hit Don Inocencio right on the head.'

'The Father Confessor?' said Pepe Rey.

'Yes.'

'Does he live in this house?'

'Of course he does.'

'And Suspiritos, the lady of the sighs?'

'She's his niece or housekeeper or something. We're always having a bit of fun at her expense because she's so nasty. But we're not in the habit of playing jokes on the Father Confessor.'

While this hasty exchange was taking place, Pepe Rey saw a nearby window in the house which was under bombardment open. Pepe Rey saw a smiling face appear, a face which he recognized and which stunned and shocked him and made him turn pale and begin to shake. It was Jacintito who, interrupted in the midst of serious academic work, had opened the window of his study and could now be seen with his pen behind his ear. His modest, fresh, ruddy face made the whole scene look like a breaking dawn.

'Good evening, Don José,' he said in a happy tone of voice.

The voice from below shouted out again:

'Jacinto! Jacinto!'

'I'm coming. I was just saying hello to a friend . . .'

'Let's go, let's go,' shouted Florentina anxiously. 'The Father Confessor is on his way up to *Don Nominavito*'s room and he'll tell us off.'

'Yes, come on. Let's close the dining room door.'

They all moved away from the terrace en masse.

'You should have foreseen that Jacinto would spot you from his temple of wisdom,' said Tafetán.

'*Don Nominavito* is a friend of ours,' one of them replied. 'From his temple of knowledge he frequently whispers sweet nothings to us and blows us kisses.'

'Jacinto?' asked the engineer. 'What devilish nickname have you given him?'

'*Don Nominavito* . . .'

All three burst out laughing.

'We gave him that name because he knows so much.'

'No; because when we were children he was a child, too. When we went out onto the terrace to play we could hear him repeating his lessons aloud.'

'Yes, and he would be singing the whole blessed day.'

'Declining, girl. That's what he was doing, like this: *Nominavito rosa, Genivito, Davito, Acusavito.*'

'I suppose I too have a nickname, then?' asked Pepe Rey.

'Let María Juana tell you what it is,' answered Florentina, hiding herself.

'Me? . . . You tell him, Pepa.'

'You haven't got a nickname yet, Don José.'

'But I will have one and I promise I'll come to find out what it is, to receive confirmation,' said the young man, getting ready to leave.

'Must you go?'

'Yes, I must. You've already wasted enough time. Back to work, girls. Throwing stones at the neighbours and passers-by is not becoming in such worthy and pretty young girls. So long.'

And without waiting for any more excuses or listening to any of the girls' compliments, he rushed out of the house and left Don Juan Tafetán there by himself.

The scene he had just witnessed; the indignity inflicted upon the canon; the inopportune appearance of the young scholar, increased the confusion, mistrust and unpleasant feelings of foreboding which disturbed the poor engineer's soul. He regretted with all his heart that he had entered the Troyas' house and, determined to make better use of his time for as long as his hypochondria remained with him, he wandered through the streets of the town.

He visited the market and went to the Calle de la Tripería where the big shops were. He observed the variety of manifestations of industry and commerce in the grand city of Orbajosa, but as he found nothing there except new sources of boredom, he made his way to the Paseo de las Descalzas. But there also he saw only a few stray dogs, because the ladies and gentlemen of the town had all stayed indoors on account of the penetrating wind which was blowing. He went to the pharmacy where ruminant progressives of diverse hues liked to gather and perpetually chew over some interminable matter. But he was bored here too. Finally he was walking past the cathedral when he heard the organ and the beautiful singing of the choir. He entered and knelt down in front of the main altar, calling to mind his aunt's strictures regarding behaviour in church. Then he visited a chapel and was just about to enter another when an acolyte or warden (whose responsibility it was to chase the dogs out of the church) approached him and addressed him in a very impolite manner, using extremely unseemly language:

'His Grace says you must get out of here.'

The engineer felt the blood rush to his head. He obeyed without saying a word. Driven out of everywhere by a superior force or his own boredom, he had no choice but to head for his aunt's place, where he found waiting for him:

First: Old Licurgo to inform him of a second lawsuit.

Second: Don Cayetano to read to him another section of his treatise on the genealogy of the families of Orbajosa.

Third: Caballuco, on some undisclosed matter.

Fourth: Doña Perfecta and her sweet smile for a reason which will become clear in the next chapter.

CHAPTER 14

The discord keeps on growing

A fresh attempt to see his cousin Rosario in the evening ended in failure. Pepe Rey locked himself away in his room in order to write a few letters, but he could not rid his mind of one particular 'idée fixe'.

'Tonight or tomorrow,' he said to himself, 'this business will end one way or another.'

When he was called for dinner Doña Perfecta walked up to him in the dining room, and said straight off:

'Pepe, my dear, don't worry. I'll calm Don Inocencio down . . . I know all about it. María Remedios, who has just left here, told me everything.'

Doña Perfecta's face radiated satisfaction like the face of an artist who is feeling proud over a painting.

'What?'

'I forgive you, my boy. Am I right in supposing that you had taken a glass or two in the Club? That's what comes of keeping bad company. Don Juan Tafetán! The Troya girls! . . . How shocking! I hope you've thought it all over?'

'I've thought about everything,' Pepe answered, determined not to get into an argument with his aunt.

'I'll be careful not to write to your father about what you've done.'

'You can write whatever you please to him.'

'Come now. Defend yourself by denying all this.'

'I'm not going to deny anything.'

'Then you admit that you were in the house of those . . .'

'I was.'

'And that you gave them a gold coin, because, according to María Remedios, Florentina went down to the Extremaduran's shop to get a gold coin changed. They couldn't have earned it from their sewing and you were in their house today; therefore . . .'

'Therefore I gave it to them. Exactly.'

'You don't deny it?'

'Why should I deny it? I believe that I have the right to do with my money whatever suits me best.'

'But surely you deny having thrown a stone at the Father Confessor?'

'I don't throw stones.'

'What I mean is that they, in your presence . . .'

'That's quite another matter.'

'And they insulted poor María Remedios.'

'I don't deny that either.'

'So how are you going to justify your behaviour? Pepe . . . for God's sake . . . You're saying nothing, you're unrepentant, you don't protest . . . no . . .'

'Certainly not, Señora.'

'And you're not even trying to make amends to me.'

'I have nothing to make amends for.'

'Come, now. The only thing left for you to do is to take this stick and beat me.'

'I don't beat people.'

'Such a lack of respect . . . Such . . .! You're not dining?'

'Yes, I am.'

There was a pause of more than a quarter of an hour. Don Cayetano, Doña Perfecta and Pepe Rey dined in complete silence. This was interrupted only when Don Inocencio entered the dining room.

'How sorry I was, my dear Don José! . . . Believe me when I say that I was truly sorry,' he said, holding out his hand to the young man and looking at him with an expression of pity in his eyes.

The young engineer did not know what to say in reply, so great was his confusion.

'I'm talking about what happened this afternoon.'

'Ah! . . . yes.'

'About your being thrown out of the hallowed portals of the cathedral.'

'The bishop,' said Pepe Rey, 'ought to think very carefully before he throws a Christian out of a church.'

'That's very true. And I can't imagine who gave His Grace the idea that you're a man of low moral standards. Nor have I any idea who told him that you broadcast your atheism all over the place and make fun of holy objects and figures or even that you intend to pull down the cathedral and use the masonry to erect a tar factory. I tried to convince him, but His Grace is rather stubborn.'

'Thank you for being so kind.'

'When you think about it the Father Confessor has no reason to be so considerate towards you. He was almost left for dead this afternoon.'

'Bah! . . . What of it?' said the priest, laughing. 'Has the news of the prank spread this far already? . . . I'll bet it was María Remedios who came here with the story. But I told her not to; I told her not to and in no uncertain terms. What happened is of no significance. Isn't that right, Señor Rey?'

'If you say so . . .'

'That is my opinion. A mere boyish prank . . . People nowadays can say what they like, but youth has always inclined towards evil and evil acts. Don José, a man of considerable gifts, cannot possibly be perfect . . . What's so unusual about the fact that those charming girls seduced him and, when they had obtained money from him, involved him in their shameful and criminal attacks on their neighbours? My dear friend, as far as my role in this afternoon's escapades is concerned,' he added, raising his hand to the affected spot, 'I am not the least offended and I have no intention of embarrassing you by referring to such a regrettable incident. I was genuinely grieved when I heard that María Remedios had come here to tell all about it . . . my niece is such a tittle-tattle . . . I'll bet she gossiped about the gold coin as well and about your frolics with the girls on the roof and how you chased and pinched each other. Then there's Don Tafetán's larking about ... really, these things should be kept a secret.'

Pepe Rey did not know which he found more embarrassing, the severity of his aunt's attitude or the condescending hypocrisy of the canon.

'Why should these things not be spoken of?' said Doña Perfecta. 'He doesn't seem to be ashamed of the way he behaved. Let everyone know about it. I'll only keep it a secret from my beloved daughter because in her nervous state an attack of anger could be dangerous.'

'Come now, it's not as bad as all that,' said the Father Confessor. 'In my opinion the matter should be dropped. And when the victim of the stone-throwing can say that, everybody else should be satisfied ... That bump on the head was no joke, Don José. I thought someone had opened a hole in my head and that my brains were running out ...'

'I'm dreadfully sorry about the whole incident!' stammered Pepe Rey. 'It really does grieve me, even though I took no part in it ...'

'Your visit to the Troya girls will attract the attention of the whole town,' said the canon. 'We're not in Madrid here. We're not in that centre of corruption and scandals ...'

'There it is possible to visit the most disgusting places,' interjected Doña Perfecta, 'without anyone knowing.'

'Here we keep a close eye on each other,' said Don Inocencio. 'We notice everything our neighbours get up to and with such a system of vigilance a high standard of public morality is maintained ... Believe me, my friend, believe me, and I'm not saying this in order to make you feel awkward: you are the first gentleman in your position who, in broad daylight ... yes, sir, the first ... *Trojae qui primus ab oris*, who first came from the shores of Troy.' Then he began to laugh, slapping the engineer on the back in a gesture of friendship and benevolence.

'It affords me much pleasure,' said the young man, hiding

his anger behind what he considered the most appropriate form of reply to the concealed sarcasm of his interlocutors, 'to see so much tolerance and generosity when my criminal behaviour is deserved . . .'

'What? Would you expect us to treat our own flesh and blood, somebody who bears the same name as ourselves, like a nobody?' said Doña Perfecta. 'You're my nephew, you're the son of the best and holiest of men, my dear brother Juan, and that's all there is to it. Yesterday afternoon the bishop's secretary came here to tell me of His Grace's displeasure at my having you here in my house.'

'He said that?' murmured the canon.

'He did indeed. I said in reply that, with all the respect I have for the bishop, and although I love and admire him, my nephew is my nephew and I cannot throw him out of my house.'

'That's another strange thing I've noticed in these parts,' said Pepe Rey, pale with anger. 'It would appear that here the bishop rules in other people's houses.'

'He's a very saintly man and he loves me so much and he imagines . . . he imagines that you'll communicate your atheism, your indifference and your strange ideas . . . I've told him on many occasions that you're a very good man at heart.'

'Concessions always have to be made in the face of superior talent,' said Don Inocencio.

'And this morning, when I was at the Cirujedas' place . . . you can't imagine what a hard time they gave me. They wanted to know if you've come to knock down the cathedral; if you've been commissioned by the English Protestants to travel around Spain preaching heretical ideas; they said that you spend the whole night gambling in the Club and that you are drunk when you leave . . . "But, Ladies," I said to them, "do you want me to send my nephew to an inn?" And moreover, as far as being drunk is concerned they are wrong, and today was the first time I'd heard anything about your gambling.'

Pepe Rey was in that state of mind in which even the most prudent of men feels within him violent passions and a wild, blind force driving him to strangle, hit, crack skulls and grind bones. But Doña Perfecta was a lady and, moreover, his aunt; Don Inocencio was old and a priest. Furthermore, physical violence is in bad taste, and unbecoming in well-bred Christians. His only option was to give vent to his repressed fury in appropriately chosen words, saying nothing unworthy of himself. But even this last option seemed premature to him and one which he should not use until the very moment when he was leaving that house and Orbajosa for good. So, resisting the furious impulse, he waited.

Jacinto arrived just as dinner was coming to an end.

'Good evening, Don José,' he said, holding out his hand to the young man. 'You and your lady friends stopped me working this afternoon. I didn't even manage to write a single line and I had so much to do!'

'I'm very sorry, Jacinto! But according to what I've been told you sometimes take part in their fun and games.'

'I!' exclaimed the young fellow, turning as red as a beetroot. 'You know that Don Tafetán never speaks a word of the truth . . . But is it true, Señor Rey, that you're leaving us today?'

'Is that what they're saying around here?'

'Yes. I heard it in the Club and at Don Lorenzo Ruiz's place.'

Rey stared for a while at the fresh features of *Don Nominavito*. Then he said:

'It's not certain yet. My aunt is very pleased to have me here. She has no time for the slanderous statements the people of Orbajosa are spreading about me . . . and she won't throw me out of the house even if the bishop insists that she should do so.'

'Throw you out? . . . Never. What would your father say?'

'Despite your kindness, dear Aunt, and despite the friendship shown to me by the canon, I may well decide to leave . . .'

'Leave?'

'Leave, sir?'

An unusual light flashed across Doña Perfecta's eyes. The
canon, despite being a man well versed in the arts of
dissimulation, could not conceal his joy.

'Yes, perhaps this very night . . .'

'But there's no need to be so impulsive . . . Why don't you
wait at least till early tomorrow morning? . . . Let's see . . .
Juan, send someone to tell Old Licurgo to get the pony ready
. . . I suppose you'll be taking a packed lunch . . . Nicolasa!
. . . That piece of veal in the sideboard . . . Librada, the
gentleman's clothing . . .'

'No, I can't believe you've made such a sudden decision,'
said Don Cayetano, feeling obliged to make some contribu-
tion to the conversation.

'But you will return, won't you?' said the canon.

'What time does the train leave in the morning?' asked
Doña Perfecta, her eyes gleaming with the feverish
impatience residing in her soul.

'Yes, I'm going to leave this very night.'

'But there's no moon.'

In the soul of Doña Perfecta, in the soul of the Father
Confessor, in the young soul of the little scholar, the words
'this very night' reverberated like heavenly music.

'Of course you'll come back, Pepe dear . . . I've written to
your father, your excellent father today . . .' exclaimed Doña
Perfecta, displaying all the facial signs which usually accompany the onset of tears.

'I shall trouble you with a few errands,' announced the
sage.

'This is a good opportunity for me to order that volume
of Abbot Gaume's which I don't have,' declared the young
lawyer.

'Goodness, Pepe, how impulsive and whimsical you can
be!' murmured Doña Perfecta, smiling and with her eyes
fixed on the dining room door. 'But I forgot to mention that
Caballuco is waiting to have a word with you.'

CHAPTER 15

It grows and grows till war is declared

They all looked over towards the door where the imposing figure of the Centaur appeared. He was a serious-
looking man with eyebrows joined in the middle and he
appeared embarrassed by his own willingness to greet everyone in a friendly manner. His rugged good looks were
disfigured by the pain caused by his efforts to smile urbanely,
to tread softly and to hold his Herculean arms in a correct
posture.

'Come in, Señor Ramos,' said Pepe Rey.

'No, no,' objected Doña Perfecta. 'He's only come to tell
you a load of nonsense.'

'Let him speak.'

'I am under no obligation to allow such ridiculous matters
to be discussed in my house.'

'What is it you want with me, Señor Ramos?'

Caballuco uttered a few words.

'That's enough, that's enough,' exclaimed Doña Perfecta.
'Don't annoy my nephew any more. Pepe, don't take any
notice of this pig-headed fool ... Would you like me to
explain the reason for great Caballuco's anger?'

'Anger? I can well imagine,' said the Father Confessor,
leaning back in his chair and guffawing expansively.

'I wanted to talk to Don José,' grunted the formidable
horseman.

'For God's sake, man, be quiet and stop bashing our
eardrums.'

'Señor Caballuco,' said the canon, 'it's only to be expected that the riders from these savage lands should have their noses put out by the gentlemen from the capital . . .'

'In a nutshell, Pepe, the point is this: Caballuco is the I don't quite know what . . .'

Laughter prevented him from continuing.

'The I don't quite know what,' Don Inocencio went on, 'of one of the Troya girls, Mariquita Juana, if I'm not mistaken.'

'And he's jealous! After his horse, the most important person in the world for him is Mariquilla Troya.'

'What a thing to say!' exclaimed Doña Perfecta. 'Poor Cristóbal! Would you have believed that a man like my nephew? . . . Now let's see, what were you going to say? Speak up!'

'Don José and I can have a talk later,' replied the local hero brusquely.

And he went out without saying another word.

A short time later Pepe Rey left the dining room to go to his room. In the hallway he came face to face with his Trojan adversary and could not suppress his laughter when he saw the grimly serious expression on the face of the offended suitor.

'A word,' said the latter, brazenly standing in front of the engineer. 'Do you know who I am?'

As he spoke he placed his heavy hand on the young man's shoulder in such a gesture of insolent familiarity that Pepe Rey could not help pushing it away violently.

'There's no need for you to crush me.'

The bully, somewhat disconcerted, recovered quickly and, staring provocatively at Pepe Rey, repeated his refrain:

'Do you know who I am?'

'Yes. And I know that you're an animal.'

He pushed the man aside brusquely and went into his room. Our unfortunate friend's state of mind at that moment was such that his choices of action could be summed up briefly as follows: break Caballuco's head without more ado; bid farewell to his aunt with stern but polite words which would go straight to her heart; say a cold goodbye to the inoffensive Cayetano and embrace him; wrap things up by giving Licurgo a good hiding; leave Orbajosa that very night and shake the dust off his shoes at the city gates.

But the thoughts of the persecuted young man could not overlook, amidst such bitterness, another unfortunate being whose situation he presumed to be more grievous and painful than his own. A maid had followed the engineer into his room.

'Did you give her my message?'

'Yes, sir, and she gave me this.'

Rey took from the girl's hand a small piece torn out of a newspaper in the margin of which were written the following words: 'They tell me you're leaving. I'll die.'

When he came back into the dining room Old Licurgo appeared at the door and asked:

'At what time do you need the donkey?'

'I don't,' Rey answered.

'So you're not leaving tonight?' said Doña Perfecta. 'It would be better to wait until morning.'

'I'm not leaving then either.'

'When are you leaving, then?'

'We'll see,' the young man said coldly, looking straight at his aunt with unflinching calmness. 'For the moment I have no plans to leave.'

His eyes offered a stern challenge.

Doña Perfecta turned red and then pale. She looked at the canon, who had removed his gold-rimmed spectacles to clean them, then stared at the other people in the room, one after another, including Caballuco who had come in a short time earlier and sat down on the edge of a chair. She surveyed them as a general fondly surveys his troops. Then she examined her nephew's serene and pensive face; the face of an enemy who had made an unexpected, strategic reappearance when everyone thought that he had been put to dishonourable rout.

Oh, blood, ruin and desolation! . . . A great battle was looming.

CHAPTER 16

Night

Orbajosa slept. At the crossroads and in the narrow streets the pitiful little lamps of the public lighting system cast forth their last rays like tired eyes fighting to stay awake. Beneath their feeble light, tramps, nightwatchmen and gamblers, wrapped in their capes, slipped past. The still peace of the historic town was disturbed by nothing more than the groans of some drunk or the song of a lover. Suddenly the *Ave María Purísima* of the wine-swigging nightwatchman rang out like the sickly wail of the sleeping town.

Silence reigned also in Doña Perfecta's house. This was interrupted only by the sounds emanating from Don Cayetano's study where he and Pepe Rey were deep in conversation. The scholar was reclining in his armchair in front of his desk, which was covered with all manner of documents bearing notes, references and jottings and about which, despite their great diversity, there was not the slightest hint of disorder. Pepe Rey's eyes were fixed on the mountain of documents; but his thoughts, no doubt, were miles away, somewhere very far from all that erudition.

'Perfecta,' said the antiquarian, 'is an excellent woman even though she does have one defect: she is easily shocked by any frivolous or insignificant deed. My friend, in these provincial towns the merest indiscretion can be very costly. I see nothing odd about your visit to the Troyas' house. And I imagine that Don Inocencio, beneath his virtuous man's cloak, is something of a mischief-maker. What's it got to do with him?'

'Don Cayetano, we've reached the point now when it's vital to act decisively. I must see and speak to Rosario.'

'Well, see her, then.'

'But they won't let me,' replied the engineer, thumping the desk. 'Rosario is locked in her room.'

'Locked in her room!' exclaimed the scholar with incredulity. 'To tell the truth I don't like the look of her at the moment, particularly the dazed look in her beautiful eyes. She is sad, she says little and she cries ... Don José, my friend, I'm very much afraid that the girl may be succumbing to the terrible illness which has claimed so many victims in my family.'

'Terrible illness! What illness?'

'Insanity ... or rather, mania. Not a single person in my family has not been affected by it. I'm the only one it hasn't touched.'

'You ... Well, never mind about mania,' said Pepe Rey, 'I want to see Rosario.'

'Nothing could be more natural. But the isolation in which her mother is keeping her is just a health measure, my dear Pepe. It's the only measure which has had any success with the members of my family. Just consider that the person whose presence and voice is bound to make the greatest impression on Rosarillo's delicate nervous system is the person whom her heart has chosen.'

'In spite of all that,' insisted Pepe, 'I still want to see her.'

'Perfecta may not be opposed to that,' said the scholar, turning his attention to his notes and documents. 'I don't want to meddle in what doesn't concern me.'

The engineer, seeing that he was not going to succeed in winning the good Polentinos over to his side, prepared to take his leave.

'You want to work and I don't wish to hinder you.'

'No; I've plenty of time. Just look at the amount of excellent information I've gathered today. Listen ... "In 1537 an inhabitant of Orbajosa called Bartolome del Hoyo went to Civitta-Vecchia in the galleys of the Marquis of

Castel Rodrigo." And another: "In the same year two
brothers, also sons of Orbajosa and called Juan and Rodrigo
González del Arco, sailed with the six ships which left
Maestrique (Maastricht) on 20 February and on the latitude
of Calais encountered an English ship together with Flemish
ones under the command of Van-Owen . . ." In brief, it was
quite a feat for our navy. I have discovered that one man
from Orbajosa, a certain Mateo Díaz Coronel, a lieutenant
in the Guards, was the man who wrote and had printed in
Valencia, *The Metrical Encomium, Funeral song, Elegiac
Lyric, Numerical Description, Glorious Harships and
Anguished Glories of the Queen of Angels*. I possess an
extremely valuable copy of this work, worth all the gold in
Peru . . . Another Orbajosan was the author of the famous
Treatise on the Different Kinds of Civet Cat, which I showed
you yesterday; and, to sum up, I never take a step through
the labyrinth of unpublished history without stumbling
across some illustrious person from these parts. I intend to
extricate all of these names from the unjust obscurity and
oblivion in which they languish. What sheer delight it is, my
dear Pepe, to restore the lustre to the epic and literary glories
of the land of our birth! No man can make better use of the
limited intelligence he might have received from Heaven or
of the inherited fortune and brief time which even those who
live longest can count on . . . Thanks to me everyone will
know what an illustrious cradle of Spanish genius Orbajosa
is. But, what am I saying? Isn't its illustrious ancestry already
recognizable in the nobility and chivalry of the present
generation of *"urbsaugustinians"*? We know of few places
showing a healthier growth of plants and shrubs of all the
virtues, free of the poisonous weeds of vice. Here everything
is peace, mutual respect and Christian humility. Charity is
practised here as in Biblical times; here envy is unknown as
are criminal passions; and if you hear talk of robbers or
murderers you can rest assured that they will not be sons of
this noble land unless they number among those sad souls
who have been led astray by the oratory of demagogues.

Here you will see our national character in all its purity: upright, noble, incorruptible, pure, straightforward, patriarchal, hospitable, generous . . . This is why I derive so much enjoyment from living in this peaceful solitude, far from the labyrinth of cities where, alas, falsehood and vice reign. This is why my many friends in Madrid have never managed to persuade me to leave; this is why I live in the sweet company of my loyal compatriots and my books, constantly breathing in the salubrious atmosphere of honesty which is gradually disappearing from Spain and now only lives on in the humble, Christian cities which have learned how to preserve it by emanating virtue. You may find it hard to believe, my dear Pepe, but this peaceful isolation has been a great help in freeing me from that dreadful illness which runs in my family. In my youth I, just like my brothers and my father, suffered from a terrible propensity to the most frightening manias. But now you see me, cured beyond belief so that I can only recognize the illness when I see it in others. That is why my dear niece worries me so much.'

'I'm delighted to hear that the air in Orbajosa has been so good for you,' said Pepe Rey, unable to contain a sense of the ridiculous which, in accordance with some strange law, was born in the midst of his sadness. 'Things have turned out so badly for me that I think I'll soon become neurotic myself if I stay here. So I'll bid you goodnight and I hope you get a lot of work done.'

'Goodnight.'

He went to his room but felt the need for neither sleep nor physical repose. On the contrary a strong impulse drove him to keep moving, walking and pondering as he paced from one corner of the room to another. Then he opened the window which looked out onto the garden and, placing his elbows on the ledge contemplated the immense darkness of the night. He could not see a thing. But a man engrossed in thought sees everything and Pepe Rey, peering into the darkness, watched his misfortunes unfold against the backdrop of the variegated landscape. The shadows prevented him from seeing either the flowers of the earth or the stars, the flowers of the sky. The almost total absence of light produced the effect of illusory movement in the abundance of trees which seemed to stretch out before him as they lazily moved away then curled back like waves in a sea of shadows. A formidable ebb and flow, a struggle between unseen forces shook the silent globe. The mathematician, contemplating the strange projection of his soul into the night, said:

'The battle will be bloody but we'll see who is the victor.'

The nocturnal insects spoke right in his ear, uttering strange words. Here, a rough chirping sound; there, a clicking sound similar to that which we make with our tongues; over there, mournful murmurings and, in the distance, a tinkling similar to that of a bell around the neck of some rogue animal. Suddenly Rey heard an odd sound, a rapid series of notes which could only have come from the tongue and lips of a human being. The utterance passed through the young man's brain like lightning and he felt the hissing sound, which lasted no more than a moment, snake its way through him again and again, with increasing intensity. He looked all around him, then to the upper part of the house where, in one of the windows, he thought he could just make out the shape of an object resembling a large white bird moving its wings. In his excited state of mind Pepe Rey thought for a moment that he saw a phoenix, a dove or a heron ... but the bird was nothing more than a handkerchief.

The engineer jumped through the window into the garden. Taking a closer look he saw the hand and face of his cousin and he thought he could make out the conventional gesture for requesting silence; a finger raised to the lips. Then the lovely shadow lowered its arm and disappeared. Pepe Rey went quickly back into his room and, trying not to make a sound, went into the corridor and moved slowly along it. He could feel his heart pounding as if he were being smitten with an axe from within. He waited a moment ... then finally he distinctly heard the faint sound of footsteps on the stairs. One, two, three . . . only dainty shoes could produce a sound like that.

He moved in the direction of the sound, surrounded by almost complete darkness, and stretched out his arms to render assistance to whoever was descending. A great swell of tender feelings arose in his heart (why deny it), and then, after that sweet sensation, there surged another, evil in origin: a terrible desire for revenge. The descending footsteps were drawing closer and closer. Pepe Rey advanced and a pair of hands, groping about in the darkness, came into contact with his. Four hands were joined together in a tight grasp.

CHAPTER 17

A light in the darkness

The corridor was long and narrow. At one end was the door to the room in which the engineer was living; in the middle, the door to the dining room; and at the other end the staircase and a large, locked door, with a step up leading to the threshold. Behind this door was a chapel containing the Polentino family devotional statues. On occasions Holy Mass was celebrated there.

Rosario directed her cousin to the chapel door and then let herself sink down onto the doorstep.

'Here?' . . . murmured Pepe Rey.

From the movements of Rosario's right hand Pepe understood that she was crossing herself.

'Rosario, my dear cousin . . . Thank you for letting me see you,' he exclaimed, embracing her passionately.

He felt the young girl's cold fingers on his lips imploring him not to say anything. He kissed them frantically.

'You're frozen . . . Rosario . . . why are you trembling?'

Her teeth were chattering and her whole body was trembling in feverish convulsions. Rey could feel the burning fire of his cousin's face against his own and exclaimed in alarm:

'Your forehead is a veritable volcano. You've got a fever.'

'Very much so.'

'Are you really ill?'

'Yes.'

'And yet you came out?'

'To see you.'

The engineer wrapped his arms around her to protect her against the cold; but it was not enough.

'Just wait,' he said quickly, standing up. 'I'm going to my room to fetch my travelling rug.'

'Put the light out, Pepe.'

Rey had left a candle burning inside his room and its faint light came through the door and lit up the hallway. He returned immediately. Now the darkness was complete. Feeling his way along the walls he managed to find the spot where his cousin was. They were reunited and he carefully wrapped her up from head to toe.

'There, my sweet, that's better.'

'Yes. Much better . . . I'm with you.'

'With me . . . and for ever,' the young man exclaimed ecstatically.

But he felt her pull away from his embrace and stand up.

'What are you doing?'

He could hear the sound of a small piece of metal. Rosario was fitting a key into the invisible keyhole and carefully opening the door on the threshold of which they had been sitting. The slight smell of dampness associated with rooms which have been shut up for a long time emanated from the tomb-black chapel. Pepe Rey felt himself being taken by the hand as his cousin said in a soft voice:

'Come on in.'

They took a few paces forward. He thought he was being led into unknown Elysian regions by the angel of the night. She was groping her way along. Finally her mellifluous voice sounded again as she said:

'Sit down.'

They were beside a wooden bench. They both sat down. Pepe Rey embraced Rosario again and at that very moment his head collided with something hard.

'What's this?'

'The feet.'

'Rosario . . . what are you saying?'

'The feet of the divine Jesus, the statue of Christ on the Cross. We all worship him in my house.'

Pepe Rey felt as though a cold shaft had penetrated his heart.

'Kiss them,' the girl said imperiously.

The mathematician kissed the ice-cold feet of the sacred image.

'Pepe,' exclaimed Rosario, ardently squeezing her cousin's hand, 'do you believe in God?'

'Rosario! . . . What are you saying? What silly things you think of!' replied her cousin, perplexed.

'Answer me.'

Pepe Rey could feel the sweat on the palms of his hands.

'Why are you crying?' he said anxiously. 'Rosario, you're killing me with your absurd doubts. Of course I believe in God. Do you doubt it?'

'I don't, but everyone's saying that you're an atheist.'

'You would go down in my estimation and lose your aura of purity and authority if you were to lend credence to such nonsense.'

'Hearing you called an atheist, and not having any reason to persuade myself of the contrary, I nevertheless protested against such a slander with all my heart. You can't possibly be an atheist. Deep down inside I have a vivid and powerful sense of your religious nature which is similar to my own.'

'Well said! So why do you ask if I believe in God?'

'Because I wanted to hear it from your own lips and to rejoice in hearing you say it. It's so long since I heard the sound of your voice . . . What could be more pleasurable than to hear you, after such a long silence, saying "I believe in God".'

'Rosario, even evil-doers believe in Him. If there are atheists, which I doubt, they are the slanderers and intriguers with whom the world is infested . . . For my part, I'm not much interested in slanders and intrigue, and if you can rise above them and close your heart to the sentiments of discord which some malevolent hand is attempting to stir up inside you, nothing will prevent our happiness.'

'But, what's happening to us? Pepe, dear Pepe . . . do you believe in the devil?'

The engineer remained silent. The darkness of the chapel did not permit Rosario to see the smile with which her cousin received such a strange question.

'One has to believe in him,' he said eventually.

'What is happening to us? Mamma will not allow me to see you. But she says nothing ill of you apart from your atheism. She tells me to wait; she says that you will decide; she says that you're going away, that you're coming back . . . Tell me frankly . . . Have you formed a bad opinion of my mother?'

'Not at all,' replied Rey, driven by his sense of tact.

'Don't you think, as I do, that she loves me very much; that she loves the two of us; that her only concern is our well-being and that in the end we are bound to win from her the consent we desire?'

'If that's what you think, then I do, too . . . Your mother adores both of us . . . But, my dear Rosario, we have to recognize that the devil has entered into this house.'

'Don't joke about it,' she replied tenderly. 'Mother is very good. Not even once has she said to me that you're not a fitting husband for me. The only thing she is adamant about is your atheism. People also say that I suffer from manias and that the current one is loving you with all my heart. In our family it is the rule not to directly confront the manias from which we suffer, because attacking them only makes them worse.'

'Well, I think that at your side you have good doctors who have undertaken to cure you and that eventually, my sweet, they'll succeed.'

'No, no; a thousand times no,' exclaimed Rosario, resting her forehead on her sweetheart's chest. 'I want to go mad with you. I am suffering because of you. Because of you I despise life and expose myself to death . . . I can see it all now . . . tomorrow I'll be worse, I'll become even sicker and then die. What do I care!'

'You're not ill,' he replied firmly, 'you're only emotionally upset and this, quite naturally, leads to slight nervous troubles. There's nothing wrong with you other than the pain caused by the dreadful treatment they're subjecting you to. Your simple and generous soul cannot comprehend this. You give in and pardon those who are harming you. You fall ill and attribute your misfortune to supernatural influences. You suffer in silence. You offer up your innocent neck to the executioner. You allow yourself to be killed and the same knife, buried in your throat, seems to you to be the thorn of some flower which pricked you as you were walking past. Rosario, get rid of these ideas. Consider the reality of the grave situation we're in. Look for its cause where it really is; don't give in to cowardice or surrender to the mortification which is being inflicted upon you and making your body and soul ill. The courage which is failing you at the moment will restore your health, because you're not really ill, my sweet. You are . . . do you want me to tell you? You've had a fright, a shock. What is happening to you is what the ancients were unable to define and referred to as witchcraft. Rosario, have courage, trust in me! Stand up and follow me. I have nothing more to say.'

'Oh, Pepe, my dear cousin! I think you're right,' exclaimed Rosario, sobbing profusely. 'Your words echo in my heart like violent blows shaking me up and breathing new life into me. Here, amidst this darkness, where we cannot even see each other's faces, an ineffable light is emanating from you and flooding my soul. What is it about you that allows you to transform me like this? I became another person the moment I met you. During those days when I couldn't see you my old insignificant self and former cowardice reappeared. Without you, dear Pepe, I live in Limbo. I'll do as you bid me; I'll stand up and follow you. We'll both go wherever you wish. Do you know how well I feel? Do you know, I no longer have a fever, my strength is coming back and I want to run and shout. My whole being is being renewed and is expanding to a hundred times its former size so that I can adore you. Pepe, you're right. I'm not ill, just suffering from a bout of cowardice or, rather, I'm bewitched.'

'That's it, bewitched.'

'Bewitched. Dreadful eyes look at me and leave me speechless and trembling. I'm afraid, but what of? Only you have the strange power to bring me back to life. Listening to you I am revived. I believe that if I were to die and you were to walk past my grave I would hear your footsteps from deep below the earth. Oh, if only I could see you now! . . . But you're here, at my side, and I have no doubt that it is you . . . I went so long without seeing you! . . . I was going mad. Each day of solitude seemed a century . . . They kept telling me tomorrow, tomorrow, always tomorrow. At night I would lean out of my window and the light from your room was my only solace. At times your shadow against the window pane was a divine apparition. I would stretch out my arms, burst into tears and cry out in my imagination because I was afraid to do it in reality. When I received your message by way of the maid; when I received your note telling me that you were leaving, it made me sad. I felt as if my soul were taking its leave of my body and that I was dying by degrees. I was falling, falling like a bird wounded in flight; falling and dying, both at the same time . . . Tonight, when I saw that it was so late but you were still awake, I couldn't resist the temptation to talk to you and so I came downstairs. I think that I used up all the courage I may have had in my whole life in this one act, and so from now on I'll always be a coward . . . But you'll give me inspiration and strength. You'll help me, won't you? . . . Pepe, my dear cousin, tell me I'm right. Tell me that I have the strength and will continue to be strong. Tell me that I'm not ill and that I won't be. I'm not ill now. I feel so well that I can laugh at my ridiculous illness.'

As she was speaking Rosario felt herself being frantically

embraced by her cousin. A cry of anguish was heard, not from her lips but from his because he struck his head against the feet of Christ when he inclined it towards her. It is in the darkness that stars are seen.

Because of his state of mind and the hallucinations which are produced naturally in dark places, Pepe imagined not that his head had struck the sacred foot but that the latter had moved, admonishing him in the briefest and most eloquent manner. Half in earnest and half in jest, Pepe lifted his head and said:

'Lord, don't hit me. I'm not about to do anything wicked.'

At the same moment Rosario took hold of the young man's hand and pressed it against her heart. A pure, serious, angelic and deeply agitated voice said:

'Oh Lord whom I adore, Lord God of all the world and guardian of my house and family; Oh Lord whom Pepe also adores; Blessed Christ who died on the cross for our sins; before you, before your wounded body; before your head crowned with thorns, I declare that this is my husband and after you he is the one whom my soul loves most; I declare that he is my husband and that I will die before I belong to another. My heart and soul belong to him. Grant that the world may not oppose our happiness and grant me the favour of this union which, I swear, the world will look kindly on, as does my conscience.'

'Rosario, you belong to me,' exclaimed Pepe, exalted. 'Neither your mother nor anybody else will prevent that.'

Rosario rested her beautiful, motionless breast on her cousin's chest. She trembled in his loving, manly arms, like a dove in an eagle's talons.

The thought flashed through his mind that the devil did indeed exist and that he was it. Rosario shuddered slightly from fear; it was as if she had experienced the tremble of surprise which presages danger.

'Swear to me that you will not give up,' Rey said in an agitated voice, calming her shudders.

'I swear to you on my father's ashes, which are . . .'

'Where?'

'Beneath our feet.'

The mathematician felt as though the flagstone beneath them was rising ... but no, it was not rising: he merely thought that it was, despite his being a mathematician.

'I swear to you,' repeated Rosario, 'on my father's ashes and in the name of God who is watching us ... May our bodies, united as they are, rest beneath these flagstones when it pleases God to remove us from this world.'

'Yes,' agreed Pepe Rey, deeply moved as his soul filled with inexplicable feelings of agitation.

Both remained silent for a while. Rosario rose to her feet.

'Already?'

She sat down again.

'You're trembling again,' said Pepe Rey. 'Rosario, you're ill. Your forehead is burning.'

'I think I'm dying,' the young girl murmured listlessly. 'I don't know what's wrong with me.'

She fainted into the arms of her cousin. As he caressed her he noticed that her face was covered in a cold sweat.

'She really is ill,' he said to himself. 'Coming out of doors was a stupid thing to do.'

He lifted her up and tried to resuscitate her, but she neither stopped trembling nor came round out of her swoon, so he decided to take her out of the chapel in the hope that the fresh air would revive her. And this, in fact, is what happened. When she had recovered her senses Rosario displayed great unease at the thought of being outside her room at such an hour. The cathedral clock struck four.

'How late it is,' exclaimed the young girl. 'Let me go, cousin. I think I can walk now. I really am very sick.'

'I'll go up with you.'

'Certainly not. I'd crawl to my room before I'd allow that ... Can you hear a noise?'

They both fell silent. Their apprehensive concentration detected only absolute silence.

'Don't you hear anything, Pepe?'

'Nothing at all.'

'Concentrate . . . Now, there it is again. It's a sound but I can't tell if it's far, far away or close, very close. It could either be the sound of my mother breathing, or the weather vane on the cathedral spire. I have very good hearing, you know.'

'Too good . . . So, my dear cousin, I'll carry you upstairs in my arms.'

'Very well, carry me as far as the top of the stairs. I'll make my own way from there. When I've had a bit of a rest I'll be as right as rain . . . Did you hear that?'

They came to a halt on the first step.

'It's a metallic sound.'

'Your mother's breathing?'

'No, it's not that. The noise is coming from far off. Could it be a cock crowing?'

'Could be.'

'It sounds like two words: I'm coming, I'm coming.'

'Yes, now I can hear it,' murmured Pepe Rey.

'Someone's shouting.'

'It's a horn.'

'A horn!'

'Yes. Go upstairs quickly. Orbajosa is waking up . . . Now I can hear it clearly. It's not a trumpet but a bugle. The army is coming.'

'The army!'

'I can't imagine why I have the feeling that this military invasion is going to be to my advantage . . . I feel happy. Rosario, upstairs, quick!'

'I feel happy, too. Upstairs.'

He carried her upstairs in an instant and the two lovers said goodnight so softly that they could hardly hear each other.

'I'll lean out of the window that overlooks the garden and tell you that I've reached my room safely. Goodnight.'

'Goodnight, Rosario. Be careful not to bump into any furniture.'

'I know my way around here well, cousin. We'll see each other again. Lean out of your window if you want me to wave to you.'

Pepe Rey did as she suggested; he waited for a long time but Rosario did not appear at the window. The engineer thought he heard agitated voices on the upper storey.

CHAPTER 18

The troops

The inhabitants of Orbajosa heard the loud bugle-call through the twilight confusion of their final moments in dream-land and, as they opened their eyes, they said:

'The troops.'

Some of them, talking to themselves, half-asleep and half-awake, murmured:

'They've finally sent that scum here.'

Others got out of bed immediately, complaining thus:

'Let's go and see the swine.'

Someone uttered the following soliloquy:

'They want us to pay in advance . . . they talk of taxes and levies, we'll talk of cudgels and more cudgels.'

In another house the following joyous words were heard:

'Perhaps my son is with them! . . . perhaps my brother is with them!'

There was much jumping out of bed, throwing on of clothes and opening of windows for a glimpse of the raucous regiment as it entered the town at daybreak. The town was all sadness, quiet and old age; but the army was all gaiety, boisterousness and youth. As the one entered the other it seemed that, as though my magic, the mummy had revived and was jumping noisily out of its dank sarcophagus in order to dance around it. What movement, what jubilation, what laughter, what joviality! There is nothing so interesting as an army. It is one's homeland displayed in all its youthful vigour. What, in one individual's opinion, that same homeland has or may sometimes possess of ineptitude, restlessness, now superstition, now blasphemy, disappears beneath the pressure of iron discipline which can turn insignificant little men into a formidable army. The soldier, or let us say the corpuscle, when he is detached from the body in which he has led a regular and at times wonderful life, frequently retains some of the qualities particular to an army. But not always. A return to civilian life tends to be followed by sudden deterioration, so that if an army means glory and honour, a soldiers' reunion can be an unbearable calamity, and those people who cry out with joy and excitement at the sight of a returning victorious battalion, groan and tremble with fear when the soldiers are on the loose.

And this is what happened in Orbajosa, for in those days there were no glorious deeds to sing about, no reason to weave wreaths, write triumphal banners or recall the valiant exploits of our brave young men. Hence fear and distrust reigned in that cathedral city which, although poor, suffered from no shortage of hens, fruit, money and young maidens, all of which treasure was immediately at risk the moment the aforesaid students of Mars arrived. In addition to this, the fief of the Polentinos, a city far removed from the hustle and bustle introduced by the traffic, newspapers, railways and other influences which there is no point in analysing here, did not like the thought of its peaceful existence being disturbed by them.

At every suitable opportunity the city showed its heartfelt determination not to submit to central authority, which, for better or worse, governs us. Remembering its ancient rights and ruminating upon them as a camel chews the cud it has eaten the day before, it got into the habit of demonstrating its rebellious independence and deplorable anarchic tendencies, which gave the Provincial Governor more than a few headaches.

Furthermore, it should be borne in mind that Orbajosa had antecedents, or rather, a seditious ancestry. There is no doubt that it harboured within its breast some of that fighting spirit which, in a bygone age, according to the

enthusiastic opinion of Don Cayetano, had driven the town
to unprecedented epic feats. From time to time, in spite of
its decadence, it still felt a passionate urge to do great things,
even if they turned out to be barbaric or unwise acts. As it
had given so many distinguished sons to the world it doubt-
less wanted its contemporary scions, the Caballucos,
Merengues and Pelosmalos, to re-enact the glorious deeds of
the epic tales of yesteryear.

Whenever there were rebellions in Spain, Orbajosa let
everyone know that it was not for nothing that it occupied
space on the face of the earth, even if it had never served as
a real theatre of war. Its genius, its situation and its history
meant that it played only a secondary role in raising insur-
gents. It provided the country with this national fruit in
1827, at the time of the Apostólicos, during the seven-year
war, in 1848, and in other talked-about epochs in the
nation's history. The rebel bands and partisans were always
popular, an unfortunate fact with its roots in the Peninsular
War, one of those good things which have spawned an
infinity of detestable things. *Corruptio optimi pessima.* The
corruption of the best is the worst corruption. The popularity of the rebel bands and partisans coincided with the ever
increasing unpopularity of anything which arrived in Orbajosa that had to do with central government. Soldiers were
always looked down on there so that whenever the old folk
spoke of some crime, be it robbery, murder, rape or some
other unspeakable outrage, they would add: 'It happened
when the troops arrived.'

Now that these important observations have been made,
it is an opportune moment to add that the battalions posted
to Orbajosa at the time of this story did not come to stroll
through the streets, because they had a very definite mission,
the details of which will soon become clear. As a snippet of
more than passing interest, we should point out that the
events referred to here took place in a year which is neither
all that far removed from the present one nor very close to
it. In just the same way it may be said that Orbajosa (*urbs*

augusta to the Romans, even if some modern scholars who have considered the ending *-ajosa* opine that it reflects the fact that the city is situated in the best garlic-growing country in the world) is neither far from nor near to Madrid, nor can anyone be certain whether its glorious origins lie in the north, south, east or west. It could be everywhere and anywhere Spaniards turn their eyes to savour the pungency of the garlic.

When the city authorities had distributed the billet allocation orders, each soldier went in search of the house to which he had been assigned. They were received with bad grace and accommodated in the least welcoming and hospitable rooms in the house. But, to tell the truth, the local girls were not all that displeased even though great vigilance was kept over them and it was not considered proper for them to reveal their delight at the arrival of such rabble. The few local boys among the soldiers were the only ones who lived like kings. All the others were treated like foreigners.

At eight o'clock in the morning a lieutenant colonel of the cavalry entered the house of Doña Perfecta Polentinos carrying his billeting order. On the orders of the lady of the house he was received by the servants. As Doña Perfecta was in such a state of emotional turmoil that she did not wish to come downstairs to greet the uncouth soldier, they showed him to the only room in the house that seemed to be available: the one occupied by Pepe Rey.

'They'll just have to sort themselves out as best they can,' said Doña Perfecta, her expression a mixture of vinegar and salt, 'and if there isn't room for the two of them they can always leave.'

Was it her intention to annoy her despicable nephew by behaving in this manner, or was there really no other room available in the house? We cannot be sure, and the chronicles from which this true story has been taken say nothing on this important point. All that we can be sure of beyond any shadow of a doubt is that the two guests were certainly not inconvenienced by being cooped up together; on the con-

trary, they were delighted as they were already old friends.
Both were greatly and pleasantly surprised when they met
and they kept on asking each other questions, letting out
whoops of joy and marvelling at the strange coincidence
which had brought them together in such a place and at
such a time.

'Pinzón . . . Fancy seeing you here! How can it be? I'd no
idea that you were so near . . .'

'I had heard that you were around here somewhere, Pepe
Rey; but I never thought I'd find you in such a dreadful and
uncivilized place as Orbajosa.'

'What a happy coincidence! . . . the happiest, most provi-
dential coincidence . . . Pinzón, you and I together will do
great things in this slum of a town.'

'And we'll have plenty of time to think about it,' the other
replied, sitting down on the bed where the engineer was
lying, 'because it seems that the two of us are going to be
sharing this room. What sort of a hell-house is this?'

'Steady on, it's my aunt's. Show a bit more respect when
you speak. Don't you know my aunt? . . . I'll get up.'

'Glad to hear it. Now I can have a lie-down. I certainly
need to . . . What a journey, my friend; what a journey and
what a town!'

'Tell me, have you come to Orbajosa to burn it down?'

'Burn it down?'

'I say that because I might help you.'

'What a town! What a town!' exclaimed the soldier,
removing his shako and laying aside his sword, swordbelt,
dispatch case and cape. 'This is the second time they've sent
us here and, if they send us back for a third time, I swear I'll
resign my commission.'

'Don't speak ill of these good people. But you couldn't
have come at a better time. God must have sent you to help
me, Pinzón . . . I have this huge project, an adventure, if you
wish to call it that; a plan, my friend . . . and it would have
been very difficult to carry out if you hadn't come along.

Only a moment ago I was going mad thinking about it and in my anxiety I said to myself: "If only I had a friend here." '

'Project, plan, adventure . . . it has to be one or the other, Mister Mathematician: either you're working out how to steer balloons or you're involved in a love affair . . .'

'It's serious, very serious. Go to bed, have a sleep and then we'll talk.'

'I'll go to bed, but I won't sleep. You can tell me all you want to tell me. The only thing I ask is that you speak as little as possible about Orbajosa.'

'But it's precisely about Orbajosa that I want to talk to you. But do you have bad feelings about this cradle of so many famous men too?'

'These garlic-eaters – we call them garlic-eaters – they can be as famous as you like, but they get up my nose just as much as the plant does. This is a town dominated by people who teach lack of trust, suspicion and hatred of the whole human race. When we have more time I'll tell you of an event . . . an incident which was both funny and terrifying and happened to me here last year . . . When I tell it to you you'll laugh and I'll explode with anger . . . But, anyway, what's past is past.'

'There's nothing funny about what's happening to me.'

'But the reasons for my hatred of this slum of a town are quite varied. You must know that my father was murdered here in '48 by some merciless partisans. He was a brigadier and had retired from service. The Government had summoned him and he was on his way to Madrid by way of Villahorrenda when he was captured by half a dozen ruffians . . . There are several guerrilla dynasties in these parts: the Aceros, the Caballucos and the Pelosmalos, and they're nothing but a bunch of convicts on the loose, as someone who knew what he was talking about said.'

'I assume that the two regiments and cavalry detachment did not come here to visit the charming gardens.'

'Far from it! We've come to search the whole countryside

for the numerous arms caches herabouts. The Government doesn't dare dissolve the majority of the town councils without posting some companies of soldiers in the towns. There's an enormous amount of rebel activity around here. Two neighbouring provinces are infested with them and the municipal district of Orbajosa has a glorious history steeped in the civil wars. For all these reasons there are fears that the local hotheads might take to the highway and rob everyone they meet.'

'A sensible precaution! But it's my belief that there will be no peace in Orbajosa until all these people die and are reborn or the rocks change their shape.'

'That's my opinion, too,' said the soldier, lighting a cigarette. 'Haven't you noticed that the rebels are the spoiled darlings of the region? All of the men who devastated the area in '48, or if not them, their sons, can be found in tax offices, collecting tolls at the city gates, in the Town Council or working for the Post Office. Some of them are constables, sacristans or tax inspectors. A few of them have become influential political leaders by rigging elections and now have influence in Madrid, deciding who gets what posting . . . In short, it's enough to make anyone sick.'

'Tell me, do you think it's likely that the rebel leaders will commit some outrage in the near future? If that were to happen you would raze the town and I'd help you do it.'

'If it were left to me . . . They'll be up to their old tricks,' said Pinzón, 'because the guerrillas in both neighbouring provinces are spreading like the plague. And, between you and me, my friend, I don't see an end to it. Some people laugh and say that another civil war like the last one would be impossible. But they don't know the country, they don't know Orbajosa or the Orbajosans. And I maintain that what's beginning now will last well into the future and there'll be another cruel and bloody struggle which will last for as long as God sees fit. What's your opinion?'

'My friend, in Madrid I used to laugh at people who spoke

of the possibility of a civil war as long and as terrible as the one which lasted seven years. But now, since arriving here . . .'

'You have to immerse yourself in this delightful countryside, observe the people from close to and listen to what they're saying if you want to understand what makes them tick.'

'Well yes . . . without being able to put my finger on the basis of my thinking, the point is that since I arrived here I've seen things in a different light and believe that there is the possibility of a long and cruel war.'

'Exactly.'

'But for the moment I'm more concerned with a private war which I declared and got involved in a short time ago than with a public war.'

'Did you say that this house belongs to your aunt? What's her name?'

'Doña Perfecta Rey de Polentinos.'

'Ah! I know the name. She's an excellent sort and the only person I've not heard the garlic-eaters speak ill of. The last time I was here I heard her kindness, charity and virtues being praised everywhere.'

'Yes, my aunt is very kind and generous,' said Pepe Rey. Then he became very pensive for a while.

'But now I remember!' exclaimed Pinzón suddenly. 'Everything's falling into place now! Yes, in Madrid I was told that you were marrying your cousin. It's all out in the open now. Is it that beautiful, divine Rosario?'

'Pinzón, it's a long story.'

'I have the impression there are obstacles.'

'More than that. There are terrible battles going on. I need powerful, intelligent friends who can use their initiative, who have great experience of difficult situations and are astute and courageous.'

'I say, all this is more serious than being challenged to a duel.'

'Much more serious. A fight with another man is no problem. But with women and invisible enemies who operate in the shadows, it's impossible.'

'Do go on; I'm all ears.'

Lieutenant Colonel Pinzón was resting full length on the bed. Pepe Rey drew up a chair and, leaning his elbow on the bed and his head on his hand, he began his lecture, consultation, briefing or whatever you like to call it, and he spoke for a long time. Pinzón listened, engrossed and without saying a word, apart from the odd little question concerning some new information or to clarify a point. When Rey finished, Pinzón looked serious. Straightening, he stretched with the pleasurable convulsion of a man who has not slept for three nights, and then said:

'Your plan is risky and difficult.'

'But not impossible.'

'Oh, no, nothing in this world is impossible. Think it through very carefully.'

'I already have.'

'And are you determined to go ahead with it? Such conduct is no longer fashionable. It usually leads to no good and the person concerned comes unstuck.'

'I've made up my mind.'

'In that case, although it's very, very serious and risky, I'm ready to help you in any way I can.'

'I can rely on you, then?'

'Till the day I die.'

CHAPTER 19

Terrible combat. Strategy

The first shots were bound to be fired soon. At the dinner hour, after reaching an agreement with Pinzón over the plan, the first requirement of which was that both friends should pretend not to be acquainted, Pepe Rey went into the dining room. There he met his aunt, who had recently returned from the cathedral where she had passed the whole morning, as was her wont. She was alone and seemed very preoccupied. The engineer noticed that the mysterious shadow of a cloud lay across her intrinsically beautiful pale, marble face. When she looked up it regained its sinister clarity; but she seldom looked up, and after a fleeting glance at her nephew's features, the kind lady's face resumed its air of studied gloom.

They waited for dinner in silence. They were not expecting Don Cayetano because he had gone off to Mundogrande. When they finally began to eat, Doña Perfecta said:

'And the big soldier-boy the Government has presented us with, is he not coming to dine?'

'I think he's more sleepy than hungry,' replied the engineer without looking at his aunt.

'Do you know him?'

'I've never seen him before in my life.'

'A fine lot of guests we're sent by the Government! We keep our beds and our table for whenever it suits those degenerates in Madrid to avail themselves of them.'

'The point is that some people fear a guerrilla uprising,' said Pepe Ray, feeling as though a flash of electricity had shot right through his body, 'and the Government has decided to crush the Orbajosans, to smash them and grind them into dust.'

'Stop, stop, sir, for God's sake, don't pulverize us,' Doña Perfecta exclaimed sarcastically. 'Poor us! Have mercy on us and let these wretched creatures live. And so, will you be one of those who help the troops in their grand task of crushing us?'

'I'm not a soldier. I'll do nothing more than applaud when I see extirpated once and for all the seeds of civil war, the insubordination, the discord, the lawlessness, the banditry and barbarity which exist here and bring shame on our times and our land.'

'God's will be done.'

'Orbajosa, my dear Aunt, possesses hardly anything apart from garlic and bandits, because bandits are what those people are who, for the sake of a religious or political idea, hurl themselves into an adventure every four or five years.'

'Thank you, thank you, nephew dear,' said Dōna Perfecta, growing pale. 'So Orbajosa possesses nothing more than that, eh? There must be something more on offer here; something which you don't have and which you've come here to look for.'

Rey felt the blow. His soul was on fire. It was difficult for him to afford his aunt the respect which her sex, position and status deserved. Violence had him in its grip and an irresistible urge was driving and goading him into conflict with his interlocutor.

'I came to Orbajosa,' he said, 'on your invitation. You came to an agreement with my father . . .'

'Yes, yes, that's true,' answered Doña Perfecta, interrupting him suddenly and trying to regain her customary sweetness of manner. 'I don't deny it. I'm the real guilty party here. I'm the cause of your boredom, of the rudeness you've shown us and of all the unfortunate things which have happened in my house as a result of your coming here.'

'I'm delighted to hear that you recognize that fact.'

'You, on the other hand, are a saint. Will it also be necessary for me to kneel down before Your Grace and beg your forgiveness . . .?'

'Señora,' said Pepe Rey gravely, taking a pause from his dinner, 'I beg you not to make such cruel fun of me. I would not be capable of descending to that level . . . All I said was that I came to Orbajosa at your invitation.'

'That's true. Your father and I agreed that you should marry Rosario and you came here to get to know her. And of course, I welcomed you like a son . . . You seemed to love Rosario . . .'

'Excuse me,' objected Pepe. 'I did love and do love Rosario; you appeared to accept me as a son. But, while receiving me with deceptive cordiality, right from the start you used all means of trickery to oppose me and to prevent the fulfilment of the proposals you made to my father. From the very first day you set out to infuriate and frustrate me. With smiles and affectionate words on your lips you have been destroying me, roasting me over a slow fire. You have ambushed me in the dark with a mass of lawsuits and had me fired from the job I came to Orbajosa to do. On account of you I am discredited in the town; you had me thrown out of the cathedral and you have kept me away from the woman whom my heart has chosen. You have tortured your own daughter with incarceration worthy of the Inquisition, which will be the death of her if God does not intervene.'

Doña Perfecta turned scarlet. But the sudden flare-up, caused by her injured pride and the realization that her intentions had been revealed, soon passed and she became pale and bilious-looking once more. Her lips trembled. Throwing down her knife and fork, she suddenly stood up. So did her nephew.

'My God! Blessed Virgin!' exclaimed Doña Perfecta, raising both hands and clasping her head in a gesture appropriate for desperation. 'Can it be that I deserve such dreadful insults? Pepe, my child, is it really you speaking? . . . If I have done as you say, then I really am a terrible sinner.'

Then she dropped onto the sofa and covered her face with her hands.

Pepe, slowly approaching her, noted her bitter sobbing and the copious tears she was shedding. In spite of his conviction he could not repress the slight feeling of tenderness which overcame him and, thinking himself a coward, felt certain remorse for all he had said and the brutal manner in which he had said it.

'My dear Aunt,' he began, placing his hand on her shoulder, 'if you reply to me with tears and sighs, I shall be moved but not convinced. I need reasoning, not sentiment. Speak to me and tell me that I am wrong in my thinking, then prove it to me and I'll admit my error.'

'Leave me alone. You are not my brother's son. If you were you would not have insulted me the way you have done. So I'm a schemer, an actress, a hypocritical harpy and a skilful weaver of domestic intrigues, am I?'

As she spoke these words Doña Perfecta had already removed her hands from her face and was looking at her nephew with a beatific expression. Pepe was perplexed. The tears, together with the sweet voice of his father's sister, could not be phenomena without meaning for the mathematician's soul. The words with which to beg forgiveness were on the tip of his tongue. Generally speaking he was a man of great fortitude, but his reactions could be childlike when his emotions and feelings were affected. Such are the weak spots of mathematicians. They say that Newton was of a similar disposition.

'I will let you have the reasons you ask for,' said Doña Perfecta, motioning him to sit beside her. 'I wish to make amends to you so that you may see if I'm kind, tolerant and humble . . . Do you think I'll contradict you or flatly deny the things you have accused me of?. . . Certainly not, I don't deny them.'

The engineer was stunned.

'I don't deny them,' Doña Perfecta repeated. 'But I do deny the malicious intentions you attribute to them. What gives you the right to set yourself up as judge of things which you know only through circumstantial evidence and conjecture? Are you gifted with that supreme intelligence which is necessary in order to judge the actions of the rest of us and to pass sentence on us? Do you know our intentions because you are God?'

Pepe was even more stunned.

'Is it not reasonable in life sometimes to use indirect methods in order to achieve a good and honourable end? What right do you have to judge my actions when you don't really understand them? I, my dear nephew, confess to you with a sincerity which you don't deserve, that I have indeed indulged in subterfuge in order to achieve something which would be beneficial both to you and to my daughter. Can't you understand that? Has the cat got your tongue?. . . Ah, so your profound knowledge of mathematics and German philosophy is not equal to the subtle workings of a prudent mother's mind.'

'You astound me more and more,' said the engineer.

'You can be astounded as much as you like, but confess your barbarism,' declared the Señora, getting carried away. 'Acknowledge your flippant and brutal treatment of me, accusing me as you have. You're nothing but an inexperienced boy with no learning other than that picked up from books which teach nothing of the world or matters of the heart. You don't understand anything except how to build roads and docks. Oh, my dear young man, the way to the human heart is not through railway tunnels and you will never plumb its depths through a mine-shaft. You won't see into another man's conscience through a natural scientist's microscope, nor can you draw conclusions concerning the culpability of your fellow-man by surveying his ideas through a theodolite.'

'My dear Aunt, for God's sake!'

'Why do you call on God if you don't believe in Him?' Doña Perfecta said solemnly. 'If you believed in Him, if you were a good Christian, you would not have dared to pass such wicked judgements on my conduct. I'm a pious woman, do you understand? My conscience is clear, do you understand? I know what I'm doing and why I'm doing it, do you understand?'

'I understand, I understand, I understand.'

'God, in whom you do not believe, can see what you don't and cannot see: the intention. I'm not going to say any more to you: I have no wish to enter into long-winded explanations because there's no need. Nor would you understand me if I were to tell you that I wished to achieve my objective without any scandal, without offending your father, without offending you and without giving wagging tongues a flat rejection to talk about. I'll say none of these things to you because you wouldn't understand them either, Pepe. You're a mathematician. You see what's in front of you and nothing more; brutal nature and that's all; lines, angles, weights and nothing else. You see the effect but not the cause. A man who doesn't believe in God will never see the cause. God is the supreme intention of the world. Anyone who doesn't know Him is bound to judge everything the way you do: like a fool. For example, in a storm such a man will see only destruction; in a fire, only ruin; in a drought, only misery; in earthquakes, desolation, but, nevertheless, my proud young gentleman, in all of these apparent calamities one must look for the goodness behind the intention . . . yes, sir, the eternally good intention of Him who can do no evil.'

This prolix, subtle and mystical dialectic failed to convince Rey. But he had no wish to follow his aunt along the bitter path of such arguments, so he simply said:

'Very well, then, I respect your intentions . . .'

'Now that you seem to have seen the error of your ways,' the devout lady continued, growing ever bolder, 'I'll confess something else to you. I'm beginning to realize that I made a mistake in the way I went about things, although my objective could not be faulted. Given your impetuous nature and your inability to understand me, I ought to have met the problem head on and said: "Nephew, I do not wish you to be the husband of my daughter." '

'That is the language you should have used with me right from the very first day,' replied the engineer, sighing with relief, like a man freed from an enormous burden. 'I'm very grateful to you for those words. After being knifed in the dark, this slap in the face in broad daylight is very welcome.'

'In that case, nephew, I'll slap you again,' said Doña Perfecta, with as much aggression as disdain. 'Now you know. I don't want you to marry Rosario.'

Pepe fell silent. There was a long pause during which they both stared at each other as though the face of each appeared as a perfect work of art for the other.

'Don't you understand what I said?' she repeated. 'It's all over. There will be no wedding.'

'Allow me to say, dear Aunt,' replied the young man, unflinchingly, 'that I am not in the least put off by your commands. As things now stand, your negative attitude is of little consequence to me.'

'What's that you say?' exploded Doña Perfecta.

'You heard. I shall marry Rosario.'

Doña Perfecta stood up. She looked indignant, majestic and awesome; an anathema in female form. Rey remained seated, calm and steady, and showed that passive courage which comes from profound belief and unshakeable determination. He did not even blink beneath the full weight of his aunt's menacing ire. That is the kind of man he was.

'You're a fool. You, marry my daughter? Marry my daughter without my blessing?'

Doña Perfecta's trembling lips articulated these words in genuinely tragic tones.

'Without your blessing! . . . She is of a different opinion.'

'Without my blessing!' repeated the lady. 'Yes . . . and I repeat: I do not wish it, I do not wish it.'

'But she and I wish it.'

'Fool! Do you think you two are the only people in the

world? Are there no parents, no society, no conscience? Is there no God?'

'It is because there is society, because there is such a thing as conscience and because there is a God,' stated Rey seriously, standing up and raising his arm towards heaven, 'that I say again that I am going to marry Rosario.'

'Conceited wretch! If you trample everything underfoot, do you think there are no laws to put a stop to your violence?'

'It is because there are laws that I say again that I'm going to marry her.'

'You have no respect for anything.'

'For nothing which is not worthy of respect.'

'And what about my authority, and my wishes. Am I nothing?'

'As far as I'm concerned your daughter is everything; the rest, nothing.'

Pepe Rey's resoluteness was like the manifestation of some immovable force which was fully conscious of its own existence. It meted out withering, heavy blows with no hint of restraint. His words resembled, if the comparison is permissible, a remorseless artillery barrage.

Doña Perfecta sank down once more onto the sofa. She was not crying but her limbs were overcome by a convulsion of nervous twitching.

'So then, for this loathsome atheist,' she exclaimed with uncontained fury, 'there are no social conventions; there are only personal whims. What base avarice! My daughter is rich.'

'If your intention is to wound me with this subtle weapon, distorting the question and twisting my sentiments in an attempt to offend my dignity, you are mistaken, dear Aunt. Call me avaricious if you wish. God knows what I am.'

'You have no dignity.'

'That is a matter of opinion. The world may consider you to be infallible, but I don't. I am far from believing that the sentences you pass can have no appeal before God.'

'Do I hear you correctly? . . . Do you persist even though I refuse my blessing? You trample on everything; you're a monster, a bandit.'

'I am a man.'

'A wretch! There's no more to be said. I refuse to allow you to have my daughter's hand, I absolutely refuse.'

'Then I will take her. And I take no more than that which is mine.'

'Get out of my sight!' exclaimed the Señora, suddenly rising to her feet. 'Fool! Do you think my daughter even remembers you?'

'She loves me the same as I love her.'

'You lie! You lie!'

'She has told me so herself. Pardon me if in this matter I place more trust in the daughter's opinion than in the mother's.'

'When did she tell you if you haven't seen her for days?'

'I saw her last night and she swore to me before the figure of Christ in the chapel that she would be my wife.'

'What scandalous, libertine behaviour! . . . But what does this mean? My God, how disgraceful!' exclaimed Doña Perfecta, pressing her head between her hands again and striding around the room. 'Rosario went out of her room last night?'

'She came out to see me. And not before time.'

'Your behaviour is despicable! You have behaved like a thief in the night! Like a common seducer!'

'I was taking a leaf out of your book. My intentions were honourable.'

'And she came downstairs . . . I suspected as much. This morning, at daybreak, I surprised her in her room already dressed. She told me she had been out for some reason . . . The real criminal was you, you . . . This is disgraceful. Pepe, I thought you capable of anything, anything apart from this outrage. This is the last straw. Get out. As far as I'm concerned you don't exist. I forgive you, as long as you go now . . . I won't speak a word of this to your father . . .

What dreadful egoism! No, there is no love in you. You don't love my daughter.'

'God knows that I adore here, and that's sufficient for me.'

'Don't speak the name of God with your blasphemous lips! And be quiet!' exclaimed Doña Perfecta. 'In the name of God (and I can invoke his name because I believe in Him), I'm telling you now that my daughter will never be your wife. My daughter will be saved. Pepe: my daughter cannot be condemned to a life in Hell, and a union with you would be Hell.'

'Rosario will be my wife,' the mathematician repeated with moving equanimity.

The pious Señora was even more irritated by her nephew's quiet determination. In a voice choking with emotion she said:

'Don't think that your threats can frighten me. I know what I'm saying. Do you think you can trample a home, a family underfoot? Do you think you can just step on human and divine authority?'

'I'll trample everything underfoot,' said the engineer, beginning to lose his calm and expressing himself with a certain amount of agitation in his voice.

'You'll trample everything underfoot! Now we can see that you're a barbarian, a savage and a man who lives by violence.'

'No, dear Aunt. I am gentle, upright, honourable and an enemy of violence. But between you and me; between you who represents the law, and me, destined as I am to obey it, stands a poor tormented creature, one of God's angels subjected to iniquitous martyrdom. This spectacle, this injustice, this unprecedented violence is what has turned my honesty into barbarity, my reason into force, my sense of honour into the sort of violent reaction associated with thieves and murderers. This spectacle, Señora, is what drives me on to have no respect for your law and to rise above it, trampling everything underfoot. What seems like folly to you is a law which cannot be denied. I am doing what societies do when brutality which is as illogical as it is exasperating stands in the way of their progress. They rise up and destroy everything in one furious attack. This is the state I'm in at the moment; so much so that I can't recognize myself. My reason has become brutality; my respect has become insolence; I was a cultured man but now I have become a savage. You have brought me to this dreadful extreme by frustrating me and causing me to stray from the path of goodness along which I was progressing in peace and tranquillity. Who is to blame, you or I?'

'You are! You are!'

'Neither you nor I can decide that. I think we are both in the wrong. In you there is violence and injustice and in me there is injustice and violence. We have both been converted to barbarism. We fight and wound each other without mercy. God allows it to be so. My blood will flow over your conscience and your blood will flow over mine . . . But enough, Señora. I don't want to vex you with useless words. It's time now for action.'

'Time for action! Fine!' said Doña Perfecta, roaring rather than speaking. 'Don't think that there's no Guardia Civil in Orbajosa.'

'Farewell, Señora. I'm leaving this house, but I'm sure we'll see each other again.'

'Get out! Get out! Get out this minute!' she yelled, pointing to the door with a violent gesture.

Pepe Rey walked out. Doña Perfecta, after muttering a few incoherent words which were the clearest expression of her anger, collapsed onto a chair as if exhausted or suffering from some nervous attack. Her maids came running to her.

'Send for Don Inocencio!' she shouted. 'Right away! Immediately! Bring him here!'

Then she sank her teeth into her handkerchief.

CHAPTER 20

Rumours and fears

The day after this terrible argument certain rumours concerning Pepe Rey and his behaviour went the rounds in Orbajosa, from house to house, club to club, from the Men's Club to the chemist's shop and from the Paseo de las Descalzas to the Puerta de Baidejos. The rumours were relayed from person to person and the commentaries increased to such an extent that if Don Cayetano were to collect and compile them they would become a rich encyclopaedia of Orbajosan benevolence. Among the varying rumours which were spreading around there was agreement on one or two salient points, such as the following. The engineer, in a state of rage at Doña Perfecta's refusal to allow Rosario to marry an atheist, had *raised his hand* to his aunt.

The young man was living in the inn run by the widow Cusco. This establishment was furnished, as they say nowadays, not in the height of, but in the depths of the most backward fashion to be seen anywhere in the country. Lieutenant Colonel Pinzón visited the inn frequently in order to discuss the plot on which the two had embarked and which the soldier appeared more than capable of bringing to a successful conclusion. He never stopped dreaming up new schemes and stratagems and hastened good-humouredly to convert his thoughts into actions, even though he was in the habit of saying to his friend:

'The role I'm undertaking, my dear Pepe, is not one from which I am likely to emerge in a good light, but I'd crawl on my hands and knees to get back at Orbajosa and its inhabitants.'

We do not know what subtle manoeuvres were employed by the artful soldier, who was a past master at worldly ruses. But there can be no doubt that within three days of being billeted in the house he had managed to make everybody like him. His behaviour pleased Doña Perfecta, who could not but be moved by his flattering praise of the splendid house and the elegance, piety and solemn magnificence of Doña Perfecta herself. He also got on very well with Don Inocencio. Neither he nor Doña Perfecta prevented his speaking to Rosario (who had been granted her freedom after her brute of a cousin's departure) and with his smooth compliments, his clever flattery and consummate skill he achieved remarkable success and was even accepted on familiar terms in the Polentinos household. But the target of all his wiles was a maid, called Librada, whom he seduced (in the chaste meaning of the word) into carrying messages and notes to Rosario, pretending that he was in love with her. The girl could not resist his bribery, which took the form of honeyed words and a great deal of money, because she did not know the course of the letters and the true purpose of the schemes. If she had known that it was just another example of Don José's devilment, even though she had a soft spot for him, she would not have betrayed the Señora for all the money in the world.

One day, Doña Perfecta, Don Inocencio, Jacinto and Pinzón were all in the garden. The conversation turned to the troops and the mission which had brought them to Orbajosa, and the topic gave the Confessor a chance to condemn the Government's tyrannical conduct. Nobody knew how, but Pepe Rey's name also crept into the conversation.

'He's still staying at the inn,' said the young lawyer. 'I saw him yesterday and he asked to be remembered to you, Doña Perfecta.'

'Who ever heard of such insolence! Ah, Señor Pinzón, you

must not be shocked to hear me use such language when speaking of my own nephew. You know him . . . the young gentleman who was staying in the room you're in now.'

'Yes, I do know him. I don't have any contact with him, but I know him by sight and have heard about him. He's a close friend of our brigadier.'

'A close friend of the brigadier?'

'Yes, Señora. He's in command of the brigade which has just arrived in these parts and been deployed to the different villages.'

'And where is he?' the lady asked.

'In Orbajosa.'

'I think he's billeted in the Polavieja house,' said Jacinto.

'Your nephew,' continued Pinzón, 'and Brigadier Batalla are close friends. They're very fond of each other and can be seen together on the streets of the village at any hour of the day.'

'In that case, my friend, the impression I'm getting concerning the brigadier is a very unfavourable one,' declared Doña Perfecta.

'He's a . . . sad case,' said Pinzón in a tone of voice appropriate to one who, out of respect, opts for the milder expression.

'Present company excepted, Señor Pinzón, as we know you to be an honourable man, one has to admit that there are all sorts in the Spanish army,' stated Doña Perfecta.

'Our brigadier was an excellent soldier before he got carried away by spiritualism.'

'Spiritualism!'

'The sect whose followers call up ghosts and goblins through table legs!' exclaimed the canon, laughing.

'Purely out of curiosity,' said Jacintillo, stressing the point, 'I've sent to Madrid for Allan Cardec's book. It's a good idea to find out about everything.'

'Do people really go in for such nonsense? . . . Jesus! Tell me, Pinzón, is my nephew also involved with this table-leg sect?'

'I think it was he who initiated our brave brigadier.'

'Jesus!'

'That's right. And when the mood takes him he can talk to Socrates, Saint Paul, Cervantes and Descartes in the same way as I can talk to Librada now when I ask her for a match. Poor Señor Rey! I wasn't wrong when I said there was something the matter with his head!'

'Apart from this,' Pinzón continued, 'our brigadier is a fine soldier. If I have any criticism of him it's that he tends to be a bit too harsh. He obeys the government's order to the letter to such an extent that if he meets much opposition here he's capable of razing Orbajosa to the ground. Yes, I warn you to tread very carefully.'

'But a monster like that will cut off all our heads. Señor Don Inocencio, these visitations by the army remind me of what I've read about the lives of the martyrs when a Roman Pro-Consul made his appearance in a Christian village . . .'

'Such a comparison is not entirely inappropriate,' said the Confessor, looking at the soldier over the top of his spectacles.

'It's rather unfortunate, but as it's the truth, it has to be said,' Pinzón remarked benevolently. 'Now, Señora, gentlemen, you're under our command.'

'The local authorities,' interjected Jacinto, 'are still functioning perfectly.'

'I think you're mistaken,' said the soldier, whose face was being studiously observed by Doña Perfecta and the Confessor, 'the Mayor of Orbajosa was relieved of his duties an hour ago.'

'By the Provincial Governor?'

'The Governor has been replaced by a Government representative who is due to arrive tomorrow. All town councils will cease work as from today. This is what the Minister has ordered because he was afraid, although I don't understand why, that support was not being given to the central authority.'

'A fine state we're in,' murmured the canon, knitting his brows and thrusting out his lower lip.

Doña Perfecta remained pensive.

'Some of the Lower Court judges have also been removed from office, including the judge in Orbajosa.'

'The judge! Periquito!. . . Periquito is no longer our judge?' exclaimed Doña Perfecta, her gestures and facial expression recalling someone who has been bitten by a viper.

'The man who was the judge in Orbajosa yesterday is not judge today,' said Pinzón. 'A new one arrives tomorrow.'

'A stranger!'

'A stranger!'

'A rogue, perhaps . . . And the other was so honourable!' said the Señora anxiously. 'I never asked him any favour which he did not immediately grant. Do you know who's going to be the new mayor?'

'They say that a *corregidor*[1] is on his way.'

'Why don't you just say that the Flood is coming, and be done with it,' commented the canon, getting to his feet.

'So we're all at the mercy of the brigadier?'

'For a few days, at least. Don't be angry with me, though; despite my uniform I'm no friend of militarism. But when we're ordered to strike, we strike. There can be no baser profession than ours.'

'I won't argue with that,' said the Señora, failing to hide her anger. 'So now it's all out in the open; we have no mayor and no judge . . .'

'Nor Provincial Governor.'

'Let them sack our bishop, then, and send us some altar-boy in his place.'

'That's all we need . . . if we let them get away with it,' murmured Don Inocencio, lowering his eyes, 'they won't stop at trifles.'

'And this is all because they're afraid of a rebel uprising in Orbajosa,' exclaimed the Señora, clasping her hands and

---

[1] Office introduced by Fernando II in 1480 as an administrative innovation for extending the King's authority throughout Spain. As the King's representatives at local level, the Corregidor combined the duties of mayor, tax collector and magistrate.

moving them up and down, from her chin to her knees. 'Frankly, Pinzón, I can't understand why even the stones don't rebel. I bear no malice to you personally, but it would serve you right if the water you all drink turned you into mud . . . Did you say that my nephew is a close friend of the brigadier?'

'So close that they're always together all day. They were students at the same college. Batalla loves him like a brother and will do anything for him. If I were in your shoes, Señora, I'd be worried.'

'Oh, my God! I fear some outrage,' she exclaimed, greatly disturbed.

'Señora,' the canon blurted out, 'before allowing any outrage to befall this honourable household; before allowing the slightest misfortune to be visited on this noble family, I . . . my nephew . . . all your neighbours in Orbajosa . . .'

Don Inocencio did not finish. His anger was so violent that he was tongue-tied. He took a few martial strides, then sat down again.

'I feel that these fears are not unfounded,' said Pinzón. 'If it proves necessary, I . . .'

'And I . . .' echoed Jacinto.

Doña Perfecta had fixed her eyes on the french window of the dining room through which she could see a graceful figure and, as she gazed at it, the dark shadows of fear seemed to pass over her face.

'Rosario, come here! Rosario!' she said, walking towards her. 'You're looking much better today and you seem happier. Gentlemen, don't you think Rosario looks much better today? She seems a totally different person.'

They all agreed that her face was the very picture of supreme happiness.

CHAPTER 21

Sword, awake!

During those days the Madrid newspapers published the following news reports:

It is not absolutely certain that rebel bands have been formed in the area surrounding Orbajosa. We have had word from the area that the countryside is so little disposed to adventures that the presence of the Batalla brigade is there considered unnecessary.

It is reported that the Batalla brigade will leave Orbajosa, because there is no need for the army to be there, and deploy to Villajuán de Nahara where several rebel bands have formed.

It has been confirmed that some riders of the Aceros gang have been active in the region of Villajuán, near the administrative district of Orbajosa. The Governor of the province of X has telegraphed the Government with the information that Francisco Acero entered Roquetas where he collected six months' taxes and demanded rations. Domingo Acero (Faltriquera) has been roaming the Jubileo mountains, actively pursued by the Guardia Civil, who have killed one of his men and captured another. Bartolomé Acero was responsible for burning the civil registry office in Lugarnoble and taking the mayor and two of the principal landowners as hostages.

Total calm reigns in Orbajosa, according to a letter which we have had sight of, and the people there have nothing on their minds other than getting the fields ready for the next garlic harvest, which shows all the signs of being a magnificent one. It is true that the surrounding areas are infested with rebel bands, but the Batalla brigade will soon see them off.

And Orbajosa was indeed calm. The Aceros, that warrior family which, according to some, deserved a mention in the *Romanceros*, had taken control of the neighbouring province. But the insurrection had not spread into the area of the cathedral city. One might have thought that modern civilization had finally won its battle with the rebellious customs of lawlessness and was now enjoying the delights of lasting peace. And it is certainly true that Caballuco, one of the outstanding figures of the rebellions in Orbajosa, proclaimed for all to hear that he did not wish to 'quarrel with the Government or poke his nose into matters' which he might have to pay dearly for.

Say what you will, Ramos's reckless character had mellowed with the years. The explosive temper which he had inherited from his Caballuco parents and grandparents, the finest fighting dynasty that ever ravaged the earth, had cooled somewhat. It is said, moreover, that around that time the new governor of the province *held a conference* with this important personage, *and heard from his very lips the binding assurances* that he would contribute to the preservation of public order and not incite any disturbances. Reliable sources confirm that he had been seen in amicable comradeship with the soldiers, as thick as thieves with some sergeant or other at the inn, and it was even reported that he was on the verge of being offered a nice little job on the Town Council of the provincial capital. Oh, how difficult it is for the historian who strives to be impartial to filter out the truth from all the opinions and thoughts of the eminent persons who have achieved fame! One does not know what

to believe, and the lack of reliable information can give rise
to terrible mistakes. When faced with such conclusive evidence as the Brumaire incident, the Bourbon sacking of
Rome, the destruction of Jerusalem, what psychologist or
historian could fathom the thinking, either prior to or sub-
sequent upon the events, that went on in the minds of
Bonaparte, Charles V or Titus? What awesome responsibility
we bear! In order to at least partially escape from it we will
quote words, phrases and even speeches of the emperor of
Orbajosa himself and by so doing each of us may arrive at
an opinion which seems the most credible.

There can be no doubt that Cristóbal Ramos left his house
at nightfall and, having crossed the Calle del Condestable,
saw three peasants on donkeys riding towards him. When he
asked them where they were going they replied that they
were on their way to Doña Perfecta's house to deliver some
of the first fruits of the harvest and some rent money. The
peasants were Señor Paso Largo, a lad called Frasquito
González and the third, a middle-aged man with a weather-
beaten face, who was known as Vejarruco, even though his
real name was José Estéban Romero. Caballuco turned back,
enticed by the good company of these fellows, with whom
he had enjoyed an open and long-standing friendship, and
they all entered Doña Perfecta's house together. According
to the most reliable information these events took place at
nightfall, two days after Doña Perfecta and Pinzón had
discussed the matters which anyone who has read the previous chapter will be aware of. The great Ramos was involved
in passing on to Librada certain unimportant messages
which a woman from the neighbourhood had entrusted to
his retentive memory. When he entered the dining room, the
three above-mentioned farm labourers and Señor Licurgo,
who happened to be there by pure chance, had struck up a
conversation about the harvest and the house. The Señora
was in a foul temper, finding fault with everything and
scolding them mercilessly, blaming them for the drought and
the barren land, phenomena for which the poor men could

not be held responsible. The Father Confessor was witness to the whole scene. When Caballuco entered the good canon greeted him affectionately and motioned to him to sit down beside him.

'The great man himself!' said Doña Perfecta disdainfully. 'It can't be true that people talk so much about a man with so little courage! Tell me, Caballuco, is it true that some soldiers knocked you about a bit this morning?'

'Me? Me?' said the Centaur, rising to his feet indignantly like a man who has just received the greatest insult of all.

'That's what they say,' said the Señora. 'Isn't it true? I thought it was, since you have such a low opinion of yourself . . . if they spit on you you think yourself honoured to receive soldiers' spittle.'

'Señora,' retorted Ramos forcefully. 'But for the respect which I owe you, you who are more of a mother to me than my own mother, my lady, my queen . . . as I say, but for the respect which I owe to the person who has given me all that I own . . . but for the respect . . .'

'What? . . . It seems to me that you talk a lot but say nothing.'

'Then let me say that, with all due respect, this business about my being knocked about is slanderous,' he said, finding it extremely difficult to get the words out. 'They all talk about me, about whether I'm coming in or going out, going away or coming back . . . Why? Because they want to consider me a figurehead so that they can get the country up in arms. Let sleeping dogs lie, that's what I say, ladies and gentlemen. So the soldiers have come, have they? . . . That's bad. But what are we going to do with them? So the mayor and the secretary and the judge have all been sacked, have they? . . . That's bad. I wish the very stones of Orbajosa would rise up against them. But I gave my word to the Governor, and up to now I . . .'

He scratched his head, knitted his gloomy brow and, with his speech becoming clumsier and clumsier, he continued:

'I may be a coarse, ignorant, dull, stubborn and untrav-

elled yokel or whatever else you care to call me. But nobody
is more of a gentleman than I am.'

'Pity the poor Cid Campeador,' said Doña Perfecta scornfully. 'Don't you think, as I do, Father, that there isn't a
single man left in Orbajosa with any shame?'

'That's a pretty extreme opinion,' replied the priest, who
neither looked at his friend nor moved the hand supporting
his pensive face away from his chin. 'But it seems to me that
this region has accepted the heavy yoke of militarism with
excessive meekness.'

Licurgo and the three peasants almost burst their sides
laughing.

'When the soldiers and the new authorities,' said the
Señora, 'have taken our last farthing and humiliated the
village we'll send all the brave men of Orbajosa to Madrid
in a glass urn so that they can be put into a museum or
carted through the streets for all to see.'

'Long live the Señora!' exclaimed the one called Vejarruco
with an animated gesture. 'Her words are pure gold. It won't
be because of me that people will say there aren't any brave
men about. I'm not with the Aceros gang on account of
having three kids and a wife, and anything could happen.
Otherwise . . .'

'But haven't you given your word to the Governor?' the
Señora asked him.

'The Governor!' exclaimed the one called Frasquito González. 'There's no greater rogue in the whole country who
deserves a bullet more than he does. Governor and Government, they're all the same. On Sunday the priest gave us
such a sermon, couched in such flowery language, about the
heresies and offences against religion that are committed in
Madrid . . . Oh! You should have heard him! . . . Then he
began shouting from the pulpit, saying that religion doesn't
have any defenders any more.'

'Here's the great Cristóbal Ramos,' said the Señora, slapping the centaur hard on the shoulder. 'He gets on his horse
and rides around the square and along the road so that the

soldiers will notice him. The moment they see him they're struck with fear at the sight of our hero's fierce looks and they run away, fearing for their lives.'

The Señora ended the sentence with an exaggerated guffaw which was made all the more shocking by the profound silence of those who heard it. The colour drained from Caballuco's face.

'Señor Paso Largo,' the lady continued, becoming more serious, 'tonight, when you go home, send your son Bartolomé back so that he can spend the night here. I need to have some good people in the house. Even so, my daughter and I could be found some fine morning murdered in our beds.'

'Señora!' they all exclaimed.

'Señora!' exclaimed Caballuco, rising to his feet. 'Is that supposed to be a joke?'

'Señor Vejarruco, Señor Paso Largo,' continued the Señora, without looking at the local hero. 'I don't feel safe in my house. Nobody in Orbajosa does, but I least of all. I live in constant fear. I can't get a wink of sleep.'

'But who . . . who would dare?'

'Come now,' Licurgo exclaimed passionately, 'you know that I, old and infirm as I am, would be prepared to take on the whole Spanish army if anyone so much as harmed a hair of the Señora's head.'

'And Caballuco,' said Frasquito González, 'is more than enough.'

'Oh, no,' replied Doña Perfecta with cruel sarcasm, 'can't you see that Ramos has given his word to the Governor . . .?'

Caballuco sat down again, crossed his legs and then placed his folded arms on top of them.

'A coward is enough for me,' added the lady implacably, 'provided that he has not made any promises. The time may come when I'll see my house attacked, my beloved daughter will be torn from my arms and I shall be trampled into the ground and vilified in the most despicable manner . . .'

She was unable to continue. Her voice choked in her throat and she burst into uncontrollable weeping.

'Señora, for God's sake, calm yourself!. . . Come now . . . there's no reason . . .' Don Inocencio blurted out, his voice and his face revealing his agitated state. 'A certain degree of resignation is required if we are to endure the calamities which God visits upon us.'

'But who, Señora . . . who would dare to commit such dreadful acts?' one of the four asked. 'The whole of Orbajosa would rise up in order to defend the Señora.'

'But who? Who?' they all repeated.

'Come now, don't annoy the lady with inopportune questions,' said the Father Confessor officiously. 'I think you should leave now.'

'No, no, let them stay,' declared the Señora, drying her eyes. 'The company of those who serve me well is a source of great consolation to me.'

'A curse on my family,' said Old Lucas, thumping his knee with his fist, 'if all these shenanigans aren't the work of the Señora's very own nephew.'

'You mean Don Juan Rey's son?'

'From the moment I saw him at the station in Villahorrenda and he spoke to me in that honeyed voice and gesticulated like a courtier,' declared Licurgo, 'I took him for a big . . . I won't say what, out of respect for the lady . . . But I saw through him . . . I summed him up that very day and I wasn't wrong. I know that you can only tell the yarn by the thread, the cloth by the sample and the lion by its claws, as someone once said.'

'Let no one speak ill of this unfortunate young man in my presence,' said the lady of the house gravely. 'However great his faults may be, charity forbids us to speak of them or make them public.'

'But charity,' declared Don Inocencio rather vehemently, 'doesn't prohibit us from guarding against dangerous men, and this is the point here. Now that character and valour have declined so much in wretched Orbajosa; now that the people seem disposed to allow four soldiers and a corporal to spit in their faces, let us find protection by uniting together.'

'I'll defend myself to the best of my ability,' said Doña Perfecta, folding her hands in a gesture of resignation. 'The Lord's will be done!'

'All this fuss over nothing . . . By the life of . . . Everyone in this house is scared to death . . .' exclaimed Caballuco, half seriously and half in jest. 'Anyone would think that Don Pepito was a *region*[1] of devils. Don't be alarmed, Señora. My young nephew Juan, who is thirteen years old, will guard your house, and we'll see which of the nephews is the better man.'

'We know how much your bragging and boasting is worth,' retorted Doña Perfecta. 'Poor Ramos, you like to play the big hero even though anyone can see that you're nothing.'

Ramos paled slightly as he glared at the Señora with a mixture of fear and respect in his eyes.

'And you needn't look at me like that, my man. You know I'm not frightened by pompous oafs. Do you want me to tell you straight? You're a coward.'

Ramos, fidgeting like a man who had been stung all over his body, showed great discomfort. His nose exhaled and inhaled air like a horse's. Inside that enormous body a passion, a storm, an apoplexy was waging war against itself, roaring and bellowing as it struggled to get out. After half articulating some words and chewing up others he got to his feet and roared: 'I'll cut Señor Rey's head off.'

'What nonsense! You're as stupid as you're cowardly,' the Señora said, growing pale as she did so. 'What's all this talk about killing? I don't want anybody killed, least of all my nephew, whom I love in spite of his wickedness.'

'Murder! How atrocious!' exclaimed Don Inocencio, shocked. 'The man's mad.'

'Kill someone!. . . The very idea of a murder fills me with horror. Caballuco,' said Doña Perfecta, closing her gentle eyes, 'my poor man! While you've been trying to show us

[1] legion

how brave you are you've been howling like a man-eating wolf. Go away, Ramos, you're frightening me.'

'Did the Señora not say that she was afraid? Did she not say that her house would be destroyed and her daughter carried away?'

'Yes, that is what I fear.'

'And all this is going to be done by one man!' said Ramos scornfully, as he sat down again. 'All this is going to be done by Pepe Pipsqueak and his mathematics. It was wrong of me to say that I'd cut off his noddle. A dummy like him should be grabbed by the ear and thrown into the river for a good soaking.'

'Yes, you can laugh now, you beast. My nephew would not commit the outrages you've mentioned and which I fear all by himself. If he alone were responsible I'd have nothing to fear. I'd just tell Librada to stand at the door with a broom . . . and there'd be nothing more to it . . . But he's not alone.'

'Who else is there, then?'

'Idiot! Don't you know that my nephew is in cahoots with the brigadier commanding these damned troops?'

'In cahoots?' exclaimed Caballuco, obviously not understanding the word.

'She means they're accomplices,' said Licurgo. 'To be "in cahoots with" means "to be an accomplice of". The Señora has confirmed what I'd already suspected.'

'It all boils down to the fact that the brigadier and the officers are hand in glove with Don José, and what he wants is what those rough soldiers want, and those rough soldiers are capable of all manner of unspeakable deeds because that's their job.'

'And we've no mayor to protect us.'

'Nor judge.'

'Nor Governor. So the truth is that we're at the mercy of these ruffians.'

'Yesterday,' said Vejarruco, 'some soldiers enticed away Old Julián's youngest daughter and the poor girl didn't dare return home. But she turned up in tears and barefoot near the old fountain, picking up the pieces of her broken ewer.'

'Poor Don Gregario Palomeque, the notary from Naharilla Alta,' said Frasquito González. 'The cunning devils robbed him of all the money he had in his house. But the brigadier, when he was told about it, said that it was just a lie.'

'No mother ever gave birth to greater tyrants,' declared the other. 'I don't mind telling you that for two pins I could join the Aceros gang . . .!'

'What about Francisco Acero?' asked Doña Perfecta meekly. 'I should be very sorry if any harm were to befall him. Tell me, Don Inocencio, wasn't Francisco Acero born in Orbajosa?'

'No. He and his brother are from Villajuán.'

'That's unfortunate for Orbajosa,' said Doña Perfecta. 'Sad times have come to this poor town. Do you know if Francisco Acero promised the Governor not to stop the poor little soldiers kidnapping young girls or interfere with their irreligious, sacrilegious behaviour and heinous crimes?'

Caballuco gave a start. He felt, not as though he had been stung, but that he had been wounded by a vicious sabre swipe. His face flamed and his eyes filled with fire, then he shouted: 'I promised the Governor because he assured me that the troops had come with good intentions.'

'Don't shout, you brute. Speak like a human being and then we'll listen to you.'

'I gave my word that neither I nor any of my friends would start an uprising in the region of Orbajosa. And I said to all those who wanted one and were itching for a fight: *"Go with the Aceros, but there'll be no rebellion here . . ."* But I've got a lot of honourable people, yes, Señora, and good people, yes, Señora, and brave, yes, Señora, who are spread out in the big houses and in the villages and the outlying areas and the woods, each in his own house, see, and the moment I say the word, see, they take down their muskets, see, and make a dash, either on horseback or on foot, to wherever I tell them to go . . . and nobody comes to

me with flowery language . . . If I gave my word, I gave my
word, if I don't go out it's because I don't want to go out,
and if I want a rebellion there'll be one, if I don't, there
won't: because I am what I am, the same man as always, as
everyone knows . . . And I say again that I don't want
anybody coming to me with their flowery language, understand? . . . or distorting the facts, understand? . . . and if
anyone wants me to leave they should tell me straight to my
face, understand? 'cos that's what God gave us tongues for,
to say one thing or the other. The Señora knows full well
who I am, just as I know full well that I am indebted to her
for the very shirt on my back, and the bread I'll eat today,
and the first peas I tasted when I was weaned, and the coffin
my father was buried in when he died, and the medicines
and the doctor who got me on my feet again when I was ill.
And the Señora knows only too well that if she says to me:
"Caballuco, go and smash your skull," I'll go into the corner
and smash my skull against the wall. And the Señora knows
that if she says that it's daytime, even though I can see that
it's night, I'll think I've made a mistake and that it really is
daytime. The Señora knows only too well that she and her
estate are more important to me than my own life and that
if a mosquito were to sting her, I would forgive it only
because it's a mosquito. And the Señora knows that I love
her more than anything under the sun. To a man with a
heart such as mine, all she has to do is to say: "Caballuco,
you great brute, do this or do that", and to hell with all this
double talk, big words, talking in riddles, poking me here
and pinching me there.'

'Come on now, calm yourself,' said Doña Perfecta graciously. 'You've got yourself all hot and bothered like those
Republican demagogues who used to come here to preach
free-thinking, free love and goodness knows what other
freedoms . . . I'll have a glass of water brought to you.'

Caballuco rolled his neckerchief into a tight ball and used
it like a floorcloth to mop his broad forehead and the back
of his neck, both of which were running with sweat. A glass

of water was brought for him and the canon, with the gentleness of manner befitting his sacerdotal nature, took it from the maid's hands and offered it to him, holding the saucer as he drank. The water poured down Caballuco's throat, making a gurling noise as it did so.

'Now bring another one for me, Señora Librada,' said Don Inocencio, 'there's a bit of a fire burning inside me, too.'

CHAPTER 22

Awake!

'On the subject of the rebel bands,' said Doña Perfecta, when they had finished their drinks, 'I'm merely telling you to do as your conscience dictates.'

'I don't understand anything about dictates,' shouted Ramos. 'I'll do whatever the Señora wants.'

'But I can't give you any advice on a matter as grave as this,' she replied with the circumspection and restraint which suited her so well. 'This is a very, very delicate matter and I cannot give you any advice whatsoever.'

'But your opinion is . . .'

'My opinion is that you should open your eyes and see; that you should open your ears and hear . . . Consult your heart . . .; I admit that you have a great heart . . . Consult that judge, that advisor which knows so much and do as it commands.'

Caballuco thought for a moment; he thought about all those things about which a sword can think.

'We in Naharilla Alta,' said Vejarruco, 'counted ourselves yesterday and the number came to thirteen, a sufficient number for any task, however great . . . But as we were afraid that the Señora would be angry with us, we did nothing. It's sheep-shearing time now.'

'Don't you worry about the sheep-shearing,' said the Señora. 'There's plenty of time for that. All these goings-on won't stop it.'

'My two boys,' declared Licurgo, 'argued with each other yesterday because one wanted to go off with Francisco Acero and the other didn't. And I said to them: gently, lads, all in good time. Wait a bit, since the bread they make here is just as good as the bread they make in France.'

'Last night Roque Pelosmalos said to me,' declared Old Paso Largo, 'that as soon as Señor Ramos gave the order, everyone would take up arms. What a shame that the two Burguillos brothers have gone to work the lands in Lugarnoble.'

'Go and fetch them,' the lady said quickly. 'Señor Lucas, have a horse made ready for Old Paso Largo.'

'If the Señora and Señor Ramos order me to,' said Frasquito González, 'then I'll go to Villahorrenda to see if Robustiano, the forest bailiff, and his brother want to go with us.'

'That seems like a good idea. Robustiano doesn't dare come to Orbajosa because he owes me a small amount of money. You can tell him I'll let him off the six and a half duros . . . These poor folk, who are capable of sacrificing themselves so generously for the sake of a lofty ideal, are content with so little . . . Is that not so, Don Inocencio?'

'Our good friend Ramos, here,' replied the canon, 'informs me that his friends are unhappy with him on account of his being lukewarm; but the moment they see that he's made up his mind they'll all put on their cartridge belts.'

'What? Have you made up your minds to take to the streets?' said the Señora to Ramos. 'I haven't advised such a step and if you do so it's entirely your decision. Don Inocencio can't have suggested anything like that to you either. But for you to decide something like that, there must be very pressing reasons . . . Tell me, Cristóbal, would you care to dine? Would you like something to drink . . . Don't be shy . . .'

'As for my advising Señor Ramos to enter the fray,' said Don Inocencio, looking over the top of his spectacles, 'the Señora is right. I, as a priest, cannot advise such a course of action. I know that some do and that some even take up arms, but that seems very, very wrong to me, and I'll never be the one to imitate them. And I carry my own scruples to the extent of never even saying a word to Señor Ramos on the vexed question of his armed rebellion. I know that this is what Orbajosa needs, I know that all the inhabitants of this noble city will bless him; I know that we are about to witness deeds worthy of being recorded for posterity; but, nevertheless, allow me to maintain a discreet silence.'

'Well said,' commented Doña Perfecta. 'I don't like priests getting mixed up in such matters. This is how a learned cleric should behave. We are all aware that under certain serious circumstances, for example when one's country or faith is in peril, then the clerics are well within their rights to incite men to fight and perhaps even take part themselves. Since God himself took part in some famous battles, in the guise of angels or saints, so his ministers can do the same. During the war against the unbelievers, how many bishops led the Castillian armies?'

'Many, and some of them were outstanding warriors. But they were different times, Señora. It's true that if we take a close look at things we can see that our faith is in greater danger than it was then ... But what do the troops who are now occupying our city and the surrounding villages represent? What do they represent? Are they anything other than a vile instrument which the Protestants and atheists who have infested Madrid intend to use for the wicked conquest and extermination of our beliefs?... We are all well aware of it. In that centre of corruption, scandal, irreligion and non-belief a handful of evil men who have been bought by foreign gold are employed in destroying the seed of faith in this Spain of ours ... So what do you think? We are permitted to say mass and you are allowed to hear it only because they retain a modicum of consideration and shame ... but one fine day ... For my part, I remain calm. I'm a man who is not moved by temporal or worldly interests. Doña Perfecta knows this very well, as does everyone who knows me. I feel calm and the triumph of the wicked does not alarm me. I know only too well that there are terrible days ahead of us and that the lives of those among us who are men of the cloth hang by a thread. This is because Spain, without the shadow of a doubt, is about to witness scenes like those of the French Revolution during which thousands of the most pious priests perished in a single day . . . But I'm not bothered. When it's time for the guillotine, I'll bare my neck. I've lived long enough. What good am I? No good at all.'

'You can throw me to the dogs for food,' exclaimed Vejarruco, waving a fist which was as hard and strong as a hammer, 'if we don't soon finish off this thieving riffraff.'

'They say they're going to start pulling down the cathedral next week,' said Frasquito.

'I suppose they'll use picks and hammers,' said the canon, smiling. 'There are craftsmen who don't possess such tools and yet they make better progress when they're building. You must be aware that, according to sacred tradition, it took the Moors a month to destroy our beautiful Sagrario chapel and then it was immediately rebuilt in one night by the angels . . . Let them destroy it, let them . . .'

'In Madrid, according to what the priest of Naharilla told us the other night,' said Vejarruco, 'there are now so few churches that some priests say mass in the middle of the street, and many are reluctant to do this because they get kicked, reviled and spat upon.'

'Fortunately, here, my children,' declared Don Inocencio, 'we have not witnessed scenes of this nature. And why not? Because they know what kind of people you are and have heard of your ardent faith and courage . . . I wouldn't change places with the first man to lay hands on one of our priests or to interfere with our faith. It has to be said, though, that if they're not stopped in time they'll wreak havoc. Poor Spain, so holy, so humble and so good! Who could have known that we would come to such a pretty pass? But I maintain that impiety will not triumph, no, Señor. There are still brave men about; there are still people like those of yesteryear, is that not so, Señor Ramos?'

'There are, yes, Señor,' replied the latter.

'And I have a blind faith that the laws of God will triumph. Someone has to come out in their defence. If some don't then others will. Someone has to raise the palm of victory and with it eternal glory. The wicked will perish, if not today, then tomorrow. He who goes against the laws of God will fall, and that's all there is to it. Whether it be in this manner or that, the point is that he will fall. No sophistry, no means of escape or fancy footwork will save him. The hand of God is raised above him and will smite him, of that there is no doubt. Let us have pity on him and desire his repentance ... And as for you, my children, do not expect me to say a word about the step which you are surely about to take. I know you are good people. I know that your generous determination and the noble end that guides you will wash away any stain of sin that may be caused by the shedding of blood; I know that God blesses you; that your victory, like your death, will exalt you in the eyes of both God and Man; I know that you deserve applause and praise as well as all manner of honours. But, nevertheless, my children, my lips will never incite you to take up arms. This is something I have never done and will not do now. Do as your noble hearts bid you. If they command you to stay indoors, stay indoors; if they command you to leave your houses, leave them with my blessing. I am resigned to being a martyr and to offering my neck up to the executioner if these wretched troops remain here. But if a noble, ardent and pious urge on the part of the sons of Orbajosa contributes to the great act of extirpating the country's misfortunes, I shall consider myself the happiest of men for no other reason than that I am your fellow countryman. And my lifetime of study, penitence and resignation will not seem as valuable to me in my aspirations to reach heaven as a single day of your heroism.'

'Nobody could have said more or said it better,' exclaimed Doña Perfecta, overcome with excitement.

Caballuco was now leaning forward in his chair with his

elbows on his knees. When the canon had finished speaking, he took hold of his hand and kissed it fervently.

'No mother ever gave birth to a better man,' said Old Licurgo, wiping or pretending to wipe away a tear.

'Long live the Father Confessor!' shouted Frasquito González, rising to his feet and throwing his cap up to the ceiling.

'Silence,' said Doña Perfecta. 'Sit down, Frasquito. You're all talk and no action.'

'Heavens,' said Cristóbal, aflame with admiration, 'you have such a golden tongue! What a pair I have before me! While you two are alive, why should I need anybody else? All the people in Spain should be like you . . . But how could they be if they're all rogues! In Madrid, the capital, where the laws and pettyfogging officials come from, there's nothing but thievery and farce. See what they've done to our poor religion! . . . There's nothing but sin . . . Doña Perfecta, Don Inocencio, on the soul of my father, on the soul of my grandfather and on the salvation of my own, I swear that I want to die.'

'Die!'

'Let those curs kill me. I say that they should be allowed to kill me because I'm not big enough to draw and quarter them.'

'You're a big lad, Ramos,' the Señora said solemnly.

'Big? Did you say big? . . . I've an enormous heart, yes. But do I have fortified positions? Have I any cavalry? Do I possess artillery?'

'That is something I don't concern myself with,' said Doña Perfecta, smiling. 'Does the enemy not possess what you lack?'

'Yes.'

'In that case take it from him . . .'

'We will take it from him, yes, Señora, and when I say that we'll take it from him . . .'

'My dear Ramos,' said Don Inocencio, 'yours is an enviable position . . . to be able to distinguish yourself, to rise above the baser crowd, to put yourself on an equal footing with the world's greatest heroes . . . to be able to say that

your hand was guided by the hand of God! Oh, what glory
and honour! My friend, this is not flattery. What bearing,
what breeding and gallantry!. . . No; men of such mettle
cannot die. The Lord goes with them and the enemy's bullets
and swords falter . . . they don't dare . . . how could they
dare when they are fired from the cannon or wielded by the
hands of heretics? My dear Caballuco, when I see you, when
I note your dashing appearance and knightly presence, I
cannot help but call to mind verses from that epic ballad
which tells of the conquest of the Empire of Trebizond:

> 'Then up came valiant Roland
> armed fully to the teeth,
> astride the powerful Briador
> his might steed,
> with the powerful Durindana
> girt firmly around his waist,
> his lance, as straight as a die
> and his stout shield on his arm . . .
> Fire shot out from his
> helmet's visor
> and quivered the length of his lance
> like a very slender reed.
> An awesome threat was he
> to the serried ranks of the foe.'

'Very good,' exclaimed Licurgo, clapping his hands. 'And
I'll say, like Don Reinaldos:

> 'Let him who loves his freedom
> never lay hands on Reinaldos!
> Whoever wants anything else
> shall be so well repaid
> that none of the rest
> shall escape from my grasp
> before I've crushed him to bits
> or taught him a lesson.'

'Ramos, you'll be wanting to eat; you'll be needing a drink, won't you?' said the Señora.

'Nothing, nothing,' answered the centaur, 'unless by chance you can let me have a plate of gunpowder.'

As he spoke he gave a loud guffaw, walked around the room a few times, watched by all as he did so, and then, coming to a halt, fixed his eyes on Doña Perfecta and, in a stentorian voice, uttered the following words:

'I say that there's nothing more to say. Long live Orbajosa! Death to Madrid!'

He then brought his hand down on the table with such force that the whole storey of the house shook.

'What tremendous spirit!' said Don Inocencio.

'Now that's what I call a pair of fists!'

Everyone looked at the table which had been split into two.

Then they turned their eyes to Reinaldos, or Caballuco, always insufficiently admired. There was no denying that there was, in his handsome face, in his green eyes, animated by some strange feline glare, in his black hair, in his Herculean body, a certain expression and air of greatness, a hint or rather a memory of the great races who have dominated the world. But in his overall appearance there was evidence of pitiable degeneration and it required considerable effort to detect the noble and heroic vestiges beneath his present brutishness. He resembled Don Cayetano's great men in the same way as a mule resembles a horse.

CHAPTER 23

Mystery

The meeting continued for a considerable time after the events we have related, but we shall omit the rest of it, as it is not necessary for a clear understanding of this story. Eventually everyone left and the last to leave, as usual, was Don Inocencio. There had not been time enough for Doña Perfecta and the canon to exchange even two words, when an old and trusted maid, Doña Perfecta's right hand, entered the dining room and, seeing her disturbed and upset, her mistress also became upset, suspecting that something untoward was happening in the house.

'I can't find the Señorita anywhere,' said the maid in reply to the Señora's questions.

'Jesus! Rosario!. . . Where's my daughter?'

'Bless me, Our Lady of Perpetual Succour!' cried the Father Confessor, picking up his hat and making ready to run after the Señora.

'Search everywhere for them . . . But wasn't she with you in her room?'

'Yes, Señora,' answered the old woman, trembling. 'But the devil tempted me and I fell asleep.'

'Damn your sleep!. . . Dear Jesus!. . . What does this mean?. . . Rosario! Rosario!. . . Librada!'

They went upstairs and downstairs and then downstairs and upstairs again, candles in hand and searching all the rooms. Finally the Father Confessor's voice was heard on the staircase, as he cried out for joy:

'Here she is! Here she is! She's turned up.'

A moment later mother and daughter stood face to face in the hallway.

'Where were you?' Doña Perfecta asked severely as she surveyed her daughter's face.

'In the garden,' replied her daughter, more dead than alive.

'In the garden at this hour? Rosario!'

'I was so hot so I leaned out of the window, dropped my handkerchief and went down into the garden to look for it.'

'Why didn't you tell Librada to fetch it for you?... Librada!... Where is that girl?... Has she fallen asleep too?'

Eventually Librada appeared. Her pale face reflected the offender's consternation and suspicion.

'What's all this? Where have you been?' asked the Señora, very much displeased.

'Well, Señora ... I went downstairs to fetch the linen from the room overlooking the street and fell asleep.'

'Everybody's sleeping tonight. It seems to me that some-body won't be sleeping in my house tomorrow. Rosario, you may go.'

Realizing that prompt, energetic action was called for, the Señora and the canon set about their investigations immediately. Questions, threats, entreaties and promises were all employed with consummate skill to root out the truth of what had happened. It turned out that the aged maid was in no way to blame; but Librada made a full confession, between sobs and sighs, of all her misdemeanours, which we shall summarize as follows:

Soon after being billeted in the house Pinzón had begun to make eyes at Señorita Rosario. He gave money to Librada, she said, in order to retain her as a carrier of messages and billets doux. Rosario did not appear offended, but, on the contrary, seemed to enjoy it, and so several days passed in this manner. Finally, the servant girl stated that Rosario and Pinzón had arranged to see each other by the window in the latter's room, which looked out onto the garden, and talk. They told the girl of their intention and she agreed not to tell anyone in exchange for a certain sum which was to be paid there and then. The plan was that Pinzón was to leave the house at the usual time and return without being seen at nine o'clock and enter his room. He would then leave his room and the house, again without being seen, and return at his usual late hour without trying to hide the fact. By acting in this manner he thought no one would suspect him. Librada waited for Pinzón, who came in all wrapped up in his cape and without saying a word. He went into his room just as Rosario was going down into the garden. Librada, while the tryst took place but at which she was not present, stood on guard in the hallway to warn Pinzón of any approaching danger. After an hour the latter left, without saying a word and all wrapped up in his cloak as before. When she had finished her confession, Don Inocencio asked the poor girl:

'Are you certain it was Señor Pinzón who went in and came out?'

The cuplrit said nothing in reply but her features revealed considerable perplexity.

The Señora went green with rage.

'Did you see his face?'

'But who else could it have been?' replied the girl. 'I'm certain it was him. He went straight to his room and he knew the way very well.'

'The strange thing is,' said the canon, 'that there was no need for him to use such subterfuge as he lives in the house . . . he could have pretended to be ill and stayed in . . . is that not so, Señora?'

'Librada,' exclaimed Doña Perfecta in a fit of rage, 'I swear to God you'll end up in prison.'

Then she clenched her hands, locking the fingers so tightly together that she all but made them bleed.

'Don Inocencio,' she exclaimed, 'let us die . . . there's nothing else to do but die.'

Then she began to sob inconsolably.

'Courage, Señora,' said the priest in moving tones. 'You

must show great courage . . . Now is the time to be brave.
What is required now is a steady hand and a stout heart.'

'I have a very stout heart,' replied Señora de Polentinos
between sobs.

'And I certainly do not,' said the canon, 'but we'll see.'

CHAPTER 24

The Confession

Meanwhile Rosario, with her heart torn asunder, unable to cry, unable to find peace of mind or tranquillity, transfixed by the cold steel of unbearable pain, her mind to-ing and fro-ing between the world and God and God and the world, stunned and driven half-mad, was in her room in the early hours of the morning, on her knees with her hands clasped in prayer, her bare feet on the ground, her passionate breast leaning on the edge of the bed, in the darkness, all alone and surrounded by silence. She was careful not to make the slightest sound to attract the attention of her mother, who was sleeping, or pretending to be asleep, in the next room. She directed her impassioned thoughts to Heaven in the following manner:

'Dear Lord, why did I not know how to lie before but now I do? Why did I not know how to deceive before, but now I deceive? Am I a wicked woman? What I feel and what I'm experiencing, is it the downfall of women who are then unable to rise up again? Have I ceased to be good and honourable?. . . I don't recognize myself. Am I the same woman, or is somebody else standing here? . . . So many terrible things have happened in so few days! So many new emotions! My heart has been consumed by all these feelings!. . . Dear Lord, can you hear my voice, or am I condemned to pray throughout eternity without being heard?. . . I am virtuous; nobody will convince me that I am not virtuous. Is it perhaps wicked to be in love, to be very much in love?. . . But no . . . this is an illusion, a trick. I am worse than the worst women on earth. I have a great viper within me and it is eating me away and poisoning my heart . . . What is it I feel? Why do you not kill me, Lord? Why do you not cast me down into Hell for eternity? It frightens me, but I confess, here, all alone, to God who can hear me, and I shall confess to the priest. I hate my mother. I cannot explain why. He has never spoken a word to me against my mother. I don't know how this came about . . . How wicked I am! Demons have taken possession of me. Help me, oh Lord, for I lack the strength to control myself . . . a terrible force is driving me out of this house. I want to escape, I want to run away from here. If he doesn't take me away I'll follow him, dragging myself along the highways . . . What divine happiness is this that combines with such bitter grief within my breast? Lord, Father in Heaven, give me a sign. All I want is to love. I was not born for this rancour which is eating away at me. I was not born to pretend to be other than I am, or to lie or to deceive. Tomorrow I'll go into the centre of the street and shout to anyone who walks past: "I love, I hate". . . . That's how I'll lift this weight off my heart . . . What bliss it will be to be able to reconcile everything, to love and respect everyone. May the Holy Virgin favour me . . . That terrible thought again. I don't want to think about it, but I do. I don't want to feel it, but I do. This is one point over which I can't deceive myself. I can neither destroy it nor lessen it . . .; but I can and do confess it, saying, "Lord, I hate my mother!" '

Finally she started to feel drowsy. During her disturbed sleep her imagination recreated all that had happened that night, distorting it but not changing it in essence. She could hear the cathedral clock strike nine. It was a delight for her to see that her aged maid was sleeping the sleep of the just, and to leave her room very softly so as not to make a noise; she was descending the stairs so quietly that she dared not move a foot until she was sure that she would not make the slightest sound. She was going out into the garden, past the servant girls' room and the kitchen. Then she paused for a moment in the garden to gaze at the dark, star-spangled sky. There was no wind. Not a sound broke the deep serenity of the night. She seemed to feel within her a silent, fixed attention, like that of eyes that stare without blinking and ears which are cocked for some important event . . . The night was watching.

Then she approached the french window of the dining room, cautiously looking in from a distance, fearing that the people inside might see her. By the light from the dining room lamp she could see her mother's back. The Father Confessor was standing to her right and his profile appeared strangely distorted. His nose was growing and starting to resemble the beak of some strange bird, while his whole figure became a foreshortened shadow, thick and black, angular in places, ridiculous-looking, scrawny and thin. Caballuco was facing her, more like a dragon than a man. Rosario could see his green eyes, like two great lanterns with convex glass panes. The glow from them together with his imposing animal figure filled her with fear. Old Licurgo and the other three looked like grotesque figurines. Somewhere, probably on the clay dolls at fairgrounds, she had seen such stupid smiles, such crude forms and such blank facial expressions. The dragon was waving its arms about but they turned like the blades of a windmill instead of behaving normally. His green lantern-like eyeballs, so like the coloured jars in a chemist's shop, rolled from side to side. His stare was blinding . . . The conversation seemed to be interesting. The Father Confessor was flapping his wings. He looked like a bird that wanted to fly but was unable to. His beak seemed to elongate and curve downwards. He ruffled his feathers furiously, then, pulling himself together and calming down, he tucked his close-cropped head under his wing. Then the adobe figurines moved about, trying to be human, and Frasquito González tried hard to pass for a man.

Rosario was overcome with an inexplicable sense of fear as she looked on that friendly gathering. She moved away from the window and advanced, step by step, looking all around her to see if she was being observed. Although she could see nobody, she felt as though a million eyes were riveted on her ... But her fears and shame suddenly dissipated. A blue man appeared in the window of the room occupied by Señor Pinzón. The buttons on his chest shone like strings of tiny lights. She went up to him. At that moment she felt a pair of arms, trimmed with braid, lift her up like a feather and, in one rapid movement, deposit her in the centre of the room. Everything changed. All of a sudden there was a crashing noise as a violent blow shook the whole house to its foundations. Nobody knew what had caused such a din. They trembled and said not a word.

It was the moment when the dragon broke the table in the dining room.

CHAPTER 25

Unexpected happenings.
A fleeting disagreement

The scene changes. Imagine now a beautiful room – bright, simply furnished, cheerful and comfortable and surprisingly clean. Fine rush matting covers the whole floor and the white walls are adorned with the beautiful prints of saints and a few sculptures of doubtful artistic merit. The ancient mahogany furniture gleams after its Saturday polishing and the altar on which an ostentatious Virgin, draped in blue and silver, receives the adoration of the household, is covered with a thousand delightful trinkets, half of them sacred and half profane. There are also little pictures made of beads, fonts for holy water, a clock-case with an *Agnus Dei*, a withered palm from Palm Sunday and more than a few vases in which stand scentless, artificial roses. A massive oak bookcase contains a rich and well-chosen library; Horace, the Epicurean and sybarite, along with gentle Virgil, in whose poems one sees the passionate heart of Dido tremble and melt for love; Ovid, with his long nose, at once sublime, obscene and ingratiating, next to Martial, that insolent yet witty rascal; the ardent Tibullus with Cicero the Great; the harsh Titus Livius, with the terrible Tacitus, scourge of the Caesars; Lucretius, the pantheist; Juvenal, who could use his pen like a dagger; Plautus, who dreamed up the best plays in the classical world while turning a millstone; Seneca the philosopher of whom it has been said that the greatest thing he did in life was to die; Quintillian the orator; Salust the rogue who speaks so well of virtue; both the Plinys, Suetonius and Varro. In a word, all the Latin writers from Livius Andronicus's first stutterings to the last breath of Rutilius.

But during the time we have been making this useless, if hasty list, we have failed to notice that two ladies have entered the room. It is very early, but in Orbajosa everyone gets up very early. The little birds are singing their heads off in their cages; the church bells are ringing for mass and the goats which are about to be milked at the doors of the houses are ringing the bells which hang from their necks.

The two ladies whom we see in the room described have just returned from attending mass. They are dressed in black and each is carrying in her right hand a prayer book and a rosary, wound around her fingers.

'Your uncle won't be much longer,' said one of them. 'He was beginning mass when we left, but he doesn't waste any time and he'll be in the vestry now disrobing. I would have stayed to hear mass, but I have a lot of things to do today.'

'Today I heard only the cathedral preacher's mass,' said the other. 'He gets through them in a single breath, and I don't think I gained much from it because I was worried and couldn't stop thinking about these dreadful things that have been happening to us.'

'But what can we do . . . We must have patience . . . We'll see what your uncle advises us.'

'Oh!' exclaimed the second woman, releasing a deep, painful sigh . . . 'It makes my blood boil.'

'God will protect us.'

'To think that a person such as yourself, a lady like you should be threatened by a . . .! And he shows no sign of giving up . . . Last night, Doña Perfecta, as you told me to do, I went back to the inn run by the widow Cusco and asked for any new information. Pepe and Brigadier Batalla are always planning something . . . My God! They're forever dreaming up their infernal plans and drinking their way through bottles of wine. They're two lost, drunken souls. They must be dreaming up some evil deed. I was so con-

cerned about you last night, when I was at the inn, that
when I saw Don Pepe go out I followed him . . .'

'And where did he go?'

'To the Men's Club. Yes, Señora, to the Men's Club,'
replied the second woman, somewhat agitated. 'Later on he
went back home. Oh, how my uncle scolded me for indulg-
ing in all this espionage till all hours! But I had no choice
. . . May the Lord protect me! I can't help it, and seeing
somebody such as you in such a dangerous predicament
drives me mad . . . But it doesn't matter, Señora, it doesn't
matter. I'm watching in case those rascals attack the house
and take Rosario away from us . . .'

Doña Perfecta, her eyes directed towards the ground,
thought for a while. She was pale and frowning. Finally she
exclaimed: 'But I don't see any way of stopping him.'

'But I do,' said the other woman in a trice. She was the
Father Confessor's niece and Jacinto's mother. 'I can think
of a very easy way: the one I've already mentioned to you
but which you didn't like. Ah! Señora, you're too virtuous.
At times like these it pays to be a little less perfect . . . put
your scruples to one side. Do you think that would offend
God?'

'María Remedios,' said the Señora haughtily, 'don't talk
nonsense.'

'Nonsense! . . . You, you may be very clever, but you've
no idea how to teach that good-for-nothing nephew of yours
a lesson. What could be simpler than what I'm proposing?
As there's no legal system to protect us any more, let's take
the law into our own hands. Don't you have men in your
house who can be used for anything? Well, then, call them
and say to them, "Look, Caballuco, Paso Largo or whoever:
get yourself well wrapped up tonight so that nobody will
know who you are. Take a trusty friend with you and stand
behind the corner on Santa Faz Street. Wait for a bit, and
when José Rey comes along the Calle de la Tripería on his
way to the Club, because he's bound to go to the Club . . .

do you see what I mean? When he comes along, jump out and give him a fright . . ." '

'María Remedios, don't be so foolish,' retorted the Señora with magisterial dignity.

'Nothing more than a fright, Señora. Listen to what I say: a fright. It's not as if I were suggesting some crime. As God is my saviour! The very idea fills me with horror and I can almost see blood and fire before my eyes. Nothing of that sort, Señora . . . A fright and nothing more than a fright, just to make that brigand understand that we're well protected. He goes to the Club alone, Señora, entirely alone, to meet up with his cronies, the ones with their sabres and helmets. Let's suppose that he gets a good fright, and perhaps a couple of broken bones, but nothing serious in the way of wounds, of course, you know what I mean?. . . Then he'll either flee Orbajosa like a coward, or they'll have to keep him in bed for a fortnight. But you'd have to tell them to make sure it was a really good fright. No killing . . . they'd have to make sure of that. Just let him know the meaning of a good drubbing . . .'

'María,' said Doña Perfecta haughtily, 'you are incapable of any lofty thought, or great and redeeming resolution. What you are advising is cowardly and beneath my dignity.'

'All right, then, I won't say another word . . . Oh, dear, what a fool I am!' exclaimed the Father Confessor's niece with humility. 'I'll save my stupid ideas so that I can console you with them after you've lost your daughter.'

'My daughter!. . . lose my daughter!. . .' exclaimed Doña Perfecta in a sudden attack of anger. 'It makes me mad just to hear you say that. No; they will not take her from me. If Rosario doesn't despise that lost soul, as I wish she would, then she soon will. A mother's authority counts for something . . . We'll uproot that passion of hers, or rather, her whim, in the same way that a blade of grass can be uprooted before it's had time to put down roots . . . No, we can't do as you suggest, Remedios; whatever happens, we can't. Even the most desperate methods aren't enough for that madman. Rather than see her as the wife of my nephew I could accept the worst that could happen to her, even death.'

'Better to see her dead, buried and food for worms,' declared Remedios, like someone at prayer, 'than see her in the power of . . . Oh, Señora, don't take offence if I say that it would be a sign of great weakness to yield because Rosario has had a few trysts with that hothead. What happened the night before last, according to what my uncle told me, seems to me like some low trick on the part of Don José to get his way by causing a scandal. Many men behave like that . . . Oh, Holy Jesus, I don't understand how any woman can look a man in the face if he's not a priest.'

'Be quiet, be quiet,' said Doña Perfecta vehemently, 'don't talk to me about the night before last. What a terrible thing to happen! María Remedios . . . I understand that anger can condemn a soul to eternal damnation but I'm burning with rage . . . How unhappy it makes me to witness all these things and not be a man!. . . But if I must tell the truth about the night before last, I still have my doubts. Librada swears blind that it was Pinzón who entered. My daughter denies everything; my daughter has never told a lie!. . . But still I have my suspicions. I think that Pinzón is a damned go-between; but nothing more.'

'That brings us back to where we were before: that the cause of all our woes is that blessed mathematician . . . My heart didn't lie when I saw him for the first time . . . So, Señora, you can resign yourself to even worse if you don't decide to call Caballuco and say to him: "Caballuco, I hope that . . ."'

'You're harping on the same thing again; but you're a simpleton.'

'Oh! I may be a simpleton, but there's nothing I can do about it. I just say what I think, without thinking.'

'Anybody could have thought up this idea of yours, this nonsense about giving him a good drubbing and a fright. You're no brainbox, Remedios. Whenever you have a serious problem to solve, you always come up with hare-brained schemes like this one. I'd expect a more dignified response from well-bred people of noble blood. A drubbing! How ridiculous! Moreover, I don't want my nephew to get even a scratch on my orders; certainly not. God will punish him in one of his own admirable ways. It only behoves us to work in a manner which will not hinder God's plans. María Remedios, in matters like these it's necessary to go directly to the root cause. But you understand nothing about causes . . . you only see insignificant details.'

'That may be so,' said the priest's niece with humility. 'But why did God make me so feeble-minded that I can't understand any of these lofty ideas?'

'You have to get to the bottom of things, the very bottom, Remedios. Do you still not understand?'

'No.'

'My nephew is not my nephew, woman. He is blasphemy, sacrilege, atheism and demagogy . . . Do you know what demagogy is?'

'Something to do with those people who set Paris on fire with kerosene and the people who destroy churches and shoot at icons . . . I understand you so far.'

'Well, my nephew is all of those things. If only he were alone in Orbajosa! . . . But he is not, my child. Through a series of misfortunes, each of which is proof of the passing evils which God sometimes visits upon us in order to punish us, my nephew is the equivalent of an army, of the Government's authority, of the mayor, of the judge . . . My nephew is not my nephew; he is the nation of officialdom, Remedios. He's that nation within the nation made up of the damned souls who rule in Madrid, which has taken control of material power; of that imaginary nation, for the real nation consists of those who remain silent, pay up and suffer; of that fictitious nation which signs decrees, makes speeches, and makes a farce of government, a farce of authority and a farce of everything. Today that is what my nephew is. You must learn to see what lies behind events. My nephew is the

Government, the brigadier, the mayor and the new judge. They all favour him because he and they all think alike; because they're as thick as thieves and all wolves from the same pack ... You mark my words. We must defend ourselves from them, for all are one and one is all. We must attack them in a group, not by beating them up as they turn a corner, but in the way that our forebears fought the Moors ... the Moors, Remedios! ... My dear child, understand this well: open your mind and let just one noble idea enter in ... let your imagination soar and raise your thoughts, Remedios ...'

Don Inocencio's niece was awestruck in the face of such loftiness of spirit. She opened her mouth to say something in keeping with these high-minded sentiments, but could manage no more than a sigh.

'Like they fought the Moors,' repeated Doña Perfecta. 'This is a question of the Moors and Christians. And did you believe that by frightening my nephew you'd put an end to everything?... How stupid you are! Can't you see that his friends are supporting him? Can't you see that we're at the mercy of that rabble? Can't you see that any of his junior lieutenants could set fire to my house if it pleased him?... Can't you see that? Can't you understand that you have to delve beneath the surface? Can't you understand the immense size and scope of my enemy? We're not talking just about one man, but a whole movement ... Can't you understand that my nephew, as he stands before me today, is not a single calamity but a whole plague?... Against it, dear Remedios, we'll raise a battalion of the Lord which will annihilate the infernal militia from Madrid. I tell you, it's going to be great and glorious.'

'If only it were, finally ...'

'But do you doubt it? This day we are to witness terrible things ...' said the Señora with great impatience. 'Today, to-day. What time is it? Seven. So late and nothing is happening!'

'Perhaps my uncle knows something. Here he is now. I can hear him coming up the stairs.'

'Thank God . . .' said Doña Perfecta, standing up in order to go and meet the Father Confessor. 'He'll have some good news for us.'

Don Inocencio came rushing in. His pained expression showed that his soul, devoted to piety and Latin studies, was not so tranquil as usual.

'Bad news,' he said, placing his hat on a chair and untying the strings to his cape.

Doña Perfecta paled.

'They're arresting people,' said Don Inocencio, lowering his voice, as if a soldier were hiding under every chair. 'No doubt they suspect that the people here will not take too kindly to their tedious games so they've been from house to house arresting anyone with a reputation for bravery . . .'

The Señora threw herself down onto a chair and gripped its wooden arms tightly.

'All we need now is to hear that they were arrested without a fight,' interjected Remedios.

'Many of them, a great many,' said Don Inocencio with approving gestures as he addressed the Señora, 'had time to escape and have arrived in Villahorrenda with arms and horses.'

'And Ramos?'

'In the cathedral I was told that he's the one they're searching for most urgently . . . Oh, my God . . . Arresting the poor wretches who have done nothing yet . . . I don't understand how any Spaniard worth his salt can remain so patient. Doña Perfecta, Señora, talking to you like this about the arrests made me forget to tell you that you should return home at once.'

'Yes, immediately . . . Are those bandits going to search my house?'

'Perhaps, Señora. These are dark days,' said Don Inocencio in solemn and emotional tones. 'May God have pity on us.'

'In my house I have half a dozen well-armed men,' replied the Señora, greatly annoyed. 'What iniquity! Are they capable of taking them away as well?'

'I'm sure Señor Pinzón will not have missed the opportunity to denounce them. Señora, I repeat that these are dark days.'

'I'm on my way. Make sure you call in to see me.'

'Señora, as soon as I've dismissed the class . . . and I have the feeling that, with all the trouble there is in the village, all the pupils will be playing truant today. But, whether there's a class or not, I'll call in to see you . . . I don't want you to go out alone, Señora. Those ne'er-do-well soldiers are strutting about the streets . . . Jacinto! Jacinto!'

'That's not necessary. I'll go alone.'

'Let Jacinto go with you,' said the latter's mother. 'He's bound to be up now.'

They heard the rapid footsteps of the young doctor of law, who was running down the stairs as fast as his legs would carry him. He entered, his face flushed and gasping for breath.

'What's the matter?' his uncle asked.

'In the Troya house,' said the young man, 'in the house belonging to those . . . well . . .'

'Spit it out!'

'Caballuco's there.'

'Up there? . . . In the Troya house?'

'Yes, Señor . . . he spoke to me from the terrace and said he was afraid they were coming to get him there.'

'Oh, how stupid!. . . That clown will let himself get caught,' exclaimed Doña Perfecta, stamping the floor impatiently.

'He wants to come down here and for us to hide him in the house.'

'Here?'

The canon and niece looked at each other.

'Let him come down,' said Doña Perfecta vehemently.

'Here?' repeated Don Inocencio, with an expression of displeasure on his face.

'Here,' answered the Señora. 'I know of no house where he could be safer.'

'He could easily jump through the window of my room,' said Jacinto.

'If he really has to . . .'

'María Remedios,' said the Señora, 'if they take that man away from us, all is lost.'

'A fool and a simpleton I may be,' replied the canon's niece, placing a hand on her breast and suppressing a sigh which was about to emerge, 'but they will not arrest him.'

The Señora ran out. Moments later the centaur was lounging in the armchair where Don Inocencio usually sat when he was composing his sermons.

We have no idea how Brigadier Batalla came to hear of it, but the fact remains that this diligent soldier received intelligence that the Orbajosans had changed their plans and, that very same morning, he ordered the arrest of those who in our rich language of rebellion are referred to as *known troublemakers*. The great Caballuco was miraculously saved by taking refuge in the Troyas' house; but believing that he was not safe there, he went down, as we have seen, to the canon's saintly dwelling, which was beyond suspicion.

All night the troops, stationed at various points, kept a close watch over those who entered or left the village, but Ramos managed to elude them by evading, or perhaps not evading, the military precautions. This put the final touches to enflaming the minds of the inhabitants, and a crowd of people gathered under cover of darkness in the houses near Villahorrenda, only to disperse in daylight and prepare for the arduous task of rebellion. Ramos ran through the neighbourhood, rallying people to arms, and as the flying columns of soldiers chased the Aceros gang in the region of Villajuán de Nahara, our chivalrous hero covered a lot of ground in a short time.

Night after night, with consummate audacity, he took the risk of entering Orbajosa, using clever tactics, or perhaps bribes. His popularity and the protection he was afforded inside the town acted as some degree of security, and it would be no exaggeration to say that the soldiers failed to display the same zeal towards the daring champion as towards the 'little men' of the locality. In Spain, and especially in time of war, which always has a demoralizing effect here, such base submissiveness to the powerful is common, while ordinary folk are persecuted without mercy. Helped, then, by his audacity, or bribery, or whatever, Caballuco went into Orbajosa, recruited more men, gathered arms, and raised money. For his own greater safety, and in order to stay within the letter of the law, he never set foot in his own house, and seldom went to Doña Perfecta's to discuss important matters. He generally had his meals with one or other of his friends, always preferring the respected home of some priest, and mainly that of Don Inocencio where he had been given asylum on the sad morning of the arrests.

Meanwhile Batalla had telegraphed the Government and informed it that he had discovered a rebel conspiracy and taken the ringleaders into custody, and that the few who had managed to escape had fled in disarray, *actively pursued by our columns.*

CHAPTER 26

María Remedios

There is nothing more entertaining than to look for the causes of those important events which astonish or disturb us, and nothing more gratifying than to discover them. When we see violent passions in hidden or open conflict, and, spurred on by the natural impulse which always accompanies human observation, we succeed in locating the hidden source whence flow the waters of that turbulent stream, we experience a sensation similar to the joy known to geographers and explorers.

God has granted us this joy now, for in exploring the hidden recesses of the hearts that beat through this story, we have uncovered a fact which is surely the progenitor of the most important events here narrated: a passion which constitutes the first drop of water of this raging torrent whose course we are observing.

So let us, then, continue with our story. Let us leave Señora de Polentinos and not concern ourselves with what may have happened to her on the morning of her conversation with María Remedios. Full of misgivings, she returns home where she is obliged to endure the apologies and courtesies of Señor Pinzón, who assures her that as long as he is alive, the Señora's house shall not be searched. Doña Perfecta answers him disdainfully, without deigning to look at him, and this causes him to ask urbanely about the reason for her displeasure. She replies by asking Señor Pinzón to leave her house, putting off until a more opportune moment an account of his treacherous behaviour in her home. Don

Cayetano arrives and he and Pinzón exchange words as one
gentleman to another. But since another matter interests us
more, let us leave the Polentinos and the lieutenant colonel
to patch up their differences as best they can, and go on to
consider the historical sources mentioned above.

Let us direct our attention to María Remedios, an estimable
woman to whom we must devote a few lines. She was a lady,
a real lady, for despite her very humble origins the virtues of
her uncle, Don Inocencio (also of humble origin, but elevated
by Holy Orders as well as his learning and respectability),
had shed extraordinary splendour on the entire family.

The love which Remedios felt for Jacinto was one of the
most vehement passions a mother's heart can contain. She
was devoted to him. She placed the well-being of her son
above all human considerations and believed that he was the
most perfect example of beauty and talent ever created by
God. To see him happy, successful and in an influential
position she would have sacrificed all her days and even part
of her eternal glory. Sacred and noble as it is, maternal
feeling is the only sentiment which is allowed exaggeration;
the only one not rendered illegitimate by excess. However,
there is a particular phenomenon which is by no means
uncommon in life: when the exaltation of maternal love is
not accompanied by complete purity of heart and by perfect
honesty, it may run wild and be transformed into a lament-
able frenzy which, like any other excessive passion, can lead
to great errors and catastrophes.

In Orbajosa, María Remedios was considered a paragon
of virtue and a model niece and, indeed, perhaps she was.
Her help was there for all who needed it. She never started
tittle-tattle or malicious gossip. She never got involved in
any intrigues. She was pious, sometimes even to the point of
being sanctimonious. She practised charity; she managed her
uncle's house efficiently; she was well received, admired and
fêted everywhere, despite the feeling of almost unbearable
suffocation she engendered with her incessant sighing and
permanently querulous tone of voice.

But in Doña Perfecta's house this virtuous lady suffered a kind of *capitis diminutio*. In days gone by, which were tragic for the whole family of the good Father Confessor, María Remedios (if it is true, why should it not be said?) had been the Polentinos' washerwoman. This is not to say that Doña Perfecta looked down on her; nothing of the sort. Her treatment of her was not based on pride; she felt a sisterly affection for her. They ate together, prayed together and shared each other's troubles. They helped each other in their charities and in their devotions, as well as in household matters . . . But, nevertheless, it has to be said that there was always something, always an invisible line that could not be crossed, between the parvenu and the born lady. Doña Perfecta used the familiar form of address with María, whereas the latter could never bring herself to dispense with certain formalities when she spoke to the Señora. Don Inocencio's niece felt so small in the presence of her uncle's friend that her natural humility took on a certain tinge of sadness. She noticed that the good canon was like a permanent royal counsellor in Doña Perfecta's house. She saw her beloved Jacintillo held in almost the same loving familiarity as Rosario, even though the poor niece and mother visited the house as seldom as possible. It should be pointed out here that María Remedios felt herself socially declassed (the word will serve) in Doña Perfecta's house. She found this very disagreeable for there was a spark of pride in that sighing soul, as there is in every living creature . . . To see her son married to Rosarito, to see him rich and powerful, to see him related to Doña Perfecta, to the Señora! . . . Ah, for María Remedios that would have been Heaven on earth, the best of both worlds, and would have made her existence supremely complete. Her mind and heart had been filled with that sweet light of hope for many years. For this she was good or bad; pious and humble or terrible and ill-behaved; for this she was whatever she wanted to be. For without such an idea, María, who was the very incarnation of her own plan, would not have existed.

Physically, María Remedios could not have looked more insignificant. Her distinguishing feature was a surprisingly youthful vigour which belied her true age. She still always wore widow's weeds, even though many a long year had passed since the death of her husband.

Five days had passed since Caballuco first entered the Father Confessor's house. Night was falling. Remedios entered her uncle's room with a lighted lamp and, after placing it on the table, sat down facing the old man who had been, since mid-afternoon, immobile and pensive in his armchair as though he had been nailed to it. His chin was supported by his fingers, which wrinkled the swarthy skin, unshaven now for three days.

'Did Caballuco say that he was coming here to dine tonight?' he asked his niece.

'Yes, Señor, he's coming. The poor folk are safer in respectable houses like this.'

'Well, I'm not completely easy in my mind, despite the respectability of my home,' replied the Father Confessor. 'What risks that brave Ramos takes! . . . And I've been told that in Villahorrenda and its environs there are many men . . . I've no idea how many men! . . . What have you heard?'

'That the soldiers are committing atrocities . . .'

'It's a miracle that those savages haven't searched my house! I swear that if I see a pair of those red breeches, I'll be struck dumb.'

'A fine mess we're in!' said Remedios, expelling half of her soul in a sigh. 'I can't stop thinking about the predicament Doña Perfecta's in . . . Oh, Uncle, you must go to her.'

'Go there tonight? . . . The troops are wandering about through the streets . . . Imagine if a soldier takes it into his head to . . . The Señora is well defended. The other day they searched her house and arrested the six armed men she had there. But they released them later on. We have nobody to defend us if there's an attack.'

'I've sent Jacinto to her house to stay with her for a while. If Caballuco comes we'll tell him to go there as well . . .

Nobody can tell me that those rascals aren't planning some terrible deed against our friend. The poor Señora! Poor Rosarito!. . . To think that this could have been avoided by what I suggested to Doña Perfecta two days ago . . .'

'My dear niece,' said the Father Confessor phlegmatically, 'we have done all that is humanly possible in order to put our sacred project into effect . . . Nothing more can be done. We've failed, Remedios. Get that into your head and don't be so stubborn. Rosarito cannot be the wife of our beloved Jacintillo. Your golden dream, your ideal of happiness which once seemed so attainable, and to which, like a good uncle, I dedicated all the resources of my mind, has become an illusion, and has dissipated like smoke. Serious obstacles, the wickedness of one man, the unquestionable passion of the girl and other things I need not mention, have turned things upside down. We were on our way to winning, and now suddenly we're beaten. Ah, niece, make up your mind to accept one thing. At this precise moment, Jacinto deserves much better than that foolish girl.'

Whims and stubbornness,' replied María with disrespectful irritation. 'That's a fine thing to bring up now, Uncle! The great minds are really coming to the fore now! . . . Doña Perfecta with her lofty ideas and you with your apprehensions; neither of you has solved anything. It's a pity God made me so foolish, giving me this brain made out of bricks and mortar, as the Señora says, because if I were not like this I'd have found a solution to the problem.'

'You?'

'If she and you had allowed me to get on with it, the problem would have been settled by now.'

'With cudgels?'

'Don't look so startled. I'm not talking about killing anyone . . . Come now!'

'A drubbing,' said the canon, smiling, 'is like scratching . . . you know what I mean?'

'Rubbish! . . . You can call me cruel and bloodthirsty, too. I haven't got the courage to kill a worm, as you well know

. . . Everyone understands that I didn't have it in mind to be the cause of a man's death.'

'To sum up, my child: whichever way you look at it, Don Pepe Rey takes the girl. There's no way of avoiding that now. He's prepared to use any means, even dishonour. If Rosarito . . . how she deceived us with her coy expression and heavenly eyes, eh?. . . I say that if Rosarito were not in love with him . . . well, then . . . everything would sort itself out. But she does love him . . . like a sinner loves the devil; she's consumed by a criminal passion and has fallen, María, into that infernal libidinous trap. Let's be honest and fair; let's turn our attention away from the ignoble couple and think no more of either of them.'

'You don't understand women, Uncle,' said Remedios with flattering hypocrisy, 'you're a saintly man; you don't understand that all this business with Rosario is nothing more than a passing whim. It's one of those whims that can be cured with a couple of good slaps round the face and half a dozen lashes.'

'Niece,' said Don Inocencio gravely and sententiously, 'when there have been serious goings-on, little whims are not called little whims, but something else.'

'Uncle, you don't know what you're saying,' replied the niece, blushing suddenly. 'Why, surely you can't be thinking that Rosario . . . how awful! I'll defend her, yes, I'll defend her . . . She's as pure as an angel . . . Come, now, Uncle, this sort of talk makes me blush and you make me angry.'

As she spoke thus, a cloud of sadness spread over the good priest's face, making him look ten years older.

'My dear Remedios,' he said, 'we've done everything that is humanly possible and everything that could or should be done in good conscience. Nothing could be more natural than our desire to see Jacintillo marry into that great family, the most important family in Orbajosa. Nothing could be more natural than our desire to see him owner of the seven houses in town, the farm of Mundogrande, the three orchards of Arriba, the colonial properties, and all the other urban and rural property which the girl owns. Your son has great merit, we all know that. Rosarito used to like him and he liked Rosarito. It seemed a foregone conclusion. The Señora herself, while not being over-enthusiastic about it, seemed well disposed to the idea, because of her high esteem and respect for me, as her friend and confessor ... Then suddenly this wretched young man turns up. The Señora tells me that she had made a pact with her brother and therefore could not reject the proposal. What a grave conflict! But what was I to do when faced with the facts? Oh, you can't imagine what it was like. I'll be frank with you: if I had seen in Señor de Rey a man of principle who was capable of making Rosario happy, I should not have interfered in the affair. But the young man seemed to me to be a calamity, and as I'm responsible for the family's spiritual well-being, I was obliged to become involved in events and I did just that. As you know, I went straight for him, as the popular expression goes. I revealed his vices; I revealed his atheism; I revealed the rottenness of that materialistic heart for all the world to see, and the Señora was convinced that he was leading her daughter into vice ... Oh, the anxiety I experienced! The Señora vacillated, but I lent fortitude to her indecisive mind. I advised her on the lawful means she could use against her nephew in order to get rid of him without causing a scandal. I suggested ingenious stratagems. And, as she frequently revealed to me how her pure conscience was disturbed, I pointed out just how far she could go legally in the battles we were waging against that ferocious enemy. I never advised violent or bloody methods, nor dreadful atrocities, but subtle subterfuge which could not be construed as sinful. My conscience is clear, dear niece. But you know that I have fought and slaved like a Trojan. My word, when I returned home at night and said, "Mariquilla, it's all going to plan", you were besides yourself with glee and kissed my hand a hundred times, and called me the greatest man in the world. So why are you so angry now, disfiguring your noble character and gentle nature? Why do you scold me? Why do you say that you're annoyed with me and make no bones about calling me a simpleton?'

'Because,' replied the woman, still irritated, 'you've suddenly turned into a coward.'

'The point is that everything is against us, woman. That cursed engineer, the darling of the troops, is capable of anything. The girl loves him; the girl . . . I don't want to say any more. It cannot be; I tell you that it cannot be.'

'The troops! But do you believe, as Doña Perfecta does, that there'll be war, and that in order to throw Pepe Rey out of here it's necessary for one half of the country to rise up against the other? . . . The Señora has taken leave of her senses and you're going the same way!'

'Her thoughts and mine are the same. Given the bond between Pepe Rey and the troops, the personal aspect is even more important . . . But, my dear niece, two days ago I had hopes that our brave men would kick the troops out, but since then I've seen the way things have turned out. Most of our men were taken by surprise before they could strike a blow. Caballuco is in hiding and it's all virtually over for us. So now I've lost faith in everything. Fine principles still lack the material strength to smash the ministers and emissaries of evil . . . Alas, María, it's a case of resignation, resignation.'

Adopting his niece's idiosyncratic mannerisms, Don Inocencio sighed noisily two or three times. María, against all expectations, remained totally silent. Outwardly, at least, there was no anger in her, or any of the superficial sentimentality which she normally displayed. There was nothing but a deep and modest suffering. A few moments after her good uncle had concluded his peroration, two tears trickled down the niece's rosy cheeks. Then some half-suppressed sobs were heard, and little by little, like the sea which roars and swells as it is being whipped up by a storm, the swell of grief in María Remedios grew and grew until it burst into uncontrollable weeping.

CHAPTER 27

A canon's torment

'Resignation, resignation!' repeated Don Inocencio.

'Resignation, resignation!' she repeated, wiping away her tears. 'Since my beloved son is destined to remain a complete nonentity, then so be it. Lawsuits are not so abundant; the day is coming when being a lawyer will count for nothing. What use is talent? What's the point of all that studying and swotting? Ah, we're paupers. The day will come, Señor Inocencio, when my son won't even have a pillow on which to rest his head.'

'My good woman! . . .'

'My good man!. . . If I'm wrong, tell me this: what kind of legacy do you intend to leave him when you close your eyes? Some loose change, six dog-eared books, poverty and nothing more . . . The times are coming when . . . What times, Uncle!. . . My poor son, whose health is not as robust as it was, won't be able to work . . . already his head swims as soon as he starts reading a book, and working at night makes him sick and gives him a bad head . . . He'll have to resort to begging in order to make a miserable living; I'll have to take in sewing, and who knows, who knows . . . we may have to beg for alms.'

'My good woman!'

'I know what I'm talking about . . . A fine time awaits us,' added the excellent woman, exaggerating the plaintive whine in her voice as she spoke. 'My God, what will become of us? Only a mother's heart is capable of feeling these things; only a mother can endure so much pain for the sake of her son's well-being. How could you be expected to understand? No; it's one thing to have children and to suffer pain for them, but it's another thing entirely to sing the *gori gori* in the cathedral and teach Latin in the Institute . . . My son is your nephew, he achieved excellent results and he is the pride and joy of Orbajosa . . . but what good will it do him?. . . He'll die of hunger, because we know what a lawyer earns, or we'll have to ask the Ministers to give him a post in Havana and then he'll die of yellow fever . . .'

'But, my good woman . . .!'

'No, I won't worry. I won't say any more. I won't bother you any more. I'm very impertinent, easily moved to tears and I'm always sighing. People find me difficult to take because I'm a loving mother and I'm concerned about my son's well-being. I'll die; yes, sir, I'll die without saying a word and choking back my anguish. I'll drink my own tears so as not to vex the canon . . . But my beloved son will understand and won't cover his ears as you're doing now . . . Woe is me! Poor Jacinto knows that I'd let them kill me for his sake and that I'd sacrifice my own life for his happiness. Poor child of my womb! To be so talented and yet be condemned to a life of mediocrity and humility. Now don't you go getting on your high horse, Uncle . . . No matter what airs and graces we give ourselves, you can't get away from the fact that you're the son of Father Tinieblas, the sacristan in San Bernardo's church . . . And I'll never be anything other than the daughter of Ildefonso Tinieblas, your brother, who used to sell pots and pans, and my son will always be the grandson of the Tinieblas . . . Darkness casts a shadow over our whole family and we can never come out from under it. Nor will we ever possess a piece of land we can call our own, or shear our own sheep or milk our own goats. I'll never be able to plunge my arms up to the elbows in a sack of wheat which has been threshed and winnowed in our own threshing barns . . . all because of your lack of guts, your foolishness and soft heart . . .'

'But . . . but my good woman . . .!'

The canon's voice increased in pitch each time he uttered this phrase, and he rocked his head from side to side, covering his ears with his hands, in a pained gesture of desperation. María Remedios's shrill wailing grew constantly sharper, piercing the brain of the unhappy and now stupefied cleric like a dart. But suddenly the woman's face changed. Her plaintive sobs were transformed into a rasping, harsh voice. Her face turned pale; her lips trembled and she clenched her fists. A few long strands of dishevelled hair fell over her forehead and the heat of fury burning within her dried her eyes completely. She rose from her chair and, not like a woman, but like a harpy screamed out:

'I'm leaving! I'm going away with my son! . . . We'll go to Madrid. I have no wish for my son to rot in this dump of a town. I'm sick and tired of seeing how he'll never amount to anything under the protection of the church. Do you hear me, Uncle? My son and I are off! You'll never see us again! Never!'

Don Inocencio had clasped his hands together and was taking the furious tongue-lashing from his niece with the consternation of a prisoner for whom all hope is dashed by the mere presence of the hangman.

'For God's sake, Remedios!' he murmured in a pained voice, 'for the sake of the Holy Virgin!'

These crises and frightening eruptions from such a gentle character as his niece were as powerful as they were rare, and as much as five or six years could pass without Don Inocencio seeing Remedios explode in anger.

'I'm a mother! I'm a mother! . . . And since nobody else is going to look out for my son I'll do it myself,' roared the improvised lioness.

'For the sake of the Holy Virgin, woman, don't get so worked up . . . See what a sin you're committing . . . Let us say a Pater Noster and an Ave Maria, and then you'll see how all this will pass.'

As he spoke the Father Confessor trembled and sweated like a poor chicken in the talons of a vulture! The woman, transformed, gave him the final mortal squeeze with the following words:

'You're a good-for-nothing; a ne'er-do-well . . . My son and I are leaving here for ever, for ever. I'll find a position for my son; I'll see him well set up, do you understand? I'm ready to sweep the streets with my tongue if that's what it takes to feed him. I'll move heaven and earth to find my son a position to help him get on and make himself rich. I want him to be somebody, a gentleman, a landowner, respected and important and all the rest . . . everything, everything.'

'God preserve me!' exclaimed Don Inocencio, collapsing onto a chair and letting his head sag onto his chest.

There was a pause, during which all that could be heard was the enraged woman's heavy breathing.

'Woman,' said Don Inocencio at last, 'you've shortened my life by ten years. You've set my blood on fire and made me mad . . . May God grant me the patience to put up with you. Patience, Lord, patience is what I need! And you, my niece, do me a favour and cry and weep, snivel and sigh for the next ten years. The skilful way you can turn on the waterworks, which I find so annoying, is preferable to these stupid displays of temper. If I didn't know that, deep down, you're a good person . . . Just look at the way you're behaving, and after having confessed and taken Communion this morning.'

'Yes, but it was because of you, because of you!'

'Because in the Rosario and Jacinto affair I advised resignation?'

'Because just as everything was going so well you turned round and let Señor Rey win Rosario.'

'And how could I have prevented it? The Señora's right when she says you're about as intelligent as a brick. Do you expect me to go out of here with my sword and, in two shakes of a lamb's tail, make mincemeat of the troops and then face Rey, saying "Leave the girl alone or I'll cut your throat"?'

'No. But when I advised the Señora to give her nephew a

fright, you were opposed to it, instead of giving her the same advice as I did.'

'All this talk about giving him a fright is madness.'

'Because "when the dog dies the rabies dies with it".'

'I cannot advise what you refer to as a "fright", which might turn into something very serious.'

'Of course. Because I'm a thug, isn't that so, Uncle?'

'You know very well that only ruffians indulge in fisticuffs. And moreover, do you think he's the kind of man who frightens easily? And his friends?'

'He goes out at night alone.'

'How do you know?'

'I know everything. And he doesn't make a move without my knowing about it. You understand? The widow Cusco keeps me informed about everything.'

'Stop this; you're driving me mad. And who's going to give him this fright? . . . Let's know.'

'Caballuco.'

'You mean to say he's agreed?'

'No. But he will if you tell him to.'

'Come, come, woman. Leave me in peace. I cannot order such an atrocity. A fright! And what exactly does that mean? Have you discussed it with him yet?'

'Yes, but he didn't take any notice of me or, rather, he refused to have anything to do with it. In Orbajosa there are only two people who could persuade him with one simple command: you and Doña Perfecta.'

'Well, let the Señora give the command if she wants to. I will never agree to the use of violent and brutal methods. Believe me when I say that, when Caballuco and his men were trying to incite an armed uprising, nobody could make me say one word to encourage them to shed blood. No, this is not the way . . . If Doña Perfecta wants to do it . . .'

'She doesn't either. I spent two hours talking to her this afternoon. She says she'll advocate war and will support it by any means necessary. But she will not order any man to

stab another in the back. She'd be right to oppose my
suggestion if it were a question of something more serious
. . . but I don't want anybody to be wounded. I just want
him to get a fright.'

'But if Doña Perfecta is unwilling to order anyone to give
the engineer a fright, and I won't either . . . you understand
what I'm saying? Nothing is more important than my
conscience.'

'Fine,' replied his niece. 'Tell Caballuco to accompany me
tonight . . . but don't tell him anything else.'

'Are you going out tonight?'

'Yes, I am. So what? Didn't I go out last night?'

'Last night? I didn't know. If I had known, I should have
been angry. Yes indeed, Señora.'

'Don't say anything to Caballuco apart from the following: "Dear Ramos, I would be very grateful if you could
accompany my niece on a certain errand which she is obliged
to undertake tonight and defend her, should she be in any
danger."'

'I can certainly do that. Let him accompany and defend
you. Ah, you rogue! You're trying to trick me and make me
an accomplice to some wicked deed.'

'Of course . . . what do you expect?' said María Remedios
sarcastically. 'Ramos and I'll cut a good few throats between
us tonight.'

'Don't jest about it! I say again that I'm not going to
advise Ramos to do anything which could smack of wickedness. I think he's here . . .'

A noise was heard at the front door. Then came the voice
of Caballuco, who was talking to the servant. Some
moments later the hero of Orbajosa entered.

'The news, let's have the news, Señor Ramos,' said the
priest. 'Come on, you must give us hope in exchange for
dinner and hospitality . . . What's happening in Villahorrenda?'

'Something,' replied the braggart, taking a seat and showing signs of tiredness as he did so, 'you'll soon see if we're worth our salt.'

Like all people who are important or who would wish to appear so, Caballuco showed great reserve.

'Tonight, my friend, if you wish, you'll take away the money I was given to . . .'

'It's about time . . . the troops won't let me pass if they get a sniff of it,' said Ramos, laughing brutally.

'Be quiet, man . . . We know you can get through whenever you want. It goes without saying. The troops are very lax . . . if they cause any trouble, just cross their palm, eh? And I notice that you're quite well armed . . . The only thing you haven't got is an eight-pounder cannon. Pistols, eh? . . . And a knife.'

'Just in case,' said Caballuco, removing the weapon from his belt and revealing its murderous blade.

'In the name of God and the Virgin!' exclaimed María Remedios, closing her eyes and turning her face away in horror. 'Be careful with that thing. It frightens me just to look at it.'

'If you have no objection,' said Ramos, putting the weapon away, 'let's eat.'

María Remedios quickly prepared everything so that the hero would not become impatient.

'Listen to me, Señor Ramos,' said Don Inocencio to his guest just as they were beginning to eat, 'have you got much to do tonight?'

'There is something I must do,' replied the braggart. 'This is the last night I'll be in Orbajosa, the very last. I have to round up some of the lads who live in these parts and then we're going to see if we can get the saltpetre and sulphur which are kept in the Cirujeda house.'

'I only asked,' said the priest jovially, replenishing his friend's plate, 'because my niece wants you to accompany her for a while. She has some errand to run and it's a bit late for her to go out alone.'

'Is she going to Doña Perfecta's house?' asked Ramos. 'I was there a little while ago but didn't want to stay.'

'How is the Señora?'

'A bit afraid. Tonight I took away the six lads she had in the house.'

'Good Lord! Didn't you think they were needed there?' said Remedios anxiously.

'They're needed more in Villahorrenda. Brave people rot inside houses. Isn't that so, Canon?'

'Señor Ramos, that house should never be left unattended,' said the Father Confessor.

'The servants are more than enough. But, Don Inocencio, do you think that the brigadier will bother attacking private houses?'

'Yes. But you surely know that this damned engineer . . .'

'There's no shortage of brooms in the house to take care of him with,' retorted Cristóbal jovially. 'In the end they'll have to let them get married . . . after all that's happened . . .'

'Señor Ramos,' said Remedios, with sudden anger, 'it seems to me that you have little understanding about people marrying.'

'I said that because earlier on tonight I saw the Señora and the girl enjoying a kind of reconciliation. Doña Perfecta was smothering Rosario with kisses and it was all affectionate and tender words.'

'Reconciliation! All this talk about weapons has made you lose your mind . . . But, anyway, will you accompany me or not?'

'It's not the Señora's house she wants to go to,' said the priest, 'but to the widow Cusco's inn. She was saying that she didn't dare to go alone because she was afraid of being insulted . . .'

'By whom?'

'You know very well. By that damned scoundrel of an engineer. Last night my niece saw him there and gave him the rough end of her tongue, so she's a bit on edge tonight. The young man's spiteful and insolent.'

'I don't know if I'll be able to go . . .' retorted Caballuco. 'As I'm now in hiding, I can't challenge José Pipsqueak. If I were not as I am, with one half of my face covered up and the other uncovered, I'd have already broken his back for him thirty times. But what'll happen if I ambush him? I'll have blown my cover and then the troops will nab me and it'll be "goodbye, Caballuco". And as for using treachery, that's something I wouldn't know how to do; it's not in my nature and the Señora wouldn't consent to it either. Cristóbal Ramos doesn't go in for premeditated beatings.'

'Have we taken leave of our senses? . . . What are you saying?' said the Father Confessor, his face showing unmistakable signs of astonishment. 'It never even crossed my mind to advise you to harm the gentleman. I'd rather cut out my tongue than suggest such a heinous act. The wicked will fall; that is true. But it is God who must decide the moment, not I. Nor is there any question of anybody getting a thrashing. I would rather be thrashed myself ten dozen times than recommend that such medicine be meted out to a Christian. I have only one thing to say to you,' he added, looking at the hero over the top of his spectacles, 'and this is that as my niece is going there and very probably . . . is that not so, Remedios? . . . may have to exchange words with that man, I'm suggesting that you might care to protect her in case she is insulted . . .'

'There are things I have to do tonight,' Caballuco replied in a dry, laconic voice.

'You heard him, Remedios. Put your errand off till tomorrow.'

'That's impossible. I'll go alone.'

'No, you will not go, niece. And let that be an end to it. Señor Ramos has things to do and can't accompany you. Just imagine what it would be like if that brute were to insult you . . .'

'Insult her! . . . a lady insulted by that . . .!' exclaimed Caballuco. 'That could never be.'

'If you didn't have things to do . . . then I'd be easier in my mind.'

'I do have things to do,' said the centaur, standing up from behind the table, 'but if you insist . . .'

There was a pause. The Father Confessor had closed his eyes and was meditating.

'I do insist, Señor Ramos,' he said finally.

'Then there's nothing more to say. We'll go, Doña María.'

'Now, my beloved niece,' said Don Inocencio, his tone of voice half serious and half jovial, 'now that dinner is over, bring me the bowl.'

He directed a penetrating stare at his niece and, matching his actions to his words, said:

'I wash my hands.'

CHAPTER 28

From Pepe Rey to Don Juan Rey

Orbajosa, 12 April

Dear father:

Forgive me if I disobey you for the first time by not leaving here and giving up my plans. Your advice and request befit a good and honourable father. My stubbornness befits a foolish son, but a strange thing is happening to me. Stubbornness and honour have become so confused in my mind that the idea of desisting and yielding shames me. I've changed a good deal. I never used to experience this fury which consumes me. Formerly, I would laugh at any violent deed, at the exaggerations of impetuous men as well as the stupid acts of miscreants. Now nothing of this sort astounds me, for I am forever finding within myself a certain capacity for the perverse. I can talk to you as a person speaks alone to God and his conscience. I can say to you that I am a wretch, for he is wretched who lacks the moral strength to rule himself, to conquer his passions and submit his life to the hard rule of conscience. I have lacked the Christian fortitude which sustains the spirit of a wronged man in a splendid state aloof from the offences he suffers and the enemies who inflict them on him. I have been weak enough to surrender to wild rage, descending to the level of my detractors, trading blow for blow with them, and trying to confound them by methods learned in their own unworthy school. How sorry I am that you weren't at my side to turn me from this path! Now it is too late. Passions will not wait.

They are impatient; they cry for their prey with the peremp-
toriness of a frightful moral thirst. I have succumbed. I
cannot forget what you have so often said to me: that anger
can be called the worst of all passions, for by suddenly
transforming our character, it breeds all the other sins and
affords them its own demonic fire.

But it was not just anger that brought me to such a state,
but also a powerful feeling: the profound and ardent love I
feel for my cousin. This is the only extenuating circumstance.
And if not love, pity alone would have compelled me to
challenge the fury and intrigues of your terrible sister since
poor Rosario, torn between an irresistible affection and her
mother, is today one of the most unhappy people on earth.
Does not the love she feels for me, and which I reciprocate,
give me the right to open the door of her house as best I
may, and to take her away from there, using the law insofar
as it is applicable, and then using force beyond the point
where the law ceases to protect me? I think that your
rigorous moral scruples would be unable to give an affirma-
tive answer to this suggestion; but I have given up being a
reasonable and pure man who faithfully adheres to the
strictures of a conscience which is as exact as a scientific
formula. I am no longer that man whom a virtually perfect
upbringing taught to regulate his emotions to an amazing
degree. Today I am a man like any other. In one leap I have
entered the common terrain of the unjust and the wicked.
Prepare yourself for hearing that all sorts of atrocities are
my doing. I shall take care to inform you of such deeds as I
commit them.

But not even the confession of my faults will relieve me of
the responsibility for the grave things which have happened
and which will occur, nor can that responsibility, however
much I may argue, be attributed entirely to your sister. Doña
Perfecta's responsibility is immense, certainly. But how great
is my own? Oh, my dear father! Don't believe anything you
may hear about me; believe only what I tell you myself. If
they say that I have committed some deliberate villainy, tell

them it's a lie. It is difficult, very difficult, for me to judge myself considering my present disturbed state of mind. But I dare to assure you that I have not brought about the scandal deliberately. You know how far passion, favoured by circumstances in its dreadful and pervasive growth, can take a man.

What most embitters my life is having used lies, deception and base dissimulation. I, who used to be truth personified! I am no longer myself at all ... But is this the greatest perversity of which the soul is capable? Am I now at the beginning or the end? I have no idea. If Rosario, with her own heavenly hand, cannot extricate me from this hell which is my conscience, then I hope you'll come to my rescue. My cousin is an angel; she is suffering for me and she has taught me many things I did not know before.

Do not be surprised at the incoherence of these lines. Various emotions are consuming me. At times I'm filled with ideas truly worthy of my immortal soul; but at others I fall into miserable depression, and I think of the weak and inadequate men whose baseness you have described to me in vivid colours in order to teach me to abhor them. In the mood I am in today, I find myself torn equally between good and evil. May God have pity on me. I understand the meaning of prayer. It is a serious and reflective supplication which is so personal that one does not approach it with formulae which trip lightly from the tongue. It is an expansion of the soul which dares to spread its wings as it searches for its origins. It is the opposite of remorse, which is a contraction of the soul, which turns in on itself and hides in the fond hope that nobody will see it. You have taught me wonderful things; but now I'm doing my practicals, as we engineers say, and as I do so my knowledge broadens and becomes more firmly established ... I am beginning to wonder if perhaps I am not so bad as I myself believe. Could that be true?

I must finish this letter as quickly as I can. I have to send it with some soldiers who are on their way to the station at

Villahorrenda, because the people here just cannot be trusted with the post.

14 April

You would be amused, dear father, if I could make you understand how the people in this dreadful town think. You will already be aware that almost the whole region is up in arms. Anyone could have seen it coming, and the politicians are wrong if they think it will all be over in a matter of days. Hostility towards us and the Government is rooted in the Orbajosans' soul and forms part of it like religious faith. Turning now to the matter of my aunt, I'll tell you a strange thing: the poor lady, who has feudalism running through her very marrow, has taken it into her head that I'm going to storm her house and kidnap her daughter, as the knights of the Middle Ages were wont to assault an enemy castle and commit similar outrages. Don't laugh. It is true. That's how these people think. I hardly need to tell you that she takes me for a monster, some kind of heretic Moorish king, and the soldiers here, with whom I have become very friendly, are no better in her eyes. In Doña Perfecta's house it is taken as read that the soldiers and I have entered into some anti-religious, satanic pact and intend to make off with the treasures of Orbajosa, as well as its faith and young women. I know for certain that your sister believes that I'm literally going to take her house by storm, and I don't doubt that there's some sort of barricade behind the door.

But it could not be otherwise. Here everyone has the most outdated ideas concerning society, religion, property and the State. The religious zeal which compels them to use force against the Government in the defence of a faith which nobody has assailed and which they themselves do not really possess, awakens in their minds unpleasant memories of their feudal past. And since they would rather settle their disputes by brute force, fire and bloodshed, slaughtering anyone who does not think as they do, they believe that there is nobody in the whole wide world who would use any other means.

Far from it being my intention to make quixotic assaults on this lady's house, I have succeeded in having her spared the annoyances which her neighbours had to endure. On account of my friendship with the brigadier, she has not been required to present a list of all her man-servants who have gone over to the rebels, as she was ordered to do. I have it on good authority that if they searched the house it was only for the sake of appearances, and if the six men who were found there were disarmed, she was able to replace them afterwards without any action being taken against her. You can see from this just how far my hostility to the Señora stretches.

It is true that I enjoy the support of the military authorities, but the only use I make of it is to make sure that I am not insulted or ill-treated by these implacable people. My chances of success rest on the fact that the authorities recently appointed by the military commander are all my friends. I draw my moral strength from them and am thus able to intimidate the Orbajosans. I don't know whether or not I shall find myself in a position where I'll have to commit some violent deed. But don't be alarmed. The idea of storming and occupying the house is a ridiculous feudal idea of your sister's. Blind chance has placed me in an advantageous position. The anger and the passion which burn within me will drive me to take advantage of it. I don't know quite how far I'll go.

17 April

Your letter has brought me great comfort. Yes; I can only attain my goal by using the resources of the law, which are totally adequate for the purpose. I have consulted the authorities here and they all back up what you say. I am glad.

Since I have sown the idea of disobedience in my cousin's mind, let it at least keep within the bounds of social law. I shall do as you tell me. That is to say that I shall give up Pinzón's rather dubious help. I will break the terrifying solidarity I have established with the soldiers; I shall cease feeling proud of my association with their power; I shall put an end to my adventures and at the right moment I shall proceed with calm, prudence and all possible benevolence. It would be better that way. My association with the army, half serious, half in jest, was formed with the intention of protecting myself from the brutality of the Orbajosans and my aunt's servants and relatives. Apart from that, I have always rejected what we shall refer to as *armed intervention*.

My friend who was on my side has had to leave the house, but my communication with my cousin has not been severed completely. The poor girl is showing heroic courage in the midst of her troubles, and she will obey me blindly.

Do not be concerned for my personal safety. I, for my part, am afraid of nothing and am very calm.

20 April

I can only write a few lines today. I have much to do. In a matter of a few days it will all be over. Do not write to me any more at this place. Your son will soon have the pleasure of embracing you.

Pepe

CHAPTER 29

From Pepe Rey to Rosario Polentinos

Give Estebanillo the key to the garden and tell him to watch out for the dog. The boy is on my side, body and soul. Don't be afraid of anything. I'll be very sorry if you can't come down as you did the other night. Try your best to manage it. I'll be there after midnight. I'll tell you what I've decided, and what you must do. Keep calm, my dear, for I have given up all my rash and violent measures. I'll tell you all about it. It's a long story and I must tell you about it in person. I can imagine your fear and distress at the idea of my being so close to you. But it's been over a week since we saw each other. I have sworn that this separation must soon come to an end, and it shall. My heart tells me that I'll see you, and I swear I will.

CHAPTER 30

Stalking the game

A man and woman entered the widow Cusco's inn after ten o'clock and came out after the clock had struck half past eleven.

'Now, Doña María,' said the man, 'I'll take you home, because I have things to do.'

'Take care, Señor Ramos, for God's sake,' she replied. 'Why don't we go as far as the Club to see if he comes out? You've already heard this afternoon Estebanillo, the lad who helps in the garden, was talking to him.'

'But are you looking for Don José?' asked the centaur morosely. 'What does it matter to us? His courtship with Doña Rosario has reached the point where all that's left now is for Doña Perfecta to allow them to marry. That's my opinion.'

'You're an animal,' said Remedios angrily.

'Señora, I'm going.'

'What? You ignorant man, are you just going to leave me in the middle of the street?'

'Yes, unless you go straight home, Señora.'

'So that's it . . . you're going to leave me alone, completely unprotected . . . Listen, Señor Ramos: Don José will leave the Club as usual. I want to know if he goes home or goes on somewhere else. This is just a whim on my part, nothing more than a whim.'

'All I know is that I've got things to do and it's already nearly twelve.'

'Be quiet,' said Remedios, 'let's hide round the corner . . .

There's a man coming along the Calle de la Tripería Alta. It's him.'

'It's Don José . . . I can tell by his walk.'

They took cover and the man walked past.

'Let's follow him,' said María Remedios, agitated. 'Let's follow him part of the way, Ramos.'

'Señora . . .'

'Just enough to see if he goes home.'

'Only for a minute, then, and no longer, Doña Remedios. Then I'm off.'

They walked for about thirty paces, maintaining a constant distance behind the man they were observing. Eventually the Father Confessor's niece stopped and said: 'He's not going into his house.'

'He must be going to the brigadier's.'

'The brigadier's house is up there, and Don Pepe's going down that way, towards Doña Perfecta's.'

'Doña Perfecta's!' exclaimed Caballuco, doubling his pace.

But they were wrong. The man under observation went straight past the Polentinos house and continued walking.

'You see; he's not going there.'

'Señor Ramos, let's follow him,' said Remedios, clutching convulsively at the centaur's hand. 'I've got a hunch.'

'Well, we'll soon find out because we've come to the edge of the town.'

'Let's not walk so quickly . . . he might see us . . . What I think, Señor Ramos, is that he's going to enter by the garden gate . . . the one which isn't used any more.'

'Señora, you've taken leave of your senses!'

'Keep on walking and we'll see.'

It was a dark night and the observers could not be certain where Señor de Rey had entered. But the unmistakable sound of rusty hinges and the fact that they did not come across the young man down the whole length of the garden wall convinced them that he had got into the garden. Caballuco looked at Remedios, stupefied. He was at a loss for words.

'What are you thinking now? . . . Do you still doubt me?'

'What should I do?' asked the hero, totally confused. 'Should we give him a fright?. . . I don't know what the Señora might say. I say this because I went to see her last night and I had the impression that mother and daughter were patching things up.'

'Don't be so stupid . . . Why don't you go in?'

'Now I remember that the armed men aren't here because I sent them away tonight.'

'And this numbskull is still wondering what to do! Ramos, don't be such a coward. Go into the garden.'

'How, if the gate's closed?'

'Jump over the wall!. . . What an idiot!. . . If only I were a man . . .'

'Over there, then . . . There are some worn bricks which the lads use when they're stealing fruit.'

'Go on, then. I'm going to knock at the front door to wake the Señora up, if she's asleep.'

The centaur climbed up although it was not all that easy for him. He sat astride the wall for a moment and then disappeared among the dark mass of the trees. María Remedios dashed off in the direction of the Calle del Condestable, and, grabbing hold of the knocker on the front door, knocked . . . she knocked three times for all she was worth.

CHAPTER 31

Doña Perfecta

Observe the tranquillity with which Doña Perfecta dedicates herself to her writing. Go into her room, despite the lateness of the hour, and you will surprise her hard at work with her mind divided between her thoughts and the long, painstaking letters she is writing with a steady pen and careful handwriting. The light from the oil lamp falls directly onto her face, breast and hands, while the lampshade leaves the rest of her body and most of the room in a sweet penumbra. She looks like a luminous figure evoked by the imagination in the midst of the vague shadows of fear.

It is strange that, up to now, we have not stated one very important fact about her. Doña Perfecta was beautiful, or to be more exact, was still beautiful, as her face retained features of consummate beauty. Life in the country, a complete absence of vanity, her simple tastes in apparel and her refusal to obey the dictates of fashion, her scorn for the vanities of the court, were all reasons why her innate beauty failed to shine, or that it shone so little. The distinctly yellowish tint to her complexion also detracted from her appearance and indicated a strong, choleric constitution.

With her dark, almond-shaped eyes, her delicate, slender nose, her broad, smooth forehead, anyone who saw her considered hers as the perfect example of the human face. But in her features there was a certain expression of hardness and arrogance which evoked feelings of aversion. Just as some people, although ugly, can be attractive, Doña Perfecta repelled. Her glance, even when accompanied by kind words, traced an impassable line of wary respect between her and strangers. But for members of her household, that is to say her dependants, friends and those with close family ties, she possessed a definite attraction. She was supreme in the art of domination, and nobody could equal her in her skill at saying the things which people wanted to hear.

Her choleric nature and her constant dealings with pious people and objects which excited her imagination without reason or result, all had prematurely aged her, and although she was young, she did not appear so. It could be said of her that because of her habits and lifestyle she had grown a shell, a stony, impenetrable covering which enclosed her within herself like a snail in its portable house. Doña Perfecta seldom emerged from her shell.

Her irreproachable conduct and public benevolence which we have observed in her from the moment she appeared in this narrative, were the reason for her great prestige in Orbajosa. Moreover, she maintained a relationship with some important ladies in Madrid and it was through these contacts that she had brought about the dismissal of her nephew from his post. Now, at this point in our story, we see her seated at her desk, the only confidant of her plans and the repository of her numerous accounts with the villagers as well as of her moral accounts with God and society. There she wrote the quarterly letters which her brother received; there she composed the notes to the judge and notary to get them to embroil Pepe Rey in lawsuits; there she hatched the plot by which he lost the confidence of the Government; there she had long conversations with Don Inocencio. To become acquainted with the settings of other acts whose effects we have seen, we should follow her to the bishop's palace and the houses of those families with which she was on friendly terms.

We cannot imagine what Doña Perfecta would have been like if she had fallen in love. When she hated she did so with the fiery vehemence of a guardian angel of hatred and discord among men. Such is the effect of religious fervour on a character which is hard and devoid of innate goodness when, instead of deriving nourishment from conscience and the truth as it is revealed in principles which are as simple as they are beautiful, it takes its vitality from narrow formulae which serve only the interests of the Church. Sanctimoniousness is harmless only in the pure at heart. Indeed, even then, it is barren as far as goodness is concerned. But hearts that are born without the seraphic purity which creates a preparatory Limbo on earth must take care not to become inflamed by what they see on altarpieces, in the choirs, in the locutories and sacristies if they have not first of all erected an altar, pulpit or confessional in their own conscience.

The Señora rose from her desk now and again and went into the adjoining room where her daughter was. Rosario had been ordered to go and sleep but she, having already crossed the precipice of disobedience, was still awake.

'Why aren't you asleep?' asked her mother. 'I don't intend going to sleep at all tonight. You know that Caballuco has taken away the men we had here. Anything could happen, so I'm keeping watch . . . If I didn't keep watch, what would happen to you and me?'

'What time is it?' asked the girl.

'It'll soon be midnight . . . You're probably not afraid . . . but I am.'

Rosarito was trembling and everything about her suggested great anxiety. Her eyes were raised to heaven as if in an attitude of prayer; then she looked at her mother, expressing real terror.

'But what's the matter?'

'Did you say that it was midnight?'

'Yes.'

'Then . . . But is it midnight already?'

Rosario wanted to say something. She shook her head as if the weight of the world rested upon it.

'There's something the matter with you . . . something's happening to you,' the mother said, fixing her penetrating eyes on her daughter.

'Yes . . . I wanted to tell you,' stammered the girl, 'I wanted to say . . . Nothing, it's nothing. I'm going to sleep.'

'Rosario, Rosario. Your mother can read your heart like a book,' exclaimed Doña Perfecta sternly. 'You're upset. I've already said that I'm prepared to forgive you if you're willing to repent, like a good, responsible girl . . .'

'What? Am I not a good girl? Oh, Mother, I'm dying!'

Anxious and heart-broken, Rosario burst into tears.

'Why the tears?' asked her mother as she embraced her. 'If they're the tears of repentance, they should be blessed.'

'I don't repent, I cannot repent,' shouted the young woman in an explosion of desperation which made her sublime.

She lifted her head and a sudden inspired energy showed itself on her face. Her hair cascaded down her back. Never has a more beautiful image been seen of an angel preparing to rebel.

'But what is this? Are you going mad?' said Doña Perfecta, placing both hands on her shoulders.

'I'm leaving! I'm leaving!' said the young woman with the exaltation of delirium.

And she jumped off the bed.

'Rosario, Rosario . . . My daughter . . . For God's sake . . .'

'Oh, Mother! Señora!' exclaimed Rosario, embracing her mother. 'Tie me up.'

'In truth, that is what you deserve . . . What foolishness is this?'

'Tie me up . . . I'm going, I'm going off with him.'

Doña Perfecta could feel the heat from her heart bubbling up to her lips. She restrained herself and only with her eyes, which were blacker than night, did she answer her daughter.

'Mother! Mother! I hate everything that isn't him,' exclaimed Rosario. 'Hear my confession, because I wish to confess to everybody, and to you first and foremost.'

'You'll be the death of me.'

'I want to confess so that you will forgive me . . . This burden, this burden on top of me won't let me live . . .'

'The burden of sin! Add God's curse to it, and then try to walk carrying that burden, wretch . . . I'm the only one who can relieve you of it.'

'No, not you, no . . .' shouted Rosario in desperation. 'But listen to me, I want to confess everything, everything . . . Then you can throw me out of this house, where I was born.'

'Me, throw you out?'

'Then I'll leave of my own accord.'

'No you will not. I'm going to teach you a daughter's duties, which you have forgotten.'

'Then I'll run away. He'll take me with him.'

'Has he told you to? Has he advised you to? Has he ordered you to?' the mother asked, hurling the words like bolts of lightning at her daughter.

'That's his advice to me . . . We've agreed to marry. We must, Mother, dear Mother. I will always love you . . . I know that I must love you . . . I'll be condemned if I don't love you.'

She wrung her hands and, falling to her knees, kissed her mother's feet.

'Rosario! Rosario!' shouted Doña Perfecta, her voice shaking. 'Get up.'

There was a short pause.

'Has this man written to you?'

'Yes.'

'Have you seen him again since that night?'

'Yes.'

'And you . . .!'

'I've written to him as well . . . Oh, Mother! Why do you look at me like that? You're not my mother.'

'If only I weren't. Enjoy the grief you're causing me. You're killing me, you're killing me for sure,' shouted the Señora with indescribable agitation. 'You say that that man . . .'

'He's my husband . . . and I shall be his wife, protected by the law . . . You're not a woman . . . Why do you look at me like that? It makes me tremble. Mother, Mother, don't condemn me.'

'You have condemned yourself, and that's all there is to it. Obey me and I'll forgive you . . . Answer me: when did you receive letters from that man?'

'Today.'

'What betrayal! What infamy!' exclaimed the mother, bellowing rather than speaking. 'Did you intend to see each other?'

'Yes.'

'When?'

'Tonight.'

'Where?'

'Here, here. I confess all, everything. I know that it's a crime . . . I'm despicable. But you, you who are my mother, can get me out of this hell. Just consent . . . Just say one word to me.'

'That man here, in my house!' cried Doña Perfecta, walking, or rather leaping, to the centre of the room.

Rosario followed her on her knees. Just at that moment three knocks, three crashes, three thunderbolts were heard. It was María Remedios's heart pounding on the door with the knocker. The house shook in a fearful tremor. Mother and daughter froze like statues.

A servant went down to open the door and, a short time later, María Remedios entered. She was no longer a woman but a basilisk enveloped in a shawl. Her face, incandescent with anxiety, exuded fire.

'He's here, he's here,' she said on entering. 'He got into the garden through the unused gate . . .'

She panted for breath with every syllable.

'Now I understand,' said Doña Perfecta, making a kind of bellowing noise.

Rosario fell to the floor, unconscious and lifeless.

'Let's go downstairs,' said Doña Perfecta, taking no notice of her daughter's fainting fit.

The two women slithered down the stairs like two snakes.

The maids and manservant were in the hallway, not knowing what to do. Doña Perfecta walked through the dining room and into the garden, followed by María Remedios.

'Fortunately we have Ca . . . Ca . . . Caballuco here,' said the canon's niece.

'Where?'

'He's also in the garden . . . he jum . . . jum . . . jumped over the wall.'

Doña Perfecta peered into the darkness with eyes full of rage. Anger lent them that vision peculiar to the cat family.

'I can see a shape over there,' she said. 'He's heading for the oleanders.'

'It's him,' shouted Remedios. 'But there's Ramos . . . Ramos!'

The colossal figure of the centaur was clearly visible.

'Towards the oleanders! . . . Ramos, towards the oleanders!'

Doña Perfecta moved a few steps forward. Her hoarse voice, shaking dreadfully, spat out the following words:

'Cristóbal! Cristóbal . . . kill him.'

A shot was heard. Then another.

CHAPTER 32

The end

*From Don Cayetano Polentinos to a friend of
his in Madrid*

Orbajosa, 21 April

Dear friend:

Please send me without delay the 1562 edition which you say you found among the books from Corchuelo's estate. I will pay any price for that volume. I have been searching in vain for it for a long time and shall consider myself the luckiest of men when I own it. You should find in the colophon a helmet with an emblem above the word 'Treatise', and the X in the date MDLXII should have the serif turning backwards. If these characteristics do appear on the volume, send me a telegram, for I am very excited ... although now I remember that, owing to these inopportune and annoying disturbances, the telegraph system is not working. I will expect a reply by return of post.

I shall soon be in Madrid, my friend, for the purpose of publishing this long awaited work on the *Genealogy of Orbajosa*. I thank you for your kind words, but I cannot accept that part of it which is flattery. My work certainly does not deserve the lavish praise you bestow upon it. This is a work of patience and study. It is an enormous and solid, yet crude, monument which I erect in honour of the greatness of my beloved country. Poor and ugly it may be in appearance, but there is something noble in the idea which begat it, which is solely to turn the eyes of this unbelieving and arrogant generation towards the marvellous deeds and unsullied virtues of our forebears. If only the studious youth of today would follow the steps I earnestly urge them to follow! If only the abominable studies and intellectual habits introduced by philosophical freedom and specious doctrines could be consigned to eternal oblivion! If only our scholars would devote themselves exclusively to the contemplation of those glorious epochs so that, once the modern age was saturated with the substance and beneficial sap of their learning, this mad desire for change and the ridiculous mania for absorbing foreign ideas, so contrary to our delicate national organism, might disappear. I am very much afraid that my wishes will not be granted, and that the contemplation of past perfections will remain limited to the narrow circle where it is now, amid the turbulence of demented youth which goes in pursuit of vain Utopias and crass innovation. What is to become of us, my friend? I fear that within a short time our poor Spain will be so disfigured that she won't know herself even when she looks into the shining mirror of her unblemished history.

I do not wish to end this letter without sharing with you a very unpleasant piece of news: the tragic death of a worthy young man who is very well known in Madrid, the civil engineer Don José de Rey, the nephew of my sister-in-law. This sad event took place last night in the garden of our house and I have not yet come to any definite conclusions concerning the causes which led the unfortunate young man to this horrible and sinful act. According to what Doña Perfecta told me this morning, on my return from Mundogrande, Pepe Rey, at about midnight, entered the garden of our house and shot himself in the right temple, dying instantaneously. Imagine the consternation and alarm this would have produced in such a peaceful and honourable house as ours! Poor Doña Perfecta was so overcome that we were quite concerned for her: but she is better now, and this afternoon we managed to get her to take some broth. We are using every means to console her, and as she is a good Christian, she knows how to bear the greatest misfortunes with edifying resignation.

Just between the two of us, my friend, I may say that to take the terrible decision to put an end to his life, young de Rey must have been greatly influenced by a hopeless passion, or perhaps by remorse for his conduct and the bitter hypochondria into which his mind had fallen. I had a high regard for him. I believe that he was not lacking in excellent qualities. But here he was held in such low esteem that I never once heard anyone speak well of him. Gossip has it that he made a display of extravagant ideas and opinions. He scoffed at religion; went into church smoking and without taking off his hat; he respected nothing and in his eyes there was no purity, no virtue, no soul, no ideal and no faith in the world, only theodolites, T-squares, rulers, machines, spirit levels, picks and shovels. Can you believe it? In honour of the truth, I must say that he always concealed such ideas from me, no doubt through fear of being demolished by the bombardment of my arguments, but a thousand stories are circulating about his heresies and outrageous behaviour.

I must draw to a close now, my dear friend, as I can hear the sound of gunfire. As I am neither a lover of battles nor a warrior, my pulse is weakening. I shall keep you informed of the progress of this war. Yours affectionately etc. etc.

22 April

My unforgettable friend:

We've had a bloody skirmish in the region of Orbajosa today. The large rebel band organized in Villahorrenda was subjected to a furious attack by the troops, and the losses on both sides were heavy. Eventually the valiant partisans were routed, but their morale is high and you may hear of their great feats. Cristóbal Caballuco, the son of the outstanding Caballuco with whom you were acquainted in the last war, commanded the rebels despite being wounded, God knows where or when, in the arm. The present chief is a man of great leadership qualities, as well as being an honourable and straightforward man. Since there has to be some sort of friendly truce eventually, I presume that Caballuco will be appointed a general in the Spanish army, an event that would be of mutual benefit.

I deplore this war which is taking on alarming proportions; but I recognize that our brave peasants are not responsible for it, for they have been incited to bloody battle by the audacity of the Government, the demoralization of its sacrilegious delegates, the systematic fury with which the representatives of the state attack that which is most venerated by the conscience of the people – religious faith and untarnished *españolismo* – which have luckily been preserved in places not yet infested by the devastating pestilence. When an attempt is made to despoil a nation in order to implant another soul; to rob it of its birthright, let us say, by altering its feelings, its customs, its ideas, it is natural that the nation should defend itself like a man halfway along a solitary road if he is attacked by murderous thieves. Let the spirit and the salutary essence of my work on the *Genealogy* be brought into the sphere of the Government (forgive my immodesty) and then there will be no more wars.

A most regrettable matter arose here today. The priest, a friend of mine, refused to grant the unfortunate de Rey a Christian burial. I intervened in the matter and appealed to the bishop to lift an anathema of such a severe nature, but he was unable to do so. Finally we buried the young man's body in a hole which had been dug at Mundogrande, where my patient explorations produced the rich archaeological finds which you already know about. It was a sad time for me and I cannot rid myself of the very painful impression it made on me. Don Juan Tafetán and I were the only people to accompany the cortège. Some time later, strange to tell, the Troya girls, as they're known, went there and prayed for a long time over the mathematician's rustic grave. Although this seemed a ridiculous display of officiousness, I was moved.

As for de Rey's death, there is a rumour going around town that he was murdered. Nobody knows by whom. According to reports he himself made this claim, as he lived for about an hour and a half. The rumour is that he remained silent on the question of the murderer's identity. I am repeating this version of events without saying either that I refute it or deny it. Doña Perfecta does not want the matter discussed and she gets very upset whenever I bring it up.

The poor woman! No sooner has she suffered one misfortune than another has befallen her, which we are all very upset about. My friend, now we have another victim of the terrible affliction which has run in our family for so long. Poor Rosario, who was getting on so well, thanks to our loving care, has lost her mind. Her incoherent words, her terrible delirium and deathly pallor all put me in mind of my mother and sister. This is the worst case I have seen in my family, because it is not simply a mania but real insanity. It is sad, very sad, that among so many I am the only one who has managed to escape, keeping my judgement sound and whole and completely free of this dreadful complaint.

I have not been able to convey your regards to Don Inocencio, for the poor man has suddenly been taken ill and is not receiving anybody or allowing his most intimate friends to see him. But I am sure he would wish to be remembered to you and I have no doubt that he will soon begin work on the translation of the Latin epigrams which you suggest . . . Shots are ringing out again. People say there will be a fight this afternoon. The troops have just marched out.

Barcelona, 1 June

I have just arrived here after leaving my niece Rosario in San Baudillo de Llobregat. The director of the establishment has assured me that she is an incurable case. She will be given the best of attention in that impressive, pleasant lunatic asylum. My dear friend, if I ever go the same way, let them take me to San Baudillo. When I get back I hope to see the proofs of my *Genealogy*. I have it in mind to add six pages, because it would be a great omission not to publish my reasons for stating that Mateo Díaz Coronel, the author of the *Metrical Encomium*, is descended from the Guevaras on the maternal side and not from the Burguillos, as the author of the *Floresta Amena* erroneously maintains.

I am writing this letter mainly in order to give you a warning. I have heard several people here speak of the death of Pepe Rey, telling it as it really happened. I revealed this secret to you when we met in Madrid, telling you of what I heard some time after the event. I am very surprised that, as I had not told anybody about it except you, the story is being told here, warts and all, explaining how he entered the garden, fired his revolver at Caballuco when he saw that he was on the point of attacking him with a knife, and how Ramos then fired with such accuracy that he dropped him on the spot . . . Finally, my dear friend, I must remind you that this is a family secret and this should be sufficient for someone as prudent and discreet as yourself.

Wonderful news! Wonderful news! I have just read in a newspaper that Caballuco has defeated Brigadier Batalla.

Orbajosa, 12 December

I have some bad news for you. We no longer have a Father Confessor. I do not mean that he has passed on to a better life, but that the poor man has been suffering from such depression since April and has been so distressed and silent that you would not recognize him. There is no trace now of that Attic wit, that attractive and classic joviality which made him so amiable. He shuns company, locks himself away in his house and has severed all connection with the outside world. If you saw him you would not recognize him as he is now all skin and bone. The most peculiar thing is that he has fallen out with his niece and lives alone, completely alone, in a mean little house in the suburbs of Baidejos. They say now that he is going to give up his place in the cathedral choir and go to Rome. Yes, Orbajosa is losing a great man in its eminent Latin scholar. I think many years will pass before we see his like again. Our glorious Spain is coming to an end, it is being annihilated and is dying.

Orbajosa, 23 December

The young man whom I recommend to you in the letter delivered to you by his own hand is the nephew of our beloved Father Confessor. He is a lawyer with ambitions to be a writer. He was educated very thoroughly by his uncle and his ideas are sound. How sad it would be if he were to be corrupted in the quagmire of sophistry and unbelief! He is honest, a hard worker and a good Catholic, which makes me think that he will have a career in a law firm like yours ... perhaps some small ambition (for he is also ambitious) will lead him onto the jousting fields of politics, and I do not believe that the cause of order and tradition would be any the worse for that, since the youth of today has been perverted and seduced by the radicals. He is accompanied by his mother, an ordinary woman who lacks social polish, but who possesses an excellent heart and true faith. Maternal love in her takes the rather colourful form of worldly ambition and she is determined that her son will be a government minister. This may well come to pass.

Perfecta sends you her regards. I'm not exactly sure what is wrong with her, but whatever it is, it's giving cause for concern. She has lost her appetite to an alarming degree and either I know nothing about illness or she is in the early stages of jaundice. This has been a house of sorrow since

Rosario left, for she brightened it with her smile and kind, angelic nature. Now there seems to be a dark cloud hanging over us. Poor Doña Perfecta speaks often of this cloud, which gets darker and darker all the time, while she gets yellower and yellower. The poor mother finds some consolation for her grief in religion and worship, which she practises every day in an ever more exemplary and edifying manner. She passes almost the whole day in church and spends her vast fortune on splendid functions, novenas and brilliant expositions of the Sacrament. Thanks to her, faith in Orbajosa has regained the splendour of former days. This never ceases to be a source of consolation in the midst of the decadence and disintegration of our nationhood . . .

The proofs go off tomorrow . . . I shall add two more pages as I have discovered another illustrious native of Orbajosa, Bernardo Amador de Soto, who was a running footman to the Duke of Osuna and served him during the vice-regency in Naples. All the indications are that he took absolutely no part in the plot against Venice.

CHAPTER 33

Now it is finished. For the time being, there is no more we can say about people who appear to be good but are not.

NOTE ON THE TRANSLATOR

Alexander R. Tulloch MA is a Senior Lecturer in Russian and Spanish with the Ministry of Defence. His translations include *The Naked Year* by Boris Pilnyak, *Arabesques* by Nikolai Gogol and *The Three-Cornered Hat* by Pedro Alarcon. He has also recently translated from Spanish a major study on the French artist Michel Duchamp.